Found in Translation

John Hastings

Found in Translation

Onwards and Upwards Publications, Berkeley House,
11 Nightingale Crescent, West Horsley, Surrey KT24 6PD

www.onwardsandupwards.org

copyright © John Hastings 2011

The right of John Hastings to be identified as the author of this work has been asserted by him in accordance with the Copyright, Designs and Patents Act 1988.

All rights reserved.

No part of this publication may be reproduced or transmitted in any form or by any means, electronic or mechanical, including photocopy, recording or any information storage and retrieval system, without permission in writing from the author or publisher.

Scripture quotations taken from the HOLY BIBLE, NEW INTERNATIONAL VERSION. Copyright © 1973, 1978, 1984 by International Bible Society. Used by permission.

ISBN: 978-1-907509-22-3

Cover design: Leah-Maarit

Printed in the UK

Contents

Contents 3
Introduction 5
The Big Picnic 7
The Pearl 13
The Coin 19
Contact 23
The Donkey 31
The Test 35
The Broken Leg 41
Teabreak 47
In the Hands of the Prophets 53
Bethlehem Towers 61
None so Blind 67
The Whole Armour 81
The Genesis Project 89
A Jar of Water 97
The Song 115
Gentled Horses 173
The Cruise of a Lifetime 179
Found in Translation 183
Three Days in Jerusalem 193
The Stowaway 277
Notes on the Stories 287

"God has given us a book of stories." The old children's hymn has it right; in the bible God has given us a treasure chest of stories that go to the heart of life as we know it. Jesus was a pre-eminent storyteller, and through the ages Christian teachers and preachers have sought to retell these stories in new ways alongside adding their own. John Hastings' work falls within this honourable line of illustrating the good news of God's love and grace in Jesus with a well told story.

Roger Standing
Deputy Principle
Spurgeon's College, London

Introduction

The Bible is a book full of stories; much more than stories, of course, but still many stories: adventure stories, love stories, travel stories, war stories; stories about kings and peasants, heroes and villains. But these stories are set in a world and a culture far removed from our 21st Century. What's more, they were originally written in ancient Hebrew or Greek, and sometimes the writers don't tell us all we would like to know.

For example, have you ever wondered what it would have been like to be there when Paul confronted Elymas the sorcerer on Cyprus (Acts 13:6-12)? Or, what would it have been like to be the boy with the packed lunch that Jesus used to feed the 5,000 (John 6:9). Have you thought, suppose Jesus was telling the parable of the 'Pearl of Great Value' (Matthew 13:45-46) today; how would he translate it into modern terms? Or, if Jesus rose from the dead today, what would the 'Emmaus Road Experience' (Luke 24:13-33) be like? Have you ever watched futuristic TV series like *Star Trek* and wondered if Christianity has a future?

That is how these stories began; with me pondering questions like these. The answers are, of course, my own. They are fiction – and not to be taken too seriously, although I have tried to be true to the Bible.

The advantage of a short story over a novel is that the short story carries more punch and can convey a single message or meaning in a way that the longer book cannot. I hope that these stories all have a message – as all Bible stories do. I have considered putting in some notes about the meaning of the stories, or even some questions for group discussion. However, experience has taught me that each one of us gets his/her own message out of a story – and not necessarily the one that the author intended.

Hence, I have not given *the* message for these stories, although I have put in some notes at the end of the book, to make sure everyone is up to speed with the background to each story. I am going to leave the message of each story to you. I simply hope that the messages you get will be compatible with the Bible passages on which many of the stories are based.

One thing I have learned, from trying out some of these stories on friends, is that adults like to listen to a story read aloud just as much as do children. So I would suggest that one way of sharing this book would be to read some of the shorter stories aloud to a small group.

I would like to thank my wife, Ann, for reading and critiquing the stories as they were being written, and many friends at Bretton Baptist Church who have read, listened to, and even enjoyed, many of these stories.

The Big Picnic

John 6:8-9
A boy's perspective on the Feeding of the Five Thousand

Sarah was surprised, as she walked down the village street, to see her sister, Ruth, standing outside the doorway of her house, staring away across the fields to the distant hills.

Ruth must have heard the sound of her footsteps, for she turned suddenly, and Sarah could see that her face was anxious and tear-stained.

"Is that you, Simon?" she exclaimed. Disappointment showed on her face as she recognised her sister and in her voice as she said, "Oh. It's you, Sarah."

"Whatever's the matter, Ruth?"

Ruth was already turning back to look across the fields as she replied, "Oh! It's Simon. He's gone off somewhere and not come back and it'll be getting dark soon and I'm so worried about him."

Sarah tried to be reassuring, "Well, I expect he's just playing with some of the other boys in the village somewhere. I'm sure he'll be home as soon as he gets hungry."

Ruth was not prepared to be reassured. "No, you don't understand. He's not in the village. He wanted to go out on his own. He's getting bigger now and he said he wanted to walk out on the hills by himself. And his father said, "Why not? He's big enough to look after himself." So I made him up a lunch in a basket, just a few rolls and a couple of sardines, and he went off. And I felt quite proud of him as I waved him off, but its hours and hours now and he's not back. He must have gone climbing on the rocks and fallen and broken his leg – or perhaps a lion's got him. And I don't know what to do."

Sarah began to feel a little anxious herself. She stood beside her sister and peered out across the fields, shading her eyes against the sun which was low in the western sky. There were some men still working out in the fields, but no small boys. Sarah tried to speak reassuringly for her sister's sake. "Well, I'm quite sure there are no lions in Galilee these days. We'd better go out and look round the village, just to make sure he isn't playing with the other boys, and then if we still can't find him, we'll have to get some of the men to..."

"Hullo, Mum, I'm back! Hullo Auntie Sarah!" A cheerful, boyish shout from behind startled them. They swung round to see a young, tousle-haired, red-cheeked boy standing in the rear doorway. He looked tired and sweaty but happy. He was carrying a small lunch basket.

Ruth rushed across the room and hugged him, "Simon! I've been so worried! Where have you *been*? Are you all right?"

Simon submitted to his mother's hug for a few moments; then, feeling that mother-love had been satisfied, he pulled away, "Of course I'm all right, Mum."

"But where *have* you been, Simon?" said Sarah.

"I just went up onto the hills, like I said I would," replied Simon, "And then I thought I would walk over to the lake. And there was this great crowd of people – must have been *thousands* of them – so I went to see what was going on."

"But it's been hours and hours!" exclaimed his mother, "What have you been *doing*?"

"Well, this crowd were all listening to this man talking," said Simon, "And I couldn't hear what he was saying so I worked my way to the front. There was this man standing up on a big rock and talking – I got up really close – and there were some more men behind him – and this entire great crowd in front of him listening. They were *really* quiet. So I listened as well. It was really interesting.

The Big Picnic

"Oh, Simon," said Ruth, "I don't believe you. You!? Listening to a man talking for all this time!?"

Sarah was inclined to agree with her sister, "What was this man talking about, that was so interesting?"

"Some of it was just grown-up talk," replied Simon, "but a *lot* of it was stories."

"Stories?" said Ruth in surprise.

"What sort of stories?" asked Sarah.

"Oh, about a farmer sowing seed, and about weeds and stones and birds," said Simon, "And one about treasure buried in a field. I wonder if our fields have got any treasure hidden in them. Can I go out and see?"

"Simon," said Ruth in her severest tone of voice, "don't you realise you're in disgrace? I don't know *what* your father will say when he hears how long you've been out and how worried I've been."

"I was quite safe, Mum," said Simon reassuringly, "There were all these thousands of people around me."

"But surely Simon," said Sarah, "you can't have been listening to stories all this time?"

"No, we had lunch as well."

"Did this man, this storyteller, give you lunch?" asked Sarah.

"Not exactly," said Simon, "I gave him *my* lunch."

Ruth would not have been surprised if Simon had said he had eaten the storyteller's lunch and his own packed lunch, but that Simon had given away his lunch was hard to believe. "You gave him *your* lunch? You must be starving."

"No," said Simon, "He gave everyone lunch."

"Simon," said Sarah, "you're not making sense."

"You're just making it all up so I won't be cross with you," said Ruth in a hurt voice.

"No. Honestly Mum," said Simon quickly, "I was starting to feel hungry and I think everyone else was too. And I thought of starting my packed lunch. And then the other men started talking to the one who was speaking. I heard them say it was getting late and he should send them away to get some food. And *he* said they should give them some food themselves. And they said they hadn't any food. So I thought, 'Well, I've got some food.' So I put my hand up and said I'd got some food and would he like one of my rolls. And he looked at me and smiled – it was a nice smile – and he said, 'Thank you,' and could he borrow my lunch basket. So I gave it to him and he told everyone to sit down. Then he opened my lunch basket and he said grace. And then he started taking out the rolls and sardines, and do you know what? He went on taking out roll after roll and sardine after sardine, and he passed them to his men, and they started passing them out to the crowd, and it just went on and on – and he gave some to me as well – and he ate some himself – and we all had plenty – and then he gave me my lunch basket back." Simon paused for breath and then finished with a rush, "But it all took a long time 'cos there were thousands of people. And that's why I'm late home."

There was a long silence while the two women gazed at their wayward son and nephew, and Simon gazed anxiously back at his Mum.

"Simon!" said Ruth at last, "I never would have thought you would have made up a story like that. What have you *really* been doing all this time?"

"But it's true, Mum, honestly," said Simon earnestly.

Ruth took Simon by the arm, while Sarah took the lunch basket. "I don't believe a word of it. You just go to your room at once, Simon. We'll see what your father says about this when he comes home."

"But Mum..." protested Simon.

"No buts. Go to your room."

The Big Picnic

Simon's protests died away as he left the room and disappeared along the corridor.

"Well!" said Ruth turning to her sister, "I can understand him rambling around in those hills and forgetting the time and coming home late. But I never would have thought he'd make up such a fantastic excuse."

But Sarah had opened the lunch basket and was staring into it. "This is funny, Ruth. Look! His basket is stuffed full of rolls and sardines."

Found in Translation

The Pearl

Matthew 13:45-46
If Jesus told the parable of the Pearl today, what would it be like?

It was five minutes past four when Simon pushed open the door of *Lorna Bateman: Jeweller and Pawnbroker*. The shop was almost empty. At one side, one of Lorna's young assistants was holding a tray of gold chains while a smartly dressed woman examined them. On the other side, Lorna's second assistant, standing behind the counter, recognised Simon immediately.

"Good afternoon, Mr Cartwright," he said. "Miss Bateman warned us to expect you. I'll tell her you're here."

He opened the door at the back of the shop and said, "Mr Cartwright is here, Miss Bateman."

Lorna came to the door at once.

"Come in, Simon, come in; take a seat." She ushered him into the office-cum-stockroom and pointed to a comfortable chair.

When they were both seated, she said, "You really are serious about that pearl collection of yours, aren't you?"

"Why, yes, I want my collection to be the very finest I can afford," said Simon.

"In that case, I've got something really special to show you."

Lorna rose, walked to the safe in one corner, worked the combination and opened the heavy door. She took out a small tray with something on it covered with a black, velvet cloth. She put the tray on her desk in front of Simon and drew away the cloth with a flourish.

Simon gasped. In the middle of the tray was an open box, and in the box, sitting in a nest of velvet, was the largest, roundest pearl he had ever seen.

"Lorna," he said in an awed voice, "it's... it's amazing. It's magnificent. It's the largest and most beautiful pearl I've ever seen."

"It's the best ever, Simon" said Lorna.

"May I pick it up?" asked Simon.

"Pick up the box. Don't touch the pearl," said Lorna.

"Of course." Simon stretched out his hand reverently and gently lifted the box. The pearl had a translucent pink lustre that told him it was an Indian pearl. It seemed to be perfectly spherical. He pulled out his jeweller's eyeglass and put it in his eye to study the pearl more closely. It had no imperfection at all that he could see. It really was the most perfectly formed pearl he had ever seen in his life.

"It's flawless," he said in hushed tones. If he had been wearing a hat, he would have uncovered his head in the presence of such beauty. He felt an odd desire to kneel on the floor in front of the pearl. Then, with a sigh, he gently placed it back on Lorna's desk.

Lorna was clearly pleased with his reaction.

"Do you want it?" she asked.

"Do I want it?" repeated Simon. He had a vision of a magnificent ballroom, crowds of beautiful women in evening gowns, partnered by men in correct evening dress, gathered round to admire the Pearl. In his mind it already had that capital letter. "Of course I want it."

Then a thought occurred to him, "Why haven't I heard about this before?" he asked. "Whoever found this Pearl has kept quiet about it. How did you get hold of it?"

Lorna looked at him, raised one finger and tapped the side of her nose. "Unusual channels," she said, "but don't worry. I haven't stolen it, if that's what you're thinking. However, I've

The Pearl

only got it long enough to show you. If you don't want to buy it, I'll have to send it back."

"It'll be too much," said Simon, regretfully. "I could never afford a pearl like that."

"I'm not so sure," responded Lorna. "It depends how badly you want it and how much you're prepared to pay."

"I do want it. It's fabulous."

"So, how much money have you got?"

"Er..." Simon hesitated and looked at the door of Lorna's office. Through the frosted glass he could see her assistants and at least one customer.

"Don't worry. It's soundproof," Lorna reassured him.

"Well, in total, in the banks, about..." he named a figure that would stagger most of us. "But surely that won't be enough."

"No, but haven't you got some investments?"

"Yes, I checked them this morning and they're worth about..." he named another, larger, figure.

"Then there's your pearl collection," said Lorna. "If you had this one Pearl, it would be better than all the others put together."

"You know as well as I do how much my collection's worth," said Simon. "But is it enough?"

Lorna got out a calculator and tapped in the figures that Simon had given her.

"Let's see," she said thoughtfully. "It's not nearly enough yet, Simon. We're talking big money for this Pearl. How much is your house worth?"

"My house? The one next door sold for..." again Simon named a very large figure, "a few months ago."

"That's better," said Lorna, tapping away at the calculator, "but you'll still need to find more."

Found in Translation

Simon was beginning to feel excited. His mouth was dry and his heart was beating faster. Was it really possible that he could become the owner of this Pearl?

"I've got a car. In fact I've got two cars." Simon swallowed uncomfortably. What would his wife say when she found out he had sold *her* car, as well as his own, for the sake of this Pearl?

"Hmm. We'll have to allow for depreciation," said Lorna. She looked at the total on her calculator. "It's still not enough."

"If you've got my house, how about all the furniture?" It was 'in for a penny, in for a pound' now for Simon.

Lorna tapped away at the calculator keys. "Yes, that's better. But I still need more."

"Wait a minute!" Simon's reason returned to him. He suddenly realised the danger he was in - of being completely swept away by his desire for this Pearl. "If I sell you my house and furniture, where will I live? What will happen to my wife and children?"

"Your family?" said Lorna, "Don't worry. I'll take them off your hands. You know," she added thoughtfully, "the one thing that the modern businesswoman needs is a wife. I'll give you a good price for yours. When I'm in the shop all day and working on the accounts in the evening, it's so difficult to keep up with the shopping, the cooking and the cleaning." She bent over the calculator again. "It's looking good, Simon, but not quite enough. Have you got anything else to offer?"

"You've got my money, my house, my cars, my family, everything. All I've got left is the clothes I stand up in," said Simon.

"Your clothes..." Lorna looked him over carefully. "Hmm. That's a *very nice* suit you're wearing – and I like the tie – and the shoes." She tapped at the number keys on the calculator

The Pearl

and then pressed the '=' key. "Yes, I think that's just about it. Do you still want the pearl?"

"Yes – yes, I really do," said Simon, with a final rush of – was it madness? Or was it really sane to want such a perfect, precious Pearl?

Lorna picked up the Pearl in its box.

"Here it is then," she passed it over the desk to Simon. Simon's hands were trembling as he carefully, still not quite believing what was happening, took the Pearl.

There was a pause, then Lorna added, "And you can keep everything else as well."

Simon could not believe what he had just heard. "I can?"

"Yes," said Lorna. "But just remember," she added firmly, "it all belongs to me. If I need any ready cash, I'll come to you; if I need a car, I use yours; if I have friends coming to stay, I put them up at your house. Remember, everything that's *yours* belongs to *me*."

Found in Translation

The Coin

Mark 12:13-17
What did the Disciples think when Jesus was challenged about paying taxes to Caesar?

Jesus was standing in Solomon's Portico; we twelve were grouped loosely behind and around him, while a crowd had gathered in front, listening as Jesus spoke about the Kingdom of God. A group of Pharisees pushed their way through to the front of the crowd. Pharisees are greatly respected by most Jews, so people in the crowd politely made way until the Pharisees were standing right in front of Jesus. Then the crowd closed in behind them and I noticed one of them look round anxiously as if he were thinking that it had been very easy getting in but getting out might be more difficult. However, the crowd were in a good mood. They had been listening respectfully to Jesus and now they could look forward to a lively and perhaps cutting debate between him and the Pharisees. There was a definite sense of excitement.

The oldest of the Pharisees began. "Teacher, we know you are a man of integrity. You aren't swayed by men, because you pay no attention to who they are, but you teach the way of God in accordance with the truth."

"Never trust a man who starts with flattery," murmured Matthew in my ear.

"I wonder what they've cooked up this time," I whispered back, and I heard Simon, who was standing on the other side of Jesus to myself, give a snort of contempt.

I glanced at Jesus and saw him incline his head forward slightly, acknowledging the Pharisee's compliment. I could only see his profile but he looked quite relaxed. I thought there

19

was even a hint of a smile at the corner of his mouth, as if he welcomed the Pharisees' interruption and question.

"Is it right," went on the Pharisee, "for we Jews to pay taxes to Caesar or not? Should we pay or shouldn't we?" He stopped, and there was definitely a smile on his face, as if he was sure he had handed Jesus an impossible question.

I thought so too and gave a silent whistle of concern. I could hear a few sharp intakes of breath from my companions. There were murmurs from people in the crowd and some of them sounded angry. I scanned their faces anxiously. The mood had changed. You could see frowns on their faces and some were looking grim. You could *feel* the tension in the air.

Of course, the Pharisees didn't really want an answer to the question. They thought they had handed Jesus a dilemma: reply 'No' and be reported to the Roman governor for sedition, or reply 'Yes' and risk having the crowd turn against him.

Jesus did not seem to be unsettled. "Why are you trying to trap me?" he said. Whatever the outcome, he wanted it to be clear to everyone that this *was* a trap, not an honest enquiry.

"Show me a coin used for paying the tax," continued Jesus, "and let me look at it."

This unsettled the Pharisees. They clearly hadn't anticipated this response. They looked at each other and debated hurriedly in whispers. At last one of them produced a small leather purse, untied the thong that secured it and fumbled around inside. He pulled out a coin, a denarius, and held it up to Jesus.

A denarius is a Roman, not a Jewish, coin. It is quite small but made of pure silver and therefore fairly heavy for its size. On one side it has the bust of the Emperor Tiberius in profile and, on the reverse, the image of some goddess or other. That makes it a dangerous coin for a Jew to handle, especially in the Temple, for the Second Commandment forbids us from

The Coin

making any idol or graven image, so this coin breaks that commandment.

The inscriptions on the coin are just as bad as the images. On one side it claims that the Emperor is the 'Highest Priest'. We Jews could never accept that a Roman could be a higher priest than the High Priest of the Jerusalem Temple. Even worse, the coin proclaims that Tiberius Caesar is the son of the 'deified' Augustus Caesar. For the Romans to claim that a man, even an Emperor, can turn into a god is the worst kind of blasphemy.

So it is not surprising that Jesus did not take the denarius that the Pharisee was offering him. There was a murmur of anger from the crowd. Several people spat on the ground and others shook their fists. The tension was rising higher. The Pharisee who was holding the coin looked round anxiously.

Jesus was the most relaxed person there.

"Whose portrait is this on the coin?" he asked innocently, "and whose inscription?"

There was a pause before any of the Pharisees replied. What sort of question was this? Everyone knew what was on the coin. Was Jesus pretending to be an ignorant peasant from Galilee who had never seen a Roman coin?

At last one of the Pharisees spoke the obvious reply: "Caesar's."

The tension went up again. I looked around me and saw that my brother Simon was standing squarely beside Jesus, to his right with his arms folded, looking, as Jesus had nicknamed him, like Peter - a rock. James and John were standing alongside Simon. To my left were the other Simon, and Bartholomew, both of them tough-looking men, ready to protect Jesus. Even Matthew, who certainly wasn't a fighting man, stood in line with the others.

The crowd was in an ugly mood by now – at least, most of them were. However, I could see people at the back starting to slip away before the real trouble began. And there were people at the front who looked as though they wanted to slip away, if only they hadn't been hemmed in by those behind. If Jesus did say 'Yes' to paying taxes to Caesar, the crowd really would riot. And if he said 'No', that would calm the present situation but the Pharisees could report him to the Romans.

Jesus still looked to be the most relaxed person there. "We-e-e-ll," he said slowly, "If this coin is Caesar's, and he wants it back, then why not give it to him?"

There was a moment of dead silence, as everyone took in what Jesus had said. Then you could *feel* the tension oozing away. Most of the crowd were smiling. There was a burst of laughter. I laughed myself with relief and around me the other disciples were relaxing and smiling. As for the Pharisees, I have never seen a group of dignified, pompous men look more foolish. There was fresh laughter as people saw their expressions: puzzled, shocked, astonished.

Jesus spoke again, "And give God what he wants as well."

Jesus raised his voice so the whole crowd could hear him clearly, "Hear, O Israel! Give to God what belongs to God."

Well, that was the end of the excitement for the moment. The Pharisees turned and made their way out of the crowd, to a few jeers and catcalls. The crowd started to break up and disperse, some talking excitedly, some looking thoughtful. Jesus stood and watched them go. And we disciples stood wondering, when *would* Jesus bring in the Kingdom of God?

Contact

> *The word "Samaritan" has changed its meaning since Jesus first told his parable. Samaritans and the Jews, to whom Jesus was speaking, hated each other's guts. So how would Jesus have told his parable today? Perhaps something like this...*

Monday 7 June 1982, Mount Vernet, Falkland Islands

We'd been on the Falkland Islands for two weeks, and we were soaking wet and freezing cold. There had been showers of snow, and the wind-chill factor was up to minus 20 degrees. We'd spent five days moving up from Port San Carlos to Mounts Vernet and Estancia. You will probably have heard from the media that we 'yomped' the sixty or so miles across the Falklands, but that isn't quite true. The Marines had 'yomped', 45 Commando, Royal marines. We, 3 Para (Third battalion, the Parachute Regiment) had 'tabbed'. And, naturally, we'd beaten the marines and been the first battalion to get into position for the assault on the capital, Stanley. But we don't speak to marines, and they don't speak to us.

I couldn't believe that two months ago we'd been in barracks at Tidworth and *hoping* that we would be sent to the Falklands to deal with the Argentine invaders.

We'd spent a few days on Mounts Vernet and Estancia, digging-in and mounting patrols south and east, towards Mount Longdon and Wireless Ridge. One morning Major Dawlish, OC of our company, called my platoon together.

"We've been given a task," he said. "About ten miles north of here is an isolated house. It's called Low Malo House. One of the SBS patrols has spotted a force of Argies occupying this house. They've counted twelve men. They're close to our rear area, and if they patrol vigorously, they could do a lot of damage, and they can certainly recce our positions. I've picked your platoon to go and clean them out."

"Thanks a bunch," was my thought.

We packed up our bergens and left them at company HQ, then set off northwards in single file, with Lieutenant Haldane leading the way and Sergeant Watson bringing up the rear. Even without our bergens we were heavily loaded. Our webbing equipment, stuffed with ammunition, food and water bottle, weighed over forty pounds. Add to that our personal weapons: the SLR with a twenty-round magazine weighed in at eleven pounds, and a bandolier with 200 rounds of ammunition for the section's GPMG was twelve pounds. I felt sorry for the lads carrying the GPMGs which weighed twenty-four pounds.

The going was typical Falkland Islands: gentle hills up and down, knee deep streams, boggy marshland, long tufts of grass that collapse when you put your weight on them, doing their best to break your ankle. Occasionally we had to cross ridges of stone; large rocks and boulders spread from west to east, right across our route, so there was no going round them. And all the time, wind and rain; that cold, wet Falkland Islands' 'wind and rain' that finds its way through and under and inside anything and everything that you're wearing.

Eventually we came in sight of a group of buildings. Lieutenant Haldane ordered us to deploy with two sections forward, in line, and the third following in reserve. We reached a rocky ridge and knelt there, taking what cover we could, while the lieutenant studied the buildings through his binoculars. There was one large building that was obviously the house, with a door and several windows. To the right of this was a second large building, windowless, that looked more like a barn. There was a small shed to the left that, even without binoculars, looked like a ruin. It was leaning drunkenly to one side, as if about to fall down. We were about six hundred metres from the buildings.

Suddenly two figures came out of the door of the house, walked across to the barn and disappeared. Presumably there was a door that we couldn't see from our position.

"Definitely Argies," said Lieutenant Haldane.

The ground was flat and open. There was no dead ground, no way to make a covered approach to the house. But there was rising ground to our right and Lieutenant Haldane now ordered our number three section to swing out to the right and take up a position looking down on the buildings. We waited until they were in position and then the lieutenant ordered us forward again, the sections moving by bounds, one section advancing while the other section took up firing positions.

In this way we got to within three hundred metres of the house without any sign that the Argies had seen us. I checked the sights on my SLR and made sure they were set to three hundred metres. The lieutenant moved the number two section further to the left and then told our section, number one, to continue to advance. Corporal Woods stood up and walked forward, so we stood up and walked with him, eight men in a ragged line abreast. It came into my mind that we were doing exactly what our grandfathers had done at the Somme in 1916: walking forward in line straight towards an enemy armed with machine-guns – and we know what happened to them. To say that I was scared would be a gross understatement. The army has an expression for how I felt that I couldn't put into print. I could feel my heart pounding away in my chest. Everything seemed to be happening more slowly than usual. That was the adrenaline starting to kick-in.

Was Corporal Woods planning to just walk up to the door of the house? I couldn't believe he would do that. If the Argies were half-trained soldiers they would be waiting now behind those blank windows with their weapons cocked. Their officer or non-com would have allocated each of them a specific target, so they could take the whole section down with one burst. It wasn't very comfortable to think that there might be an Argentine rifle aimed at my chest right now. The fact that we had one section behind us to our left and another on the slope to our right ready to give covering fire was no comfort. By the time they opened fire we would all be dead.

At two hundred metres Corporal Woods halted us and we knelt down, covering the house with our SLRs, while the GPMG team set up their weapon on the right of our line. Corporal Woods signalled us to spread out more and, as I was on the extreme left, I found myself opposite the shed that was falling down. Perhaps when the firing started I could sprint up to that building and take cover behind it. I could now see the end wall of the house. It had one window, so I covered that with my SLR.

There was still no sign of the Argies. Were they so bad at soldiering that they hadn't seen us coming? Were they really going to let us walk up to their front door and take them prisoner?

Then the door of the house opened and two Argies came out. They had simply walked out casually, and you could see them halt in surprise. They stood still, trying to understand the scene in front of them. At last they realised that the line of camouflaged figures in front of them were British soldiers. One of them let out a warning shout; they both turned back towards the door. Corporal Woods shouted, "Open fire!" and we did.

One of the Argies fell; the other made it back through the door. I fired two rounds at the window I was covering and saw the glass shatter. Then our covering sections joined in with bursts of GPMG fire. I fired more shots through the window. It seemed an age before the Argies started to return fire, but then I heard rounds passing near me – they make a nasty *zipping* sound. Vaguely, from a long way away, I heard Corporal Woods shouting, "Rob, lie down!" but I didn't take in that he was shouting to me.

All at once another Argie ran out of the door and knelt beside the fallen man. I looked at him closely and could just make out a red cross on the front of his helmet. A medic; I hoped no-one would shoot him. Indeed, the firing did seem to die down. Two more Argies came out and they began to drag the wounded man inside.

The firing became more intense. I suddenly realised that rounds were being aimed at me. I could hear them zipping past quite close. They were coming from the falling down shed! There must have been at least one Argie inside and he had now woken up and joined the fire-fight. I heard a long burst from one of our GPMGs and saw splinters fly from the shed. Then something hit my leg with a blow like a sledge-hammer.

Without quite knowing how I got there, I realised I was lying on my back. My left leg was aching. I tried to sit up, and that brought a sharp jab of pain from my leg, so I flopped back down again. "So this is what it's like to be wounded," I thought.

There were still rounds zipping overhead and I could hear someone shouting, "Rob! Rob!" I waved a hand in reply; somehow I didn't want to shout back.

"I'll just lie here quietly until someone comes to sort me out," I thought.

Then I heard someone running. His boots squelched on the wet Falklands Island grass. He dropped down beside me. I looked up to see which of my mates had come to help me and all I saw was a round helmet with a big red cross on a dirty white background. It wasn't one of my mates; it was the Argie medic.

He said something in Spanish which meant nothing to me, then got into a kneeling position and started pulling at my leg.

Found in Translation

I gritted my teeth as the pain came again. I could feel him put a field dressing on my leg and bandage it tightly. The fire fight was still going on around us, and people were shouting in both English and Spanish, but it all seemed a long way away and not very important.

The Argie medic lay down beside me. I could just see his grinning face. Then there were more stabs of pain from my leg, and I couldn't stop myself groaning. The medic said something I couldn't understand. I shook my head and he spoke again. This time I caught the word 'morphine'. Of course! Why hadn't I thought of that? We all carried a syrette of morphine taped to the cord of our dog tags. I put my hand up to the neck of my smock and pulled on the cord. The medic understood and pulled out my tags and the syrette of morphine. His face disappeared out of view, but I soon felt it as he jabbed the syrette into my right leg. Not that it made any immediate difference. We had been told that it might be half-an-hour before the morphine took effect.

The medic's face appeared over me again. He pulled me into a sitting position and then, by a combination of unintelligible Spanish, gestures and heaving on his part, got me standing on my right leg. He pulled one of my arms over his shoulder and tried to walk me. It was no good. As soon as I put any weight on my left leg, pain shot through it and the leg collapsed. I was down on my knees. The medic bent and, before I realised what he was doing, he had hoisted me onto his shoulders in a fireman's lift. Then he began to walk.

Every step sent a jab of pain through my leg. In between I thought, "This is great. Not only have I been wounded but now I'm being captured."

The medic halted and let me slide off his shoulders, and once again I flopped onto my back. I saw his face again and his grin and a "thumbs up" signal. I managed to give him the thumbs up and then he disappeared. In his place Sergeant Watson's face loomed over me.

"You *** fool," he said, "Why didn't you lie down when Corporal Woods told you to?"

"Thanks, Sergeant," I thought. "Nice to see you too."

"What happened to the Argie medic?" I said out loud.

"He's running back to the house," said the Sergeant.

"Don't shoot him," I said, for intense firing was still going on.

"Don't worry. The lads are being careful."

How long I lay there I'm not sure, but the morphine began to dull the pain in my leg, and I started to feel cold lying still on the wet ground. At last I heard someone shout, "The Argies are pulling back!" and then Lieutenant Haldane, "Let them go. Cease fire!"

Presently Lieutenant Haldane himself came over to look at me.

"I've called for a med-evac helicopter," he said, "It should be here in about half-an-hour." He knelt beside me, "We should really have shot the Argies to pieces as they retreated, but after what that medic did for you, it didn't seem right, somehow."

Found in Translation

The Donkey

What happened between Mark 11:3 and Mark 11:4? Perhaps something like this...

"What I don't understand, Bart," said Phil, "is, why?"

"Why what, Phil?" I said.

Phil and I were near Bethany. We had come with Jesus and the other ten disciples from Galilee to Judea in order to keep the Passover in Jerusalem, as all good Jews are supposed to do, if they possibly can.

"All these weeks we've been walking everywhere. We've walked all over the country, into every village in Galilee…"

"I know. I've cut a notch in my staff for every village we've been into."

I held up the staff to show Phil. I'd cut so many notches in it that it was uncomfortable to grip firmly, so it wasn't much help for walking any more.

"But," said Phil, impatiently, "everywhere we've been, we've *walked*. Why does he suddenly decide he needs transport?"

I had to think about that for a few moments. At last I said, "It'll be in fulfilment of another prophecy, you'll see."

"You mean Jesus will be setting out to fulfil a prophecy deliberately?" There was doubt as well as questioning in Phil's tone.

"That's what I *think*, Phil."

"Won't that sound like a put-up job?" said Phil, even more doubtfully. "I always thought that the prophecies would be fulfilled sort of naturally, as if they just happened. Doesn't it seem a bit hypocritical if Jesus sets out to do what the prophecies say? Sort of play-acting?"

I had to ponder that one for quite a while.

"Well, Phil," I replied at last, "perhaps it does, this time; but he couldn't set out to fulfil *all* the prophecies, could he? I mean, he couldn't set out to be born where the prophets said he would be born, could he now?"

Phil looked puzzled. "Just run that one by me again, Bart," he said.

"One of the prophets said that the Messiah would be born in Bethlehem." I paused, remembering the Scripture lessons we'd had as children, years ago. "*You, O Bethlehem, in the land of Judah,*" I recited in a loud, clear voice, as we'd been taught in the synagogue. "*You, O Bethlehem, out of you will come a ruler, who will be the shepherd of my people Israel.* Right?"

I was glad to see that Phil was impressed. "That's good, Bart. Who said that?"

"I just did, Phil."

"No!" said Phil, tetchily. "I mean, which *prophet*?"

"Oh. Micah, I think. Anyway, the point is, no one could *arrange* to be born in a certain town, could they?"

Phil had been frowning, but now he brightened up. "I see what you're getting at. No one could; but *God* could arrange it for them."

"Exactly," I said. "Here's another one. The prophet Isaiah said, '*He took up our illnesses and carried our diseases.*'"

"Right?" Phil looked puzzled again.

"Don't you get it? That's a prophecy about healing, and Jesus has healed dozens of people. But a man can't just set himself up as a healer; he needs the power to do it – and the power has to come from God."

"Of course!" said Phil, smiling again as the light dawned.

I was beginning to feel that I was on a roll. "In another place, Isaiah says, '*The Spirit of the Lord is on me, because he has anointed me to preach good news to the poor. He has sent me to proclaim freedom for the captives and recovery of sight for the blind.*'"

The Donkey

"So Jesus healing people is proof that he is the Messiah – the Anointed One," said Phil. "But, Bart, that still doesn't explain why he suddenly wants transport."

"It'll be another prophecy, if we could only remember which one." I started to rack my brains. "He's going into Jerusalem" (thinking aloud) "and the Messiah is also the King. A King ought to ride into his capital city."

"But not on a donkey! That's stupid. A king ought to ride on a horse, a warhorse - an Arab stallion at least."

Suddenly inspiration came. "Wait a minute. I've got it! The prophet Zechariah."

"What about him?"

"He wrote, '*Rejoice, Jerusalem. Your king is coming to you, gentle and riding on a donkey.*' He meant that the Messiah would be a king of peace, not of war."

"So you think," said Phil, "that Jesus is going to ride a donkey to show that he really is a man of peace and he's not going to start a war against the Romans."

I grabbed Phil's arm. I had just seen something. We had reached the outskirts of Bethany, and there it was, tethered to a post at the door of the first house: a donkey, ready for us, just as Jesus said it would be.

"There it is!" I exclaimed.

"Let's go and collect it," said Phil. Then he added, with increasing excitement, "This is going to be good. The people all love Jesus and there's crowds going to Jerusalem for the Passover. He'll ride into the city and they'll all be cheering him and waving and we'll be there with him and we'll have him installed in the Temple as Messiah and…"

"Wait a minute!" A serious thought had just struck me.

"What?"

"All these prophecies are coming true," I said, "about Jesus' birthplace and about him healing and about riding on a donkey into Jerusalem – but remember that Jesus told us he was going to Jerusalem to die there. Is that prophecy going to come true as well?"

The Test

Matthew 4:1-11, Luke 4:1-13

"Who are you?"

The young man looked round from the flat rock on which he was seated. A second man was standing a few paces away. Silhouetted against the light of the sky, it was hard to make out any details. The second man was little more than a dark shadow.

"Well? Who are you?" the man repeated.

"That's what I came here to find out," replied the young man.

"Many come here to find out who they are," said the other man. "They do not always like what they find."

The young man looked around him. They were on a bare, rocky hilltop. The sun was close to the zenith and the day was hot. The rock on which he was seated was hot to the touch. The sky was a hard, bright blue. The horizon was a vague, blurred line, shimmering in the heat haze.

"This is a good place to think things out," said the young man.

"Oh yes," said the other, "a lonely place, a quiet place, a high place, a place where a man might hear the voice of God. No one to disturb your thoughts."

"Until you came along."

"Until I came along. I can help you put your thoughts in order."

"Can you?" asked the young man.

"Of course," said the other. "I can ask you the hard questions. Like, why don't you stay at home and work your father's land?"

"My father is dead, and he had no land."

"So... how do you make your living?"

"I work with my hands."

"What could be better than that?"

"I feel there is more that I should be doing," said the young man.

"Many think that. Most achieve nothing."

"What is it to you what I do with my life?"

"I hate to see a young man throwing his life away."

There was a short pause.

"You're not a priest or a Levite," continued the other, "unless your father was; and then your course would be set. Perhaps you see yourself as a prophet?"

"Perhaps."

"*Perhaps...*" said the other scornfully. "You must be *sure* before you set yourself up as a prophet." He pointed with his staff to a round, flattish stone. "Turn this stone into bread. That is what Elijah would have done; or Elisha."

The young man looked down at the stone for a long time. He suddenly realised that he was hungry. He was used to fasting, of course; that was a normal part of worship and prayer. But he had never fasted for so long at one stretch. Now that the other man had drawn his attention to it, he realised that he had never felt so hungry in his life. Never had he felt the pain of hunger before, never such a longing. He could imagine giving the command. He knew it would work. He could *see* the stone turning into bread - a new round loaf, fresh out of the oven. He could *smell* it; and in his hunger it seemed the most delicious fragrance he had ever smelt...

Words came into his head. He had often heard them read on the Sabbath. He had read them himself more than once. He could *see* the scroll on the lectern, unrolled at the very place.

"It is written, '*Man does not live on bread alone, but on every word that God speaks.*'"

The Test

"Good Scripture," said the other. "A prophet needs to know the Scriptures. So, what is your prophetic message?"

"I will tell people about the Kingdom of God."

The young man thought that the other shook his head, but it was hard to tell, for he was still little more than a shadow against the sky.

"Where will that get you? People will listen, certainly, but they will do nothing. You have to lead them; or drive them."

"I do not want to drive people."

"Well then," said the other, "You will have to find a way of leading people. Give them a demonstration that will show them that God is with you." He turned and pointed across the barren hills. "On the horizon, you can just make out the city and the Temple. You can see the gold shining in the sun."

The young man looked. It was just possible to make out, on the horizon, a whiter, squarer shape than the curving hills, and something was certainly shining in the sunlight.

"If you were to go to the highest place on the Temple walls and throw yourself down into the courtyard, God would make sure that you landed safely, and people would see that He was with you. They would follow you then."

The young man thought. He had been to the Temple at least once a year since he was twelve as every boy and man did. He knew the buildings, the courtyards, the stairways, the high walls and colonnades, the crowds of worshippers, the smell of wood smoke and roasting meat of the sacrifices. He could see himself, standing there among the crowds. He could look up and see, over the roof of the colonnade, the corner where two of the high walls came together. A man could stand up there and look down into the courts at the crowds. Behind him would be the much greater drop into the Kidron valley. Almost he felt giddy with the thought of being there. He could stand looking down on the heads of the people. At first no-one would notice. Then one or two heads would turn. People would point and shout; everyone would look up. He could launch himself into space and float gently down; or perhaps he would fall like a stone until the very last moment when he would land safely. There would be gasps of fear as he jumped, then gasps of wonder as he landed. People would gather round and push and shove to get near enough to see, to touch. They would want to touch him and yet be afraid to do so. Some, he was sure, would kneel at his feet. They would clamour for him to bless them. Others who hadn't seen properly would ask him to do it again...

"They would only follow me to see more wonders. It would make no change to what was in their hearts."

"But it would give you an opening, make them pay attention to what you tell them."

"No," said the young man. "I would have to go on performing wonder after wonder to keep their interest. I don't think that's the way to lead people."

"You can't know until you try it out. But perhaps you are afraid to make the attempt. You don't need to worry. It is written, *'He will command his angels and they will hold you in their hands, and guard you in all your ways.'*"

That was from the Psalms. In his mind he could see the words on the scroll. But then the scroll in his mind turned backwards. There were fresh words on the page; fresh but very familiar.

"It would be putting God on trial. And it is written, *'Do not put the Lord your God to the test.'*"

"Perhaps you are right. We can go on quoting Scripture and counter-Scripture but it will not get you very far with your 'Kingdom of God'." The other man flung out an arm in a grand gesture. "Over there is the Roman Empire: Asia, Greece, Italy, Spain, Gaul and more besides. Up there" (he swung his arm round) "are the great plains where the nomads live with their horses and their petty kings. Then that way lies

The Test

the kingdom of Parthia, then India and, beyond the mountains, peoples of which you know nothing. Down there" (he pointed in the direction of the sun) "is Egypt, a much older civilization than yours, and beyond, the desert, the plains and the forests, with kingdoms that rise and fall within a man's lifetime." He turned back to the young man. "I can give you all this, all authority over these lands, for it is mine to give, and you can turn all these kingdoms into your 'Kingdom of God'."

New pictures came into his mind: fields with men ploughing and reaping; shepherds and herdsmen; men gathering olives and grapes and making wine; rivers with cargo ships and the boats of fishermen; mines of silver and gold and precious stone; cities filled with men buying and selling; potters and metalworkers, stonemasons and woodworkers, weavers and dyers; temples with statues of strange gods and goddesses; marching armies, weapons gleaming in the sun, their standards lifted high at the heads of their columns. He could see himself marching out, leading his armies to conquest, establishing the Kingdom of God; marching, marching, marching to – who knows where?

"What must I do for you to give me these kingdoms?"

"The merest trifle. Just kneel down and pledge your loyalty to me, and it will all be yours."

There was a long silence. It would be so easy, a mere gesture, a symbol, to kneel and make a promise. It wouldn't be a promise that anyone could be expected to keep...

But there was the scroll in his mind and the words standing out black and clear.

"It is written," said the young man at last, "*'Worship the lord your God and serve only him.'*"

The other hissed with frustration. The young man looked around the horizon again.

"I think you should go now," he said.

Found in Translation

The Young Man looked back at the Other, but the place where he had been standing was empty.

The Broken Leg

John 7:53-8:11
A modern woman caught in adultery

I moved into sheltered accommodation about six months ago. It's a very well designed, modern building. Each resident has their own one-bedroom flat, with sitting-room, kitchen and bathroom, and there are communal rooms as well: sitting room, TV room, function room with its own kitchen, even a small library and a games room with chess, draughts and a pool table. Mind you, a lot of the residents just stay in their rooms and don't want to socialise, even though Janet (our Warden) is very good at arranging events.

One evening as I walked down to the common rooms I heard the sound of the piano being played in the function room. I'm no musician but I knew it was being well played - a hymn tune, which surprised me. I looked through the doorway. The piano is an upright one that was donated to the complex, I believe, and at first the pianist was hidden from me. I went closer and saw that the piano was being played by a man whom I did not know. He looked up as I approached and went on playing, changing to a new tune. I could see that he was playing without music and without looking at the keys. There was a quiet smile on his face. He came to the end of the tune and stopped.

I gave a little clap. "That was very good."

"It's a good piano," he replied modestly.

"*When I survey*, wasn't it? And the second one was a hymn tune as well?"

He nodded. "*Crimond*. The twenty-third Psalm. I used to be church organist - St Joseph's Church, in Northborough. Now I've had to move in here."

"It's not so bad," I said, "for sheltered accommodation. My name's Avery, William Avery."

I held out my hand and he took it. A strong handshake, but I noticed that his fingers were long and slender.

"You have the hands of a pianist," I said.

He gave a slightly embarrassed laugh. "Do you judge everybody by their handshake?"

"I was a nurse before I retired" I said by way of explanation. "You get used to noticing that sort of thing."

"I used to teach. My name's Lennox."

"There's a local church here that sometimes arranges services for us. I'm sure they could use a piano player – they can't always get one during the day."

He shook his head. "Not any more. My church playing days are over."

"I'm sorry to hear that. How come?" I asked.

"I just used to swallow everything the Vicar said and everything in the Bible. Then I started reading and thinking for myself."

"Reading?"

"Come up to my flat and I'll show you."

We went up in the lift together to the second floor. His sitting-room was neatly furnished and perfectly clean. There was a large bookcase, reaching to the ceiling, which took up half of one wall and was full to over-flowing. That surprised me; none of the residents that I knew (not that I had been in many rooms) had that many books. I could see that there was a whole shelf of books of music and there were quite a few paperback novels. But there were others: history books and travel books and others I couldn't identify without examining more closely.

Lennox pulled out a thick paperback from one of the middle shelves. I recognised it at once - a book by a well-known scientist, arguing the case for atheism.

The Broken Leg

"See what this chap says about the Bible," he said, offering me the book.

"I have read it," I replied, "and most of what he says about the gospels is half-truth and half-baked. He just didn't do his homework before sitting down to write."

"How do you mean?" asked Lennox, with a frown.

"Well, he says the gospels were copied over and over and this had a 'Chinese Whispers' effect on them. So we can't know what the original authors wrote. But there are so many manuscripts of the gospels, written over hundreds of years, that we know that there was no Chinese Whispers effect."

"What about before they were first written down? They must have been passed on by word of mouth, so they could have been changed then."

"The whole point of the Chinese Whispers game," I pointed out, "is to *whisper* the message and not repeat it and not let the listener ask questions. So naturally the message gets distorted. But when people were telling stories about Jesus they were trying to make sure their hearers *got* the message right."

"Hmm." Lennox looked thoughtful for a moment. Then he brought another book from his shelves.

"What about this one? The author's a professor of religious studies. You can't say *he* hasn't done his homework."

"Well?" I said cautiously, although I guessed what he was about to say next.

"He says that the ending to Mark's gospel isn't original." Lennox was flipping through the pages as he spoke and now handed me the book with his slender forefinger pointing at a particular paragraph. "He says that Mark originally stopped at verse 8 of chapter 16 and that the last twelve verses were added later."

"Yes," I agreed, "that's perfectly true, but it's not a new fact. It's been known for, oh, I don't know, a hundred and fifty years, maybe. I've got a copy of the Revised Standard Version of the Bible – it was published in 1952, I think – and that ends Mark at verse 8, and adds the other verses as a footnote."

Lennox frowned. "Well, why isn't that better known?" he said.

I shrugged. "I suppose people don't bother to find out about that sort of thing. But it's in all modern translations of the Bible. I've known about it since I was in my twenties. And that author ought to have known as well; he's about ten years younger than me."

"Still, somebody made up that ending to Mark."

"It depends what you mean by 'made up'. Nearly all of it comes from the other gospels and from Acts."

Lennox looked as if he was not convinced. He held out the book again. "So what about the woman taken in adultery? He says that's not original either."

"No, it isn't," I agreed, "but that's not news either. It's obviously a well-known story about Jesus that didn't make it into any of the gospels, so some scribe decided to add it in. In fact, it was added more than once – to Luke's gospel and to the end of John – as well as the middle of John."

Lennox was looking carefully down at the pages of his book. "What about these questions he raises? What happened to the man who was with her? He should have been stoned as well. What did Jesus write on the ground? Why did Jesus just let the woman go? Surely she ought to have been punished in some way?"

I took a deep breath, for I was feeling pretty anxious and sweaty under the armpits. This was the first time I'd really talked, face to face, with anyone about these issues, and I wondered how Lennox would react if I told him...

"I can't answer all your questions," I said carefully, "but can I tell you a story of my own?"

The Broken Leg

Lennox looked up at me. I wasn't sure from his expression if he was interested or not, but he said, "Go ahead. Maybe we should sit down."

I sat down, gratefully, into a very comfortable armchair. Lennox sat in its twin a few feet away and looked at me expectantly.

"A long time ago," I began, "I was a student nurse in my second year of training and I was sent to Casualty for eight weeks' experience. We still called it 'Casualty' in those days; there was none of this 'Accident and Emergency' business. I was very anxious on my first morning, not knowing what to expect, and I was very surprised to get there and find no casualties, no patients at all.

"Anyway, one of the Staff Nurses began to show me around and explain what my duties would be. Suddenly an ambulance arrived with a *real* casualty! I couldn't do anything, of course, just hover around and observe while the staff went to work.

"The ambulance crew brought in a young woman; I suppose she was about thirty and she had on a skimpy, purplish nightie. She had a broken leg, and it was about the nastiest break I've ever seen. Below the knee her leg was bent – well, perhaps I'd better not go into all the details. The doctors and nurses got to work and I watched while they sorted her out. The ambulance crew told us what had happened. She had been in bed with someone who wasn't her husband. Her husband came home unexpectedly. She panicked and jumped out of the first-floor window and landed on the concrete path. Anyway, she was seen by the orthopaedic surgeon and transferred up to theatre. That was all I saw of her."

"I see," Lennox nodded.

"I can't tell you her name. I don't know what happened between her husband and the man she was sleeping with. I don't know what happened between her and her husband. But if you ask me, 'Did Jesus meet a woman caught in adultery?' I can say, 'I've met a woman caught in adultery, and I believe Jesus did too.'"

Teabreak

Luke 24:13-32
If the Resurrection happened today, what would the 'Road to Emmaus' incident be like?

Joan put her head out of the canteen door. "Tea's up!" she called, loud enough to be heard over the hum of machinery. "Come and get it!"

As always, the response was slow as the workers waited for the right moment to stop or switch off the various machines they were operating. Pat was the first to arrive, carrying a folded newspaper under her arm. Then came Ken and, one by one, the other workers straggled in from different parts of the Machine Room of Blake's Systems. Joan busied herself pouring mugs of tea. The staff settled themselves on the not very comfortable chairs scattered around the small canteen. Pat and Ken took two of the bar stools at Joan's tea counter.

"Just the job," said Ken, taking a big swig of tea. "I needed that. Thanks, Joan."

"What's on the news?" Pat pressed the 'On' button of the radio on the counter.

From a local radio studio, not so very far away in the small town, came the voice of the newsreader. "... took five hours to clear the overturned lorry but police report that southbound traffic is now flowing freely again...

"...The mystery deepens surrounding the death of the young preacher who was murdered last week. This morning his grave in the town cemetery was found to be open and the coffin was empty."

"Turn that thing off," said Ken.

"Several followers of the preacher have claimed that they saw him alive in the cemetery," continued the voice of the newsreader.

Ken reached over and pressed the 'Off' button firmly, cutting off the voice in mid-sentence. "Load of nonsense!" said Ken, crossly.

"Why did you do that?" asked Joan. "I think it's very interesting."

"Rubbish!" retorted Ken. "All this talk of a man being murdered and then coming back to life. People seeing ghosts in broad daylight. Load of..." He stopped himself just in time, remembering there were women present and that his favourite expletive would be too fruity. "...rubbish," he finished, lamely.

"It's here in the paper as well," said Pat. She held out the paper to show Ken the front page. "Look, there's even a photo of the empty grave."

Ken almost snorted with disgust. "Anyone can dig up a grave. B***** vandals! The man's dead now. Why can't they leave him in peace?"

Joan took the paper from Pat and studied the front page. "Well, I don't know," she said at last. "Drink up your tea."

A young man in work overalls looked into the canteen. "Is this where we come for our tea break?"

"Yes. Sit yourself down here," said Pat, indicating the third bar stool, which happened to still be empty. The young man seated himself shyly between Pat and Ken.

"Here's a mug of tea - and there's the sugar," said Joan.

"Thank you very much," said the young man. "That's a good cup of tea," he added after taking his first mouthful.

"You're new here, aren't you?" said Joan.

"Yes, just started this morning. Mr Blake's been showing me around."

"You'll soon settle in," said Pat. "It's only a small place. Do you know which machine you'll be working on?"

Teabreak

"Not yet."

"The boss will probably put you on Tom's machine," said Ken. "He left at the end of last week."

"What were you talking about when I came in just now?" asked the young man.

"About this young preacher who was murdered," explained Joan, "and they're saying he's come back to life."

"It's all a big con. You'll see," maintained Ken.

"Well, I think it might be true," said Pat, waving the newspaper under the young man's nose. "Look, this photo shows the grave and the empty coffin in the bottom of it."

"I don't know," repeated Joan. "What do you think?" she asked the young man.

"We-e-l-l," he responded slowly. "I think that if God decides to bring a dead man back to life, why shouldn't He do it?"

Ken gave a snort of disgust.

"But things like that just don't happen," said Joan, firmly. "Do they?" she added, a note of uncertainty coming into her voice.

"You know," said the young man thoughtfully, after taking a drink from his mug of tea, "it says in the Bible that God will not leave the man He has chosen in the grave."

"Does it really?" said Joan

"It also says in the Bible," the man continued, "that God will send a man who will have to die for all the wrong that everyone has done and then God will raise him from the dead."

"Well," said Joan, "I never knew that."

"So do you think that this preacher might have been the man God sent?" asked Pat.

"I'm sure of it," said the young man. He drained his mug. "Thanks for the tea. I must be getting back to work."

Found in Translation

He slid himself off the bar stool, stood up and walked out of the canteen.

Joan, Ken and Pat watched him go. None of them spoke for several seconds. Then Joan pulled herself together. "Right. Come on you lot. Tea-break's over. Back to work."

The other workers began finishing their mugs of tea, standing up and drifting back to their workstations. Ken and Pat went on sitting at the counter.

"Strange bloke that," said Ken thoughtfully. "Who was he anyway?"

"Didn't you hear him say he'd just started today?" said Joan. "I've certainly not seen him before."

"We should have asked him his name," said Ken. "Oh well, we're bound to see him in the Machine Room. There isn't anywhere you can hide in this place."

"What's up, Pat?" said Joan to Pat.

Pat had opened her newspaper and was now staring at one of the inside pages with wide eyes and open mouth.

"Look!" she exclaimed. "There's a photo of him in the paper."

"Photo of who?" said Joan.

"The preacher who was murdered."

"So what?" said Ken.

"Look!" Pat held out the paper so the others could see the page she had been staring at. "Don't you recognise him?"

"He looks familiar," said Joan. "I expect there have been pictures of him in the paper before now."

"It's that man who was sitting here talking to us!" said Pat.

Joan took the paper and studied the photograph carefully. "Why, you're right!" she said. "So he really is alive."

Ken took the paper in turn and looked closely at it. "Well, it looks like him, but I don't..."

"Of course it's him," said Pat. "He really is alive. And he was sitting here drinking tea and talking to us."

Teabreak

Joan took the paper from Ken and headed for the door.

"Where are you going, Joan?" Ken called after her.

"To phone the newspaper, of course," replied Joan over her shoulder. "If a dead man really has come back to life, that's news! Everyone ought to be told about it!"

Found in Translation

In the Hands of the Prophets

Matthew 2:16
Herod tries to prevent a prophecy coming true

"WHAT DO YOU MEAN, THEY'RE NOT COMING BACK?"

Herod sounded furious, and when King Herod was furious the only safe thing to do was to keep quiet and keep out of his way. As his Secretary, of course, I couldn't simply disappear, but I kept my mouth shut and tried to merge into the wall hangings of the throne room.

Nadab, the chief *explorator* (spy or scout), was remarkably calm, considering that his life depended on the whims of an unstable, absolute monarch.

"My agents followed them to Bethlehem, discreetly, as instructed, your Majesty," explained Nadab, calmly. "They didn't go into the town but waited on the outskirts. It would have been impossible for them to stay under cover in such a small place. After two days they became suspicious, so they searched the town anyway. There was no sign of these men who called themselves *Magi*. They must have slipped away to the East or South. One of my agents returned to report to me while the others started to search all the roads out of Bethlehem."

"At least they have that much initiative!" sneered Herod. "Why didn't they watch all the roads from the first?"

Nadab didn't have an answer to that question. Instead he said, "I have sent out the rest of my agents to join in the search."

"Good. Did your spies manage to learn anything about this new king?"

"The inhabitants are reluctant to talk to my agents. They gave evasive answers to their questions. The innkeeper denied that there had been any babies born in his inn. There is a rumour that some shepherds saw a vision of angels telling them that the Christ had been born. One of my agents is questioning all the local shepherds, but they are so scattered over the hills it will take some time to track them all down. There is also a rumour of a baby being born in a stable but I hardly think the Christ..."

"HE IS NOT THE CHRIST! There is only one king of the Jews and that's me. Do you understand? And after me one of MY sons will be king of the Jews – provided Caesar approves."

Nadab fell silent and Herod paced up and down the throne room. His face was pale as well as angry and there was sweat on his brow.

"Go down to Bethlehem," he ordered at last. "Take charge of the search."

"At once, your Majesty." Nadab turned to leave.

"Oh, and Nadab," said Herod.

"Yes, your majesty?"

"If you don't catch those Magi, it would be safer for you not to come back to Jerusalem."

"Of course, your Majesty." Nadab went out.

"SHAMMAI, SHAMMAI!" shouted Herod.

"Here, your majesty," I said, stepping forward nervously.

"Send for that High Priest," ordered Herod, "and my astrologer."

"Yes, your Majesty." I was glad of a reason to hurry out of the room myself. In the anteroom I quickly ordered one messenger to find the court astrologer, another to go to the Jewish temple to summon the High Priest and a third to the house of the High Priest in case he should not be in the temple. Then I went cautiously back into the throne room.

In the Hands of the Prophets

Herod had resumed his pacing but I was relieved to see that he seemed to have calmed down. He looked more worried than angry.

"Shammai," he said, "I'm getting too old for this sort of thing."

"Surely not, your Majesty," I ventured to reply.

"Yes I am," he said. "Do you know how old I am? Sixty years and then some; that's how old I am. This is my thirtieth year as king of Judea."

"It's a great achievement," I said, politely.

"I've got more than enough sons to succeed me as king, if only they weren't so stupid. Surely one of them can persuade the Roman Emperor to confirm him as king. And I don't want some Jewish upstart baby creeping in and stealing the throne from my sons!" Herod had started with a note of bitterness in his voice but the last sentence was spoken in a growing tone of anger.

It was a relief when a steward came quietly into the room and announced the arrival of Jether, the court astrologer. I gestured to him to come in and he did so, bowing deferentially to the king. Clearly, he had been warned that Herod was in a foul temper. However, Herod ignored him and continued pacing up and down.

There was a long silence, during which I moved quietly back against the wall hangings and Jether stood stock-still. Neither of us wanted to disturb Herod as he continued his pacing.

It took some time for the High Priest to arrive. When he did so, he was accompanied by one of his Scribes, the men who were responsible for copying the Jewish holy books and were therefore knowledgeable as to their contents.

"Tell me all about this Jewish *Christ*, this *Messiah*," said Herod, using first the Greek word, then the Jewish.

55

"There is no more to tell except what we told you last time we spoke together. The word *Messiah* means *Anointed One*," explained the High Priest. "Our prophets have foretold that there will come a man who will be King of the Jews, who will be God's Chosen One - hence the term *Anointed* – and who will restore the independence of the Jewish nation. His reign will last forever and will be a reign of peace."

"But *I* am King of the Jews," said Herod, ominously.

"Of course," said the High Priest smoothly. "The prophecies do not say when the Messiah will come."

"And Judea is part of the Roman Empire."

"Of course, your Majesty, but, with all due respect, no earthly empire lasts forever."

"And you can tell your Messiah that a reign of peace is pie in the sky. You can't rule by peace; you can only rule by force and by fear. I should know. I fought for ten years to become king of Judea, and I've held the land by force for thirty years."

"But the Messiah will have God on his side, and it is only by the power of God that we Jews gained this land in the first place."

"Well, where is this Messiah to be born?"

The High Priest looked at his Scribe. "I think that Berekiah, our chief Scribe, is perhaps the best person to answer that question."

"Then let him answer it," growled Herod.

"As we told you before, your Majesty," said Berekiah, "the prophet Micah foretold that the Messiah will be born in Bethlehem. Let me quote." Berekiah closed his eyes and said, in a sing-song voice, *"But you, Bethlehem, though you are small among the clans of Judah, out of you will come for me one who will be ruler over Israel, whose origins are from old, from ancient times."*

"No more than that?" said Herod. "No date, no family name?"

In the Hands of the Prophets

"It is expected that the Messiah will be a descendant of David, our greatest king," said Berekiah. "The prophet Isaiah wrote: *A shoot will come from the stump of Jesse; from his roots a Branch will bear fruit. The Spirit of the Lord will rest upon him.* Jesse was the father of King David, so this is interpreted to mean that David will be an ancestor of the Messiah. Bethlehem is the ancestral home of the family of Jesse and David; many of their descendants still live in Bethlehem, so that is the natural birthplace for the Messiah."

"And that's all you can tell me?" asked Herod.

"There are many other prophecies concerning the Messiah, but that is all the Scriptures tell us about where he will be born," said Berekiah.

Herod turned to Jether and the man gave a sort of shudder. "Now you, court astrologer, you know what those Magi from the East said they had seen in the stars. What do *you* think?"

"I think, your Majesty," stammered Jether, "that, er, they are right in their, ah, observations of the heavens."

"Go on," said Herod.

"In the constellation of *Pisces*, er, that's the Fish, your Majesty, there has, ah, been a conjunction of the planets Jupiter and Saturn. Er, *Pisces* can be interpreted as relating to the Jews," he coughed nervously. "Saturn is the oldest of the gods while Jupiter is the kingly planet. Therefore this conjunction could, ah, be interpreted that God has caused a..." He hesitated and Herod frowned at him. "KingoftheJewstobeborn." He finished with a rush.

"And so the Magi saw this conjunction in the East and came here looking for a king," said Herod, thoughtfully. "Do the stars tell you that this king will be born in Bethlehem?"

"No, your majesty," said Jether, "but... but... from Jerusalem, *Pisces* appears in the southern sky at this time of the year, and Bethlehem is South of Jerusalem."

"So the stars agree with your prophets," said Herod to the High Priest.

"It would appear so; however..."

"However!" snapped Herod. "The key question now is, how do we get rid of this child?" He turned to me. "Call the Captain of my Guard."

I hurried into the anteroom and was pleased to see that the Captain of Herod's Bodyguard was already there. Someone must have had the good sense to alert him.

He came into the throne room and gave Herod a military salute.

"Call out my Idumaean Guard!" said Herod. "Take them to Bethlehem. Blockade the place. No one is to enter or leave until I give permission. *No one*, do you understand?"

"Yes, sir" said the Captain.

"Then take your troops into Bethlehem; search out every male child, from the baby born today up to two years old, *every* male child, and kill them."

I was shocked. The High Priest made a sound as if he had taken a sharp, deep breath. Berekiah started to say something, then turned it into a cough. The Captain was a veteran soldier, as hard a man as you could find in any army in the world, but even he looked shocked. For the first time in his life, perhaps, he questioned an order.

"*Kill* all the male children?"

"You heard the order."

"Your majesty," interrupted the High Priest. "I don't think you quite understand..."

You think *I* don't understand?" said Herod, ominously.

"Perhaps," began Berekiah, "your Majesty has not quite taken in the implications..."

"You think I'm not capable of taking in the political implications of a rival king?"

In the Hands of the Prophets

"What my colleague is trying to convey to your Majesty," said the High Priest, "is that if there is a child, born by the will of God, according to what the prophets have spoken, you will not be able to kill him. You are in danger of setting yourself in opposition to God – a dangerous thing to attempt."

"So I'm in the hands of your Jewish prophets am I? I have to stand by and let this *boy* usurp my throne, do I? Well, I'm not a Jew, am I? I won this throne by fighting for it and I'm going to fight to keep it. Do *you* understand?" Herod turned to the Captain of the Guard. "Captain, carry out your orders."

"Yes, sir!" The Captain saluted smartly once more, turned on his heel and marched out.

The High Priest tried to make one final protest, "Your Majesty..."

"GET OUT!" shouted Herod. "All of you, get out!"

Jether promptly scurried out of the throne room. The High Priest kept his dignity and walked out slowly, with Berekiah following. I stayed where I was, against the wall hangings.

Herod walked to the doorway and shouted into the anteroom.

"I WANT HIM DEAD! KILLED! DO YOU HEAR! THERE IS ONLY ONE KING OF THE JEWS! I AM HEROD. *I* AM KING OF THE JEWS!"

Suddenly Herod turned, walked back to his throne and sat down. He seemed to shrink inside his robes; his shoulders slumped, his head drooped. All the anger, all the energy had drained out of him.

"And I'm scared," he whispered.

59

Found in Translation

Bethlehem Towers

> *Fawlty Towers was a BBC sitcom set in the worst hotel in England, that ran for two seasons in 1975 and 1979. The hotel was run by Basil and Sybil Fawlty (played by John Cleese and Prunella Scales) aided (or hindered) by Spanish waiter Manuel (Leonard Sachs) and waitress Polly (Connie Booth), who was the only sane member of staff. What if the inn at Bethlehem had been like Fawlty Towers? Would it have been something like this...?*

The phone rang at Reception and Sarah picked up the receiver.

"Bethlehem Towers, how can I help you?" she said in a high-pitched, slightly sing-song voice, "... Yes, this is a hotel ... yes, we do have rooms ... No, we can't give you a room for the night ... We have rooms, but they're all occupied. ... You're welcome ... Goodbye."

She put down the phone and turned to the mirror, patted a stray lock of hair into place and examined her make-up closely. Her husband Benjamin came hurrying out of the Dining-Room on his long legs, shouting as he came, "Mattenai! Mattenai!"

There was no answer. Benjamin paced to and fro, muttering complaints about his errant staff. Presently Mattenai came shambling down the stairs with that peculiar round-shouldered gait that made him a butt of ridicule for the guests and source of exasperation for his employers.

"Mattenai!" snapped Benjamin.

"Si?" responded Mattenai, putting his head on one side.

("Why," thought Sarah, "did Ben have to employ a waiter from, where was it, Idumaea, who couldn't even speak good

Aramaic? He was cheap, of course, but this was a Jewish hotel in a Jewish town and their guests expected Jewish staff.")

"Mattenai," said Benjamin, in his usual rapid manner, "have you put clean linen on all the beds, set the dining room for dinner, restocked the bar and swept out the stable?"

Mattenai looked puzzled, as he usually did when Benjamin spoke to him, but he began to check off on his fingers, "Beds, si. Dining room, si. Bar, si. Stable, no."

"Well get on with it!" ordered Benjamin. "We have a lot of guests; the hotel is full tonight. And remember Mattenai, these are all Jews so whatever you do, don't mention the Romans."

The front door of the hotel was pushed open and a young couple made their way cautiously into reception. Benjamin glanced at them and thought of directing them to the tradesmen's entrance at the rear. They were dressed in ordinary working clothes; the man wore jeans and the woman had a denim skirt, and they came in nervously, as if they weren't used to a posh hotel.

"Romans?" said Mattenai, questioningly.

Benjamin turned back to him, "I said, don't mention the Romans!"

"Si, si. No mention the Romans," said Mattenai, hastily.

"Don't even think of..." began Benjamin when he was interrupted by the young man ringing the reception desk bell. "With you in a moment," he said, waving a hand in the couple's direction.

"We'd like a room," said the young man.

"I said I'd be with you in a moment," said Benjamin sharply. "A mo – ment. Which syllable of moment do you not understand?"

"We'd like a room for ..."

"You're not Romans are you?" interrupted Benjamin, "This is a Jewish hotel. We're not going to mention the Romans, are we?"

Bethlehem Towers

"My wife's going to have a baby," explained the young man.

Benjamin looked at the young woman; she was clearly heavily pregnant. "A baby? Well she's not going to have it here," he snapped. "We're not a Maternity Hospital, you know. There's a perfectly good one in Jerusalem."

"We had to come to Bethlehem to register because of the census," said the young man. There was a note of desperation in his voice. "My family comes from Bethlehem, so we have to be here. That's what the Romans..."

"Don't mention the Romans!"

"Look, this is an inn, isn't it?" said the young man.

"No," said Benjamin scornfully. "It's a hotel."

"But you have rooms where people can come and stay?"

"Yes, we do," admitted Benjamin, reluctantly.

"Well, have you got a room that we can stay in?" asked the young man.

"Let me see," said Benjamin. "We've got Major Gideon in number one, Miss Gera and Miss Tabitha in two and three," he continued, reckoning them off on his fingers, "some Pharisees in numbers four, five, six and seven, Levites in eight and nine; and Priests in ten, eleven and twelve. No. We have no room. No room at all. They're all full. Try somewhere else. Goodbye."

"Oh, Ben!" exclaimed Sarah, who was feeling sympathy for the young mother-to-be. "Of course we can fit them in somewhere."

"Where can we fit them in?" demanded Benjamin. "In the dining room? In the kitchen? Behind the bar?"

"There's always the stable," said his wife.

"Right! The stable, of course!" said Benjamin, smiting his brow. "Stupid of me not to have thought of the dirty, mucky, cold, stable. The perfect place to have a baby. Stable it is then. Mattenai, go and set up a bed in the stable."

"Qué?" said Mattenai, sounding even more puzzled than usual.

"A bed," said Benjamin, enunciating his words slowly and clearly, "in the stable, stay-bell, where all the cattle and sheep and horses and camels are – and straw. Stable. Comprenez vous?"

"Si," Mattenai nodded. "Stable. You want to sleep in the stable?"

"No," said Benjamin patiently. "We want our guests to sleep in the stable."

"Sleep in the stable. Not in a room, no?"

"No. No room. All rooms full up. Take these two to the stable." Benjamin waved his hand towards the young couple.

"Si." Mattenai waited while the man and his pregnant wife signed the hotel register that Sarah pushed in front of them, then led them off down the corridor that led to the back door of the hotel.

"There," said Sarah. "Another little problem solved."

However, before she and Benjamin could begin to relax, the main door opened again and an older man entered. He was tall but stoop-shouldered. He had a neatly-trimmed beard that was almost white and he wore a robe of brilliant blue, embroidered with gold stars and crescents.

"If you're looking for a room," snapped Benjamin, "we're full up."

"No," said the newcomer, in a dreamy sort of voice. "I'm looking for a king."

"A king?" exclaimed Benjamin. "A king! Oh, a king. Does this place look like a palace? This is a hotel. We have rooms where people sleep. We don't have any kings."

"He isn't king yet," replied the stranger. "He'll only be a baby. Newly born."

Bethlehem Towers

"Oooh!" exclaimed Sarah. "That'll be that young couple." She looked down at the register. "Mary and Joseph. They're in the stable. But the baby hasn't been born yet, you know."

"Not been born yet?" The man pulled a diary out of the folds of his robe. "What is the date today?"

"Twenty-fourth of December," said Sarah.

"Ah!" said the man, turning the pages of his diary. "I see where I've gone wrong. I thought it was the sixth of January. I was wondering where my two friends were. Silly old me."

"Silly old you," said Benjamin sincerely.

"You can go and see if he's been born yet," said Sarah, helpfully. "The stable's down that corridor and through the door at the end."

The old man, humming a cheerful little tune to himself, walked off down the corridor.

"Fancy that!" said Sarah. "A king – born in our stable." She thought for a moment, then added, "The Romans won't like it."

"Don't mention the Romans!" snapped Benjamin.

Found in Translation

None so Blind

Acts 13:6-12
What led up to the Christians' confrontation with Elymas the sorcerer?

> *There's none so blind as those who will not see (sixteenth century proverb).*

"And I am happy to report, your Excellency," continued Elymas, "that the current positions of the planets in relation to the signs of the zodiac indicate that your governorship will continue to prosper and that your rule here will continue to be a time of peace and increasing prosperity to our island of Cyprus. I foresee good harvests and profitable trade for our people under your esteemed governance."

"You're laying the oil on thick," I thought to myself. But I did not speak my thought out loud, for I knew that the Proconsul respected Elymas and placed great reliance on his predictions.

You can call me Titus. I had just completed the usual three years' service as a Military Tribune with the XVth Legion in the province of Lower Germany when my father heard that Sergius Paulus was about to take up the post of proconsular governor of the island of Cyprus. Paulus and my father were old comrades from their own military service, so my father promptly asked Paulus to take me with him to gain experience in provincial administration. He said it would be good experience for me and good for my career!

So I had come to Cyprus with Paulus and he had done his best to give me experience. I had learned about the finances of the island, sources of wealth and collection of taxes. I had

67

inspected town water supplies and aqueducts and learned about the disposal of sewage. I had learned about town amenities and observed the building of the public baths in Salamis. I had sat beside Paulus when he sat as judge in court. He discussed cases with me, asked me for my opinion and did his best to make sure I had a good grasp of law. Mind you, the cases were mostly land disputes and cases of unpaid debt. The only interesting case was our one murder trial.

After a year of this I was getting bored and the thought of two more years was disheartening. Elymas was a pleasant diversion. He usually performed a few conjuring tricks for the Proconsul. I was sure that they were conjuring tricks (plus a bit of alchemy to make different coloured smoke and different smells). Even if I couldn't work out how he did them, I didn't believe for a moment that he had any real magic. However, Paulus seemed to believe in Elymas, and he was my boss, so I played along and made admiring comments in the right places.

Elymas was still speaking. "However, the spirits have revealed to me that a group of men will come to Paphos spreading a new superstition that has arisen in the East. If they are allowed to continue, they will cause unrest amongst the people and threaten the peace that we enjoy under your governance and the overlordship of the mighty Caesar Claudius."

Paulus was clearly concerned. He sat up straight and asked, "How many men? What are their names?"

"The spirits do not concern themselves with such details," replied Elymas, with a dismissive gesture of one long, bony hand, as if he thought it was impertinent of Paulus to ask.

"Do you know when these men will arrive in Paphos?" asked Paulus.

"Very soon, your Excellency," said Elymas, unhelpfully to my mind.

"Well, I will set a watch for them and arrest them when they do arrive," decided Paulus.

"Of course," said Elymas. "Your Excellency is a model of discretion and authority. If it pleases you, I will now return to my chambers. It may be that the spirits will give me further information about this superstition."

Paulus made a gesture of dismissal. Elymas bowed and withdrew. Paulus spoke to one of his attendants: "Send for Centurion Fabius."

Cyprus, as a peaceful proconsular province, had no regular troops, but Paphos did have a body of Vigiles (a police-cum-fire service) commanded by Centurion Lucius Fabius, a veteran of the IInd Legion. The Centurion was out doing his morning rounds of the town, so it took some time to find him and bring him back to the Proconsul's palace. Paulus explained to him the warning that Elymas had given.

Fabius frowned; that is, the vertical lines between his eyebrows grew deeper. He thought for a moment. "There is a group of Jewish teachers, rabbis as they call them, from Syria - three of them. They landed in Salamis about fifteen days ago. They've been teaching in the Jewish synagogues across the island. They arrived in Paphos yesterday."

"If they've been here fifteen days," I said, "Elymas didn't need any spirits to tell him about these men. All he needed was an agent to spy on them."

Paulus looked at me with an expression I couldn't quite interpret. Was he pleased with my observation? Or was he annoyed because I had cast doubt on his beloved Elymas? He turned back to Fabius. "Do these men seem dangerous?"

"I really could not say, Sir," replied Fabius. "I don't know if they are teaching something new or just the usual Jewish religion. But," he added, "they certainly haven't caused any trouble so far."

"You must find out what they are teaching so we can decide if it is dangerous."

"Yes, Sir. Tomorrow is the Jewish holy day, the Sabbath. They'll gather in the synagogue, and these teachers are sure to be there. I'll go and listen to what they have to say."

"Do that," said Paulus. Then he looked at me again. "And take young Titus here with you. It will be good experience," he added with a smile, before I could object.

. . . .

So the next morning found me standing beside Centurion Fabius in the street opposite the Jewish synagogue.

I had had no idea how many Jews there were in Paphos. If you had asked me, I might have said, "A handful." It was now clear that there were perhaps fifty or sixty men and a similar number of women, with small children, crowding into the synagogue.

What surprised me was that many of them seemed to know Fabius and he knew them.

"Shalom," several of them greeted him, and he responded, "Shalom."

"That means 'peace'," he explained to me.

"A good greeting," I said.

"Those are the men we're looking for," said Fabius, pointing.

I looked and saw three men: one older, one about thirty and a younger one who clearly could not yet grow a full beard. By their clothing, it was obvious that they were Jews. Otherwise there was nothing special about them that I could see. I mentioned this to Fabius.

"That's the most dangerous kind," he said.

Presently, when most of the Jews had gone into the synagogue, Fabius led me across the street and into the

None so Blind

building. When my eyes had become accustomed to the dimness after the bright sunshine of the street, I was able to look around. The synagogue was simply a large hall at the far end of which was a table and, at one end of the table, an oil lamp was burning. There was a broad aisle leading up to this table, and the Jewish men were seated on benches that faced each other across the aisle. The women, with their children, were crammed into an area to the right that was fenced off from the rest of the hall. At the back, on the left of the doorway, were a couple of benches on which men who were not dressed as Jews were sitting. Fabius indicated that he and I should sit here.

"These seats are for enquirers," he explained, "People who aren't Jews but want to find out about their religion."

There were richly embroidered tapestries on the walls and I now noticed, to the left of the table, a set of shelves on which there were a large number of scrolls; at least two dozen, I thought.

"The Jewish sacred texts," said Fabius, noticing where I was looking.

The thing that most surprised me was that there was no statue of the Jewish god and no altar for sacrifice or burning incense. At that time I knew almost nothing of the Jews and their religion. I knew that they were considered to be atheists, because they insisted that there was only one God, not the dozen or so principal gods and goddesses that we Romans, and all civilised peoples, venerated.

Presently the service began, and I hardly understood a word of it since it was almost entirely in Hebrew, the Jewish language. I stood up when the Jews stood up and sat down when they sat down. There were prayers spoken by one of the older men. At one point everyone sang a song called, in their language, a psalm. Then one of the scrolls was taken reverently from its shelf, laid carefully on the table and unrolled. One of the oldest men read a passage from the scroll, after which it was rolled up and placed, with equal reverence, back on its shelf. However, there was no sacrifice, no burning of incense, not even the pouring of a libation of wine. I was impressed with the simplicity of it all. I had often wondered what the immortal gods actually did with the sacrifices and libations that Roman priests offered to them.

Then the man who had been leading the service announced in Greek, "Brothers, today we have three honoured guests who have travelled a great distance to be with us and have news of things that have been happening in Jerusalem and Judea in recent times." Then he spoke to our three suspects who had been given seats near the front: "Brothers, our people are ready to hear your message."

The oldest of the men stepped up beside the table and, turning, began to speak in Greek: "Men of Israel, I am Joseph. I was myself born in Cyprus, but some years ago I travelled to Judea because my family owns land there. There I heard about Jesus of Nazareth in Galilee. He was a man accredited to us by God by means of healings, signs and wonders. Our leading men handed this man over, by God's foreknowledge and purpose, to the Roman governor in Jerusalem, who put him to death by crucifixion. But God raised him from death, and he was seen by chosen witnesses for many days. The God of our fathers has glorified his servant Jesus and made him both Lord and Messiah. This is how God fulfilled what he had foretold through the prophets, that the Messiah would suffer. And now He commands you to repent so that your sins may be wiped out and that times of refreshing may come from the Lord."

I couldn't follow a lot of this. The word 'messiah' was quite new to me. But I did get it clear that this man Joseph was claiming that a man had been executed and then come back from the dead. If they believed that, either they were mad, or something extraordinary really had happened in Jerusalem.

None so Blind

Now a second man, the thirty-year-old, stepped to the front.

"Brothers and men of Israel, I am Saul, born in Tarsus, but as to our religion I belonged to our strictest sect. I was a Pharisee. I thought it my duty, under God, to destroy the followers of this Way that Joseph has explained to you. But God in his mercy met me on the road between Jerusalem and Damascus. There I saw this Jesus, raised from the dead and glorified by God, as was shown by the blinding light that fell about me and my companions. At once I joined the followers of the Way and began to proclaim the message of Jesus, the Messiah, crucified and raised by God from the dead. In his name, repentance and forgiveness of sins must be preached to Jews everywhere. And not only Jews but to all peoples everywhere. For God shows no favouritism but accepts men from every nation who fear him and do what is right. Already this good news has been proclaimed in Judea, in Galilee and in Syria.

"We ourselves (Joseph, our companion Jonathon and I) have been sent out from Antioch, commissioned by God's Holy Spirit, to bring this good news of Jesus the Messiah to you here in Cyprus."

After the men had spoken there was a lot of discussion, most of which I couldn't follow. One point that was made strongly, by more than one person, was that this man Jesus couldn't possibly be the Messiah because he had been crucified. As I still didn't know what a Messiah was, this meant nothing to me. However, Joseph and Saul apparently tried to respond by quoting from the Hebrew sacred texts.

Eventually, the meeting came to an end and people began to leave the synagogue. Fabius led me out and across the street once more.

"We'll just check on where they are staying," he said.

We had to wait some time. Apparently Joseph and Saul were still discussing their message with some of the locals.

"What do you make of them?" I asked Fabius.

"I've heard some tall stories in my time," he replied, "but I've never heard anyone claim that a man has come back to life. Ghost stories, yes, but never a man coming back in a living body."

"Do you think they're dangerous, like Elymas claimed?"

"They could be dangerous," said Fabius cautiously. "If they're claiming that this Jesus is 'Lord', they could be claiming that he is greater than Caesar. But they don't sound like rebel-rousers."

A thought occurred to me, and I mentioned it to Fabius. "If that man Saul was born in Tarsus, then he must be a Roman citizen." The city of Tarsus was the provincial capital of Cilicia, and Pompey the Great had granted citizenship to the men of Tarsus a hundred years ago.

Another idea occurred to me. "I wonder what Aphrodite will make of this new teaching," I said. The goddess Aphrodite (Venus as we Romans call her) was believed to have risen from the sea near Cyprus. Because of this, Paphos is a great centre of her cult and has a magnificent temple dedicated to her.

"If she really is a goddess, she can take care of herself," said Fabius, who was clearly a practical man.

Presently the three men came out of the synagogue and walked up the street. We followed at a distance until they turned into a modest house on the outskirts of town.

"That will do," said Fabius. "I'll get some of my vigiles to check out that house and keep an eye on our three suspects. You and I ought to report back to the Proconsul."

. . . .

None so Blind

Sergius Paulus listened to our report carefully and questioned us both closely. At last he said, "I would like to talk with these men. Have them brought to me, Fabius."

"Shall I arrest them, Sir?"

"No. Just tell them that I wish to see them. If they refuse to come, you can arrest them."

"Your Excellency," said Fabius, "today is the Jewish holy day that they call the Sabbath. These men will consider that coming into your palace makes them ritually impure."

The Proconsul thought for a moment. "Very well," he said. "Tell them to come tomorrow, at the third hour. Set a watch to make sure they don't slip away tonight."

"Of course, Sir." Fabius saluted, turned about smartly and marched out.

"An interesting story, Titus," said the Proconsul. "Either this is all nonsense and superstition, as Elymas said, or there is some real power here."

"Yes, Sir," I agreed, "and if there is truth in their story, then it is Elymas who has been telling us nonsense and superstition."

The Proconsul looked at me shrewdly. "You have a head on your shoulders, young Titus, when you care to use it," he said. "We must decide which party is teaching the truth."

After a pause, Sergius Paulus called in his secretary to read aloud some legal papers and required me to give an opinion on them. However, it was clear that his mind was only half on the task, for he accepted my opinions without question and told the secretary to act on them. Usually he pointed out to me where I was wrong and corrected me on points of law. After a time he gave this up and told me to carry on working with the secretary, while he withdrew to the palace gardens. He had never trusted me to work alone before. Clearly, he was greatly disturbed.

Found in Translation

. . . .

At the third hour next morning, an attendant came to call me to the Proconsul's audience chamber. The three Jewish rabbis were already standing there, as was Fabius.

Presently, Sergius Paulus entered and took his seat on the tribunal. I took my place to his left and slightly behind him.

"Sir, these are the three men you wished to see," said Fabius, then announced, "His Excellency Sergius Paulus, Proconsular Governor of Cyprus."

The three men bowed respectfully and, as they straightened up, I was able to get a clearer view of them than had been possible in the synagogue. The oldest of the three looked calm, and even cheerful, as if he was glad to be able to speak with the Proconsul. The youngest looked nervous; he was little more than a boy - about eighteen, I judged. The third man looked more serious. His beard was black, his eyes dark and he had thick, black eyebrows. He looked, I thought, like a man preparing to face a battle. I had seen that expression, once, on the faces of the legionaries of the XVth, just before we went into action.

"Bring seats for my guests," ordered the Proconsul.

When the Jews were seated, he said, speaking in Greek, "Tell me your names."

"I am Joseph, nicknamed Barnabus, a native of Cyprus," said the oldest man, also in fluent Greek.

He indicated the serious man. "This is Saul Paulus, of Tarsus," he gestured to the young man, "and this is Jonathon Marcus, from Jerusalem."

"You two are Roman citizens?" said the Proconsul, looking at Saul and Jonathon.

"Your Excellency is correct," replied Saul.

"My family name is also Paulus," said the Proconsul.

None so Blind

"It is an honourable name," said Saul. "You have famous ancestors."

"And you are the leader?" said the Proconsul to Joseph.

"Your Excellency, we are all equal," replied Joseph.

"What is this new teaching that you are bringing to Cyprus?"

It was Saul who answered. "Not just to Cyprus; the Gospel is for the whole world."

"What is this 'Gospel'?" asked the Proconsul.

Again it was Saul who spoke. "The God who created the world gives to man life and spirit and everything that man needs. He does not dwell in temples, nor on mountain tops. Nor can man make any image of the divine being in gold or silver or stone. In the past, God in his mercy has overlooked our ignorance, but now he calls all men everywhere to repent, to turn back to Him, who made us, and to live holy lives. He has made a way for us to turn back to Him by sending His Messiah, Jesus. God has given us proof that Jesus is Lord and Messiah by raising him from the dead."

"Explain this word 'Messiah'," said the Proconsul.

"In Greek, we might say Christ," said Saul. "It means the Anointed One. Kings and priests are anointed by men but our Jewish prophets have long foretold that God would one day send a man who would be anointed by God Himself. This Christ would call all Jews and all nations back to God. What greater sign could there be that a man is God's Christ but that he should rise from the dead?"

"What greater sign indeed?" said the Proconsul, thoughtfully.

"Is this Lord and Christ greater than Caesar Claudius, Emperor of Rome?" I asked.

"Yes, he is, because he has been anointed by God Himself and because he rules over all nations, even beyond the borders of the Roman Empire."

77

"That sounds like treason," I said carefully, well aware that this was a most serious accusation to make and that these men did not appear to me to be traitors.

"The Christ does not come to overthrow earthly emperors, rulers and kings," said Saul. "He calls on them, as on all men, to repent and to lead holy lives."

"What do you mean by a 'holy life'?" asked the Proconsul.

"A holy life," replied Saul, "is a life of joy, peace, patience, goodness, gentleness, self-control and good faith. Jesus the Christ sends to us, his followers, the Holy Spirit to enable us to live a holy life."

"Your Excellency! Forgive me!"

We all looked round at this interruption. Elymas had swept grandly into the room with his dark-blue cloak, covered with astrological symbols, trailing behind him

"Forgive me, your Excellency," he repeated. "I was in my secret chamber, meditating on the meaning of certain ancient scrolls, when the spirits revealed to me that these men had come, seeking to disturb your mind and spirit with their false superstition. I came at once to protect you from their cleverness and deceit."

"Humph!" I thought to myself. "If it were really the spirits, why didn't they tell you before the men arrived here? I bet it was just one of the slaves you have in your purse that ran to tell you who was with the Proconsul."

"These men do not appear to me to be deceitful," said the Proconsul.

"Not deceitful!" said Elymas, scornfully. "When they tell you that they follow a man who has risen from death?"

"We follow Jesus the Messiah, whom God raised from the dead," said Saul. "Why should you think it impossible for God to raise a man from the dead?"

None so Blind

"What god has ever raised a man from the dead?" retorted Elymas. "Since the beginning of the world such a thing has never been heard of."

"God has done a new thing in Jesus," said Saul.

"So why isn't your risen Messiah here?" demanded Elymas.

"He died on the cross and was laid in a tomb," said Joseph. He said this quietly, but it startled me because he had not spoken for several minutes. "On the third day, God raised him from the dead. He appeared to chosen witnesses, most of whom are still alive. He appeared to his eleven closest disciples, whom we now call apostles. On one occasion he appeared to five hundred of his followers together. He appeared to his own brother, James. He even appeared to certain women. After forty days, God took him up to heaven, like Enoch and Elijah."

"How very convenient," sneered Elymas. "So he appeared only to his followers - not to Pontius Pilate, the governor who justly crucified him as a rebel, nor to the Jewish priests who very properly handed him over to Pilate."

"You are well informed about the Way that we follow," said Joseph. "Why do you not turn to Jesus the Messiah?"

"Turn to a crucified rebel?" said Elymas. "I, who have the wisdom of the Ancients at my fingertips, who understand the influence of the stars and the planets on human fortunes? What would I have to do with your peasant Messiah?"

Saul stood up. He was clearly angry. I have seen men lose their temper and storm and shout, but this was different. This was controlled anger.

"You are a child of the devil!" His voice was clear and steady. If ever a man believed he was speaking the truth, it was Saul at that moment. "You are full of deceit and trickery. The hand of the Lord is against you."

"Oh, is it?" said Elymas. "The hand of your crucified Messiah, I suppose? Well, where is he? Where is his power? Why can't I see him?" He walked up to Saul and looked straight into his face. "Why can't I see him?" he repeated. "Is there something wrong with my eyes?"

"Yes," said Saul quietly. "There is something wrong with your eyes."

Suddenly a change came over Elymas - something about the way he stood, something about the way he held his head. He looked uncertain. He moved his head from side to side, up and down. He made a sound that was something like a cry of surprise and despair. "I – I – can't see!"

"Yes," said Saul, "you are going to be blind, and for a time you will be unable to see the light of the sun."

"Help me," gasped Elymas, turning and stretching out his hands. He stumbled. One of the attendants stepped forward and grasped his arm.

"He has bewitched me. Take me to my chamber."

The attendant led him out and we heard his final words: "Must find a counter spell."

There was dead silence in the audience chamber. I let out a long breath. I hadn't realised I had been holding my breath. Saul sat down again. He looked tired, even shaken, as if what had happened had taken him by surprise as much as it had taken us.

At last the Proconsul spoke. "I see that this teaching comes with real power."

"The power of the Holy Spirit of God," said Joseph, "not the devil's power used by this sorcerer. It is God who has judged him, not Saul, for we are only men like yourselves."

"I want to know more of this God and this Messiah you speak of," said the Proconsul. "Tell me everything."

The Whole Armour

How did Paul come to write Ephesians 6:10-17?
Perhaps something like this...

"... and masters, treat your slaves in the same way. Do not threaten them, since you know that he who is both their Master and yours is in heaven and there is no favouritism with him."

"No favouritism with him," repeated Tychicus, scribing away frantically, as he tried to keep up with Paul's dictation.

"Finally..." Paul began, hesitated, and then his voice died away.

"Finally," repeated Tychicus and looked up expectantly.

Paul, however, was lost in thought. At last he said, "That will do for now, Tychicus, thank you. I am sure the Lord wants me to say something more; I just don't know what it is. I must have some time to pray and meditate."

Tychicus rose, gathering up his papers, pen and ink. "I'll get on with making a fair copy of this so far." He walked out of the room.

"Would you like to be left alone?" asked Timothy, who had been sitting opposite Paul at the table, listening eagerly to the letter as Paul dictated.

Paul glanced at Julius Valens, seated on his left. He gave a wry smile. "Perhaps it would be good if I was as alone as possible," he agreed. There was no chance of being really alone when the chain that bound him to the soldier was only six feet long.

Timothy, together with Luke (who had been sitting in one corner of the room), went out of the room. Paul was left with Valens.

Found in Translation

After a few minutes Paul rose and walked to the window, Valens rising and following him. It was not much of a view. They were on the first floor and the window opened onto a narrow street with a four-storey tenement block opposite. The street was crowded and noisy as people went about their business. How was the small church supposed to make an impact on these crowds? All those people. Roman citizens, most of them; slaves and freedmen, many of them. All worshipping the gods of Rome: Jupiter "best and greatest" (as they called him) and Juno his consort; Apollo, Minerva, Vesta and countless others. The Romans had a god or goddess in charge of everything, every aspect of human affairs. They had a contract with each one of them. "We carry out this sacrifice/ceremony and you give us a good harvest/freedom from plague/success in war/peace." But they had no idea of a God of grace – a Father God who loved to give gifts to His children.

And there were cities like this all over the Empire, smaller than Rome, of course, but full of people worshipping false gods. Like Ephesus, where was the little group of Christians he was writing to and where they had the great temple of Artemis (Diana, the Romans called her). Paul remembered the riot started by Demetrius, the silversmith, against the Christian preaching of one God. The Way, the life of a Christian, was not easy; sometimes it was like a battle - a war against false gods, against evil spiritual forces. And to fight a battle and win, you needed to be a soldier (a trained soldier at that) like this Valens standing stolidly beside him. Guarding a prisoner, being chained to one man for a day and a night, must be the most boring (even if the easiest) duty that a soldier had to do. Yet Valens did it because he was trained and disciplined. His officer gave him orders, and he carried them out.

It wasn't enough to be well-trained either. A soldier needed good weapons. Paul didn't know much about armies,

The Whole Armour

but he did know that Rome made sure her soldiers had the best possible weapons and armour.

And Valens here had done some real soldiering. He had been in real battles; he had a scar on his right forearm to prove that. If anyone knew what a soldier needed in battle it was this Valens.

"Valens," said Paul, "what does a soldier need to fight and win a battle?"

Valens gave a start of surprise. Clearly his thoughts had also been far away, thinking of whatever soldiers do think about when they have time to day-dream.

Paul repeated the question.

"Boots," said Valens, decisively.

"Boots?" Paul was surprised.

"Boots," repeated Valens. "You need good, well-soled boots. Comfortable boots, so you can march all day and day after day. It's no good being a soldier if you can't even get to the battlefield. And when you're on the battlefield, you need boots with a good grip. You can't afford to slip when you're face to face with a charging Barbarian with a sword. And you can't use your own sword and shield if you can't stand firm on the ground."

"I see," said Paul, thoughtfully. "I've heard about that thing you make with your shields - the tortoise, is it called? I can see you would need to stand firmly together to make that."

"Testudo," said Valens. "Yes, we're trained to fit our shields together like the plates on a tortoise-shell. That's where the name comes from. When you've formed testudo, with all your mates of course, the enemy can throw pretty well anything at you and you won't be touched - not by arrows or slingstones, or any sort of javelin or dart. But it takes a lot of practice to hold that formation and move together without leaving gaps."

"The shield for protection and the sword for attacking," said Paul.

"Oh, we can use our shields for attack as well as defence," responded Valens. "Look," he continued, "you hold your shield like this." He held out his left forearm, horizontal, keeping his upper arm close to his chest. His left hand, palm downwards, was clenched around the imaginary hand-grip of a shield.

"You hold the shield close to your body for protection during the charge," he explained. "In front of your hand is the metal boss." He made a graphic gesture with his right hand, conjuring up, in Paul's mind, a picture of the dome-shaped shield boss. "When you get really close to your enemy, you punch with your shield like this." Valens thrust his left hand forward, forcefully. "With any luck, you knock him over, or at least knock him off balance. Then you follow-up with your sword."

Paul nodded. "And then you have body armour, and a helmet?"

"Lorica is the body armour," said Valens. "I don't know the Greek word for it. But your lorica and your helmet are the most important equipment for protection. You can't rely on being able to block every weapon and every missile when you're fighting with sword and shield."

"Boots, sword, shield, helmet and lorica," said Paul, thoughtfully. "Is there anything else that a soldier needs?"

"All sorts of things," said Valens. "Cloak, provisions, water bottle, skillet, kettle, mess pan, entrenching tools, rope. And we carry all those things on our backs. They don't call us Marius' mules for nothing," he added with a laugh.

Paul smiled. "I doubt if I can put all those things in a letter."

"You want to write about a soldier's kit in your letter?" said Valens, in a puzzled tone.

The Whole Armour

"I was thinking that sometimes a Christian is like a soldier," explained Paul.

"I thought you Christians claimed to be men of peace," said Valens, suspiciously.

"Yes, we are," said Paul hastily, "but we are in a war against evil powers - spiritual powers," he explained. "Not a war against lawful government but against rebellious spirits that set themselves up against God."

Valens still looked suspicious.

"We're not arming ourselves with real weapons," said Paul. "We're not rebels against the Emperor. But there are evil forces trying to control men - spiritual forces - and we need to be a spiritual army armed with spiritual weapons to fight against them."

Valens looked less suspicious, but still puzzled.

"We need to stand firm against immorality, against witchcraft, against envy and selfish ambition, against rage and factions and hatred."

Valens nodded his head slowly. He was a member of the Praetorian Guard and he was no fool. He knew how the Emperor Tiberius had been manipulated by the Prefect Sejanus; he knew about the madness of Gaius Caligula and how Claudius had been poisoned and his wife had schemed to bring her son Nero to the throne while Claudius' own son had been done away with.

"An army needs a standard to rally around," said Valens.

"We have the cross," said Paul. "The cross of Christ," he added, seeing Valens puzzlement.

"How can a cross – an execution post – and for rebels at that – be a standard? How can it be a symbol of anything but shame and defeat?"

"For us it is a symbol of victory. Jesus died on a cross and he nailed sin to the cross; he was buried and on the third day

God raised him from the dead. He had defeated death and God made Jesus Lord."

Valens frowned again. "That sounds like treason against the Emperor."

"I am speaking of God, the one true God, who created Heaven and Earth. He has the authority to appoint one Lord over all – even one Lord over the Emperor. That does not mean he takes away Caesar's authority. But even Caesar must submit himself to God's authority."

Valens nodded. "This God you speak of – is he the one we call Jupiter?"

"No. I mean the God who made the world and everything in it, the God who does not need temples built by human hands."

Valens said slowly, "If you want to do away with temples, I'd say you have got a fight on your hands."

Paul laughed. "Remind me to tell you what happened at Ephesus and the temple of Artemis sometime. But, go on, what else is important for a soldier?"

"One thing a soldier does need," said Valens, "is an emblem, a badge - something that marks him out as a soldier."

Now it was Paul's turn to look puzzled.

"Look at me," said Valens. "What about me tells you that I am a soldier?"

Paul looked. Valens wore a tunic of dark red, his sword in its scabbard hung on a baldric at his right side and his tunic was caught in at the waist by a broad leather belt with an apron of leather strips. A chain ran from an iron manacle on his left wrist to a similar manacle on Paul's wrist.

"You have your sword," said Paul, "and me as your prisoner."

"I am only allowed to wear my sword when on duty."

Paul looked carefully. Valens' tunic was simply that - a tunic such as worn by any man in Rome. But the belt...

The Whole Armour

"Your belt is very distinctive," he said.

"Exactly," said Valens. "It's a military belt. No one except a soldier is permitted to wear a belt like this. And I wear it when I'm off-duty – so everyone can see that I'm a soldier. They can see I'm not a slave, or a potter, or a wine-seller, or a rubbish-sweeper. I'm a soldier, and I can hold my head up in any public place."

Paul looked again at Valens' belt. There were little square plates of bronze sewn to the leather and round plates sewn to the apron strips. It was indeed instantly recognisable. Anyone seeing it would know that they were in the presence of a soldier of the Roman Empire. So: belt, boots, shield, sword, helmet and lorica. What were these things pictures of? What did a soldier of Christ need to be fully-equipped for spiritual warfare? What was the badge that a Christian should wear to mark him out as a soldier of the Lord Jesus?

Paul turned back into the room.

"Tychicus!" he called. "I'm ready to finish the letter."

Found in Translation

The Genesis Project [1]

In several places on the Old Testament (Job 1:6-12, Job 2:2-6, I Kings 22:19-22) we learn that the LORD sometimes holds council meetings in heaven in order to make decisions about what is to happen on Earth. So is it possible that the LORD held a council meeting right at the beginning, before Creation and before Genesis 1:1? If he had done so, might it have gone something like this...?

"Joy to you, Metatron."

"Glory to you, Sir," I replied.

I was just completing the layout of the Creation Room for the scheduled Planning Meeting when J.C. walked in. Five copies of the Works Operational Requirements Directive were set out on the table and nameplates for the various participants: at the head of the table, the General Operations Director; to his right, J.C. and then the representative from the Association of Cherubim, Angels, and Seraphim; to his left, the Senior Adviser for Terrain, Atmosphere and Nature; and to his left, a seat for myself as heavenly Scribe, Typist And Recorder (or S.T.A.R. as I like to be known).

"Thank you for these copies of the W.O.R.D.," said J.C. "Have you loaded the presentation onto the projector?"

"Just about to do that, Sir," I responded, switching on the projector and inserting the memory stick.

As I was adjusting the projector, the General Operations Director walked in.

"Joy to you, J.C.," he said, "and to you, Metatron."

---

[1] This story is meant to be light-hearted but I realise that the subject matter will be regarded by some as not suitable for humour. To those people I apologise; my target is bureaucracy, not Scripture.

Found in Translation

J.C.'s "Joy to you, Director" and my "Glory to you, Sir" came out together and collided in mid-space, but the Director didn't seem to mind. He simply walked to his chair at the head of the table and sat down.

"What's on the Agenda for this meeting, Metatron?" he asked.

"The main item is the Genesis Project, Director. We have to decide whether or not to give it the final go-ahead."

Gabriel walked in and said, "Glory to you, Director, Glory to you, J.C. and joy to you, Metatron."

"Joy to you, Gabriel," said J.C. "I understand you're representing the Association of Cherubim, Angels and Seraphim."

"That's correct, J.C.," replied Gabriel.

"Now we just need the Senior Adviser for Terrain, Atmosphere and Nature," said J.C.

At that moment, the door opened and a young angel walked in.

"I'm here as his representative, Director," he said. "The S.A.T.A.N. couldn't come and he has asked me to tender his apologies."

"And you are?" said the Director.

"I am the Deputy Adviser for Terrain and Atmosphere," said the young angel, producing an identity badge marked 'D.A.T.A.'

"This is a very important meeting, D.A.T.A.," said J.C., with a frown. "We were expecting the S.A.T.A.N. to be here in person."

"He's recovering from an accident," explained the D.A.T.A. "Our department has been experimenting with fire and brimstone. There was an explosion..."

"We understand," said the Director, generously. "I am sure you will represent his views quite adequately, and please wish him a speedy recovery from myself and J.C." He paused for a

The Genesis Project

moment and then said, "I think, J.C., that we should begin the meeting."

"Of course, Director," replied J.C. He picked up the remote control and brought the first slide onto the screen. "This is the Works Operational Requirements Directive for the Genesis Project. Now as you can see," he flicked to the second slide, "the Project calls for the creation of a standard Class A Universe with the usual laws of nature. There will be a range of galaxies, stars and planets - a proportion of the planets to have life forms, both plant and animal. The work to be completed in six days, followed by one day of testing to see that everything is good, after which we let it run according to its inbuilt laws of nature."

"That all seems quite straightforward so far," commented the Director.

"The particular interest of this project is that on one of the planets..." J.C. went to the next slide, which showed a blue-green planet, with a cloudy atmosphere and about three-quarters of its surface covered by oceans. There were large ice-caps at the North and South Poles, as well as several continents and numerous islands of different sizes. "...we are creating a Site of Special Scientific Interest, here." He brought up the fourth slide, showing two large continents, separated by an inland sea and two large ocean gulfs. An arrow pointed from the label 'SSSI' to a tiny area of land at one end of the inland sea. "We are installing a full range of plant and animal species, but the special item will be the people. Initially, we intend to place two people into this S.S.S.I. The expectation is that they will multiply, of course, but we fully expect them to develop a high level of intelligence and wisdom to the extent that they will be able to form a close personal relationship with us."

"Excellent presentation, J.C.," said the Director. "I don't like this 'Site of Special Scientific Interest' stuff, though.

Found in Translation

Clumsy title. We need to think of something more snappy, something with bite. Any suggestions?

"National Park?" offered J.C.

"No, we used that in the last universe," said the Director.

"Ferry Meadows?" suggested Gabriel.

"No," said the Director. "I know; we'll call it a 'Garden'. Yes, I like that. The Garden of - what were we going to call the place?"

"We were going to call it 'Eden'," said J.C.

"The Garden of Eden," said the Director. "Good, that's settled then. Now, anyone got any comments?"

Gabriel raised a hand. "At A.C.A.S. we are a little concerned about the stability of this planet. You've put a lot of water into it. I know that a lot of it is going to be frozen into those polar icecaps but we're worried about the number of volcanoes you've left in. With all that atmospheric pollution from the volcanoes you could get a greenhouse effect. Melt all the ice and you'd have a great flood which would wipe out most of the life forms."

"We have taken that into account," responded J.C. "A great flood is one of a range of options built into this project as a contingency plan."

Gabriel nodded, as if satisfied with this explanation, but now the D.A.T.A. broke in, and he was clearly unhappy.

"Our Office has some fundamental objections to the whole scheme," he said. "If you would permit me to make a presentation of our case....?"

The Director seemed a little surprised. "Of - er - course, Mr - er – D.A.T.A."

The D.A.T.A. moved to the projector and, after a few moments, brought up a fresh slide.

"In the first place," he began, "you are proposing that these "people" would be mammals. The S.A.T.A.N. thinks that they should be reptiles - specifically, snakes."

The Genesis Project

The slide showed the words 'Mammals' and 'Reptiles' side-by-side and, below them the words 'Humans' and 'Snakes'. At the bottom of the slide was the word 'Competition'.

"Snakes! Why snakes?" exclaimed J.C., putting my own thought into words.

But the Director said, "Interesting idea, D.A.T.A. Let him go on, J.C."

"We also think," continued the D.A.T.A., "that the whole idea is too tame. Strength comes from competition. You have made these people so intelligent they will have no problem dominating the other animals."

"There will be male and female people," put in Gabriel. "That leaves room for competition."

The D.A.T.A. was not to be put off. "We think that you should have intelligent mammals against intelligent reptiles. That will be a real test to find out which is superior."

"Actually, Director," said J.C., "we were intending that there should be co-operation rather than competition."

"Yes, of course we were," said the Director, "so no intelligent reptiles, D.A.T.A. Interesting idea, though. We might try them in the next universe - on their own - see how it works out."

However the D.A.T.A. was not yet finished. "In the S.A.T.A.N.'s department we also feel that you have made these creatures too intelligent. It seems likely that as they grow in wisdom and power they will become the equals of and perhaps superior to angelic beings. We strongly object."

"But the whole idea was to see if these intelligent mammals would exceed the angels," protested J.C.

"We in ACAS have no objection to this aspect of the project," said Gabriel, hastily.

"It's disgusting!" exclaimed the D.A.T.A. "The idea of creatures made out of ordinary matter, dust of the earth, dirt, being superior to angelic beings made of pure spirit!"

"Don't forget you're a creature yourself, D.A.T.A.," said J.C. warningly, "even if you are pure spirit."

"And what happens when it all goes wrong?" demanded the D.A.T.A.

"How do you mean?" asked J.C.

"It won't just be angels," said the D.A.T.A. "Once these creatures get a taste of real power they'll want to challenge you and the Director. They'll want to be totally independent, selfish and wicked. What will you do then, J.C.?"

"Well, as I said before," replied J.C., "contingency plan A is the great flood. We choose a few of the best people to save and drown the wicked ones."

"And if that doesn't work?" the D.A.T.A. persisted. "If the ones you save from the flood become wicked?"

"We do have a contingency plan B," said J.C., trying to be reassuring, "but it does involve a personal commitment from me to the Director and I would prefer not to discuss it here."

"Involving some great personal sacrifice no doubt," sneered the D.A.T.A. "Director, I have to say that the S.A.T.A.N. and his department are totally opposed to this project."

"Thank you for your comments, Mr D.A.T.A.," said the Director. "May I remind you that you are here as an adviser. The decision on whether or not to proceed with this project is for me alone."

"In that case," said the D.A.T.A., gathering up his papers, "there is little point in me staying. I have given our advice. I think that if you go ahead with the Genesis project, the S.A.T.A.N. will withdraw himself completely from your service."

So saying, the D.A.T.A. stood up and stalked out of the meeting. I wondered how I was to record this in the Minutes. Such a serious disagreement and potential rebellion had, to my

The Genesis Project

knowledge (which is, of course, eternal) never happened before.

"Pity about that," said the Director. "I thought the S.A.T.A.N. was quite an enlightened fellow. But he's right about one thing, J.C. This project is risky and it involves a lot of personal risk for you. Do you still want to go through with it?"

"Yes, Director," said J.C. "I've thought through the risks, and I want to go ahead."

"In that case," said the Director, "the final decision is mine." He paused for a moment in deep thought; then he proclaimed, "Project Genesis is to proceed immediately. LET THERE BE LIGHT."

Found in Translation

A Jar of Water

II Samuel 23:13-17
How did the incident come about in which three of David's followers made their way through the Philistine lines to Bethlehem? Perhaps something like this...

My first battle was over! I was hot, sweaty and tired, as much from fear as from exertion. I scarcely had strength to hold up my spear and shield. But we had won! Relief and triumph swept over me – we had won! Of course, under David's leadership – David who as a boy had slain the giant Philistine, Goliath – we never thought we would lose. But a real battle is a dreadful thing. Every young man wants to fight in a battle, hand to hand, up close and personal. Those who get their wish, and survive, rarely want to fight another.

All around me, the men of Israel were cheering, brandishing their weapons, clapping each other on the back. But all around there were bodies lying on the ground – and not all dead. Many were writhing, groaning in pain, coughing. Not far away someone was screaming. There were dark stains on the ground – real blood. Near me were the two young men, no older than I, who had stood next to me in the battle-line. Just before the battle, we had been told to form up in lines and we had done so without much thought as to who we were standing alongside. I didn't even know their names. But now we looked at each other and I could see relief on their faces - relief that we had survived. I was glad to see that they were alive and uninjured, although one of them had a hand covered with blood.

"It's all right," he said, seeing my anxious look. "It's Philistine blood, not mine."

Suddenly we were all three hugging each other – a dangerous thing to do, since we were all still holding our weapons. I have always remembered that hug. We had fought side-by-side and we knew we were comrades – more than that; we knew we were friends.

"What are your names?" I asked when I felt able to talk again.

"I am Shammah and this is Elika," said one. "We're both from Harod."

"I'm Elhanan, son of Dodo, from Bethlehem," I responded.

"Bethlehem!" exclaimed Elika. "That's Commander David's home town."

"Do you know him?" asked Shammah, eagerly.

I would have liked to say 'yes', that I knew David well, and enjoy the reflection of his reputation, but "Not really," I confessed. "He's a few years older than me. I knew him by sight when we were children, but I haven't seen him since he left Bethlehem until today when he gave his orders to the army."

The other two looked at me as if they thought I must know David and he must know me, so I said, "Didn't you kill some Philistines today?"

"One each, I think," said Shammah. "Let's have a look."

When the Philistines had given way and turned to flee, our whole army had pursued them until the trumpet call told us to halt and rally. We had run perhaps four or five hundred paces, and we now walked back to where we had stood in the battle-line.

"This one's mine," said Shammah eagerly, looking down at a Philistine body. "And this is his blood on my hand," he added, more soberly.

"This is mine," said Elika. "Just look at that belt he's wearing." He stooped down, unbuckled the belt, dragged it off

A Jar of Water

the corpse and held it up. It was made of polished leather with burnished discs of bronze attached along its length, each of them embossed with little symbols.

"Pagan images," said Shammah, taking the end of the belt and examining it closely. "You'd better not be seen wearing this."

Elika's face fell, then, after a moment, cheered up. "Perhaps I could dedicate it to the Ark of Yahweh," he said.

"That sounds better," said Shammah, looking down at another dead Philistine. "Is this one yours, Elhanan?"

"Yes," I said. It ought to have been my moment of triumph – my first enemy killed in battle. Actually what I felt was that I needed to be sick. I hadn't really killed the man. He had charged at me, I had managed to hold my spear straight and level and firmly, and he had run straight on to it. Also I had somehow remembered to hold my shield up, and it had caught the blow from his sword. Otherwise my first battle would have been my last. My shoulder was aching from the force of his blow and there was a chip in the upper rim of my shield.

"Here are some young warriors of Israel, Jonathan," cried a voice behind me.

It was a cheerful, loud, confident voice. We turned and there in front of us was Commander David, son of Jesse, himself. And with him was Jonathan, son of King Saul, no less. We tried to pull ourselves to attention, holding our spears smartly upright, but David would have none of it.

"Relax," he said. "The battle's won - time for warriors to enjoy the victory. Have you had success? I see blood on your hand, young man." This last was spoken to Shammah.

"We have each slain one Philistine," replied Shammah as modestly as he could manage.

"Excellent," said David. "I only slew one Philistine in my first battle."

"The giant Goliath," said Elika, eagerly.

"Yes, and I'm not going to tell that story again," said David. "Are these your enemies?"

He bent down and dragged the sword from the hand of the Philistine whom I had killed.

"Who killed this one?"

"That was Elhanan," said Elika.

"This is an excellent sword," said David, examining it closely. "Look at the metal of the blade, Jonathan"

Jonathan took the sword and looked it over keenly. "This is as sound and as sharp a blade as you will find on any sword," he said. He gripped the hilt and swung the blade experimentally. "It has a sure grip and is well-balanced." He turned the sword, handed it to me hilt first and said, "Keep this and bring it to your next battle. Wave it in the faces of the Philistines. When they see you already have one of their swords, half the fight will go out of them."

"Thank you, Sir," I replied.

Just at that moment a man came up to us carrying a water jar. He handed it to Jonathan who, without drinking, handed it to David, and David, also without drinking, handed it to me. I suddenly realised how thirsty I was. My mouth had been dry before the battle began. Now I was parched so that talking was difficult. I drank deeply, and that water, cold and clear, was the finest drink I had ever had in my life. I handed the jar back to David but he gave it straight to Shammah and, after he had drunk, to Elika. Only after we had quenched our thirst did David and Jonathan drink.

David said, "Blessed be Yahweh, God of Israel, for giving us victory over His enemies and for this life-giving water."

I couldn't believe that we three young men, hardly more than boys, were standing talking and drinking with Israel's two greatest warriors and leaders. And they had made us drink first. These were great men; I would follow them anywhere.

A Jar of Water

Any hope that my first battle would be my last was to be disappointed. The war with the Philistines grumbled on, first one side then the other gaining an advantage but with neither side being able to force the other to submit. For we Israelites, the problems were made worse by other nations taking advantage of our conflict with the Philistines to launch raids into Israelite territory. So we found ourselves marching the length and breadth of the Promised Land and across the Jordan into Gilead as we tried to counter raids from Moab and the Amalekites in the South, Ammon to the East and the Aramaeans in the North. There were skirmishes and battles, pursuits and retreats.

Through it all, Shammah, Elika and I stuck together. We became skilful fighters; we trained with sword and spear, shield and sling. We learned to patrol and scout, to set ambushes and to detect enemy ambushes. Our young bodies hardened. We could stand cold and heat. We could march all day and still fight at the end of it. We learned to go hungry and thirsty – and to eat and drink our fill when the opportunity offered. We learned to stay awake and alert on guard duty all night. We learned how to find our way and to move quietly at night. And we learned the lie of the land, every hill and valley, every town and village, every well and spring and stream.

Then one day came terrible news. We had driven out an Ammonite raiding party and were camped near Jabesh in Gilead when a swift runner from Gibeah brought a message for our Captain. The news he brought went round the camp like a whirlwind: "King Saul has driven David out of his court!"

We were shaken. David, our great Commander, exiled by the King! Worse still, King Saul had tried to kill David with a

Found in Translation

spear! There had been rumours that Saul had grown jealous of David and that the King had become unstable in mind, but we had never expected anything as bad as this! Apparently Jonathan had spoken up for David at the court, so the King and his son were now at loggerheads. With David and Jonathan commanding our armies, we felt that no-one could defeat us, but if those two had quarrelled with the King, who should we follow? The army might fall apart.

Our Captain called the company together and we marched back across the Jordan, to Shechem and then on to Gibeah. There we learned that King Saul had summoned us to Ramah. Scarcely had we reached Ramah when we were ordered back to Gibeah. We camped there for a few days until the time of the New Moon, when we ate a sacred meal in honour of Yahweh. There was talk that the King hoped to be reconciled to David at this festival. Sadly that did not happen.

The next thing that we heard was that David had fled the court once more and that Jonathan had helped him to escape. As if things could not be worse, we next learned that David had gone for help to the priest Ahimelech at Nob, a man called Doeg had betrayed him and, although David escaped, King Saul had had Ahimelech and all his priests slaughtered.

Now Abner, who was Commander of the Levy (that is, all the men of Israel who could be called up to fight in an emergency, as compared with ourselves, who were full-time soldiers) took command of the whole army and, with King Saul, led us South into the wilder lands of Judah to hunt down David. Jonathan stayed in Gibeah.

We didn't catch David, of course. I guess most of us didn't really want to. So we marched around getting hot, dusty and thirsty. David had collected a few followers of his own, and they were obviously watching us. Twice David spoke to King Saul, or rather shouted to him from a safe distance, and at first the King decided to give up the hunt, then changed his mind,

A Jar of Water

then turned back towards Gibeah, for news had come of a fresh Philistine incursion into Israel. However, Saul did not lead us against the Philistines. He simply kept us under arms, encamped near Gibeah. Soon we heard that the Philistines had advanced into Judah and taken Bethlehem – my home town! David's home town!

Shammah, Elika and I talked things over.

"I can't bear the thought of those Philistine dogs in Bethlehem," I said. "What they might be doing to my family, I daren't imagine."

"Why doesn't the King lead us against the Philistines?" said Elika.

"Or let Jonathan lead us against them, or even Abner?" said Shammah.

"He's too concerned about David," I said, "and he doesn't trust Jonathan. He just doesn't know what to do."

"I can't really believe that David is a traitor to the King," said Shammah.

"Nor I," said Elika, "especially if Jonathan doesn't think so. After all, if David were to become King after Saul, it would be Jonathan who would lose the chance to succeed his father."

"They say that the King is sick," I said, "that an evil spirit from Yahweh is tormenting him."

"Perhaps it is so," said Shammah. "It seems that Yahweh is on David's side and is against Saul. Otherwise we would have been able to capture David and his men."

"How can we be sure of that?" said Elika. "David is a skilled Commander. He knows those Judean hills thoroughly. Perhaps Yahweh is on neither side."

"But that means Yahweh has deserted Israel," I said.

"It may be that Yahweh supports Jonathan," suggested Elika.

"Elhanan is right," said Shammah. "If King Saul goes on leading us round in circles, the Philistines and these other nations will simply overrun our land while we chase our tails."

"Do you think Yahweh is punishing Israel?" I asked.

Shammah shrugged. "How should I know? We need a prophet like Samuel to tell us that."

"If we have no prophet and no word from Yahweh, I think that tells us that He is punishing Israel," suggested Elika.

"But what have we done? What sin have we committed?" I said.

"My father told me that years ago, when the people first asked for a King, Samuel said they were rejecting Yahweh as King of Israel," said Shammah.

"But He still gave us a King – Saul," I said.

"Yes, and then Saul went wrong," said Shammah. "I don't know all the ins and outs of it, but they say that Samuel himself told Saul that Yahweh had rejected him as King."

Something from the past came into my mind at that moment. "You know, in Bethlehem they used to say that Samuel had anointed David as King over Israel – secretly – when he was still only a boy – even before he killed Goliath."

There was a long silence. I believe we were all thinking the same thing, but it seemed too terrible to put into words.

At last Shammah said, "If Yahweh has rejected Saul and chosen David to be King, we ought to join David."

"That would be desertion – and treason," said Elika.

"It would be treason against Saul," said Shammah, "but to fight against David would be treason against Yahweh."

There was another long silence.

"I think we know what we have to do," I said.

The others nodded. We still did not want to put our thought into words.

That same evening, as the sun was setting, we gathered up our weapons and equipment and slipped away from the camp.

A Jar of Water

. . . .

"We should be able to see Bethlehem from here," I said.

From Gibeah, we had gone south-east, down to the edge of the Salt Sea, in order to avoid Philistine patrols. We had continued south and then struck off westward, heading for a place called Adullam, where we knew there was a cave that made a good hideaway for a small band of men.

Fortunately we had guessed right, and David was there. He made us welcome although we thought that Joab and his brothers Abishai and Asahel (who were David's nephews) were suspicious of us. The cave was at the head of a narrow ravine. A strong force of men could only come at us through the ravine, where we could ambush them. If we were defeated, there was a narrow path leading up from the ravine over the hills by which a small band such as ours could escape. David had sentries posted in the ravine and a look-out post on a steep hill at one side.

We three had been posted to this look-out position. At mid-day we climbed to the peak of the hill and relieved the three men on duty.

I shaded my eyes and looked away to the north-east. There were hills, valleys, rocky crags and gentler slopes. There were patches of yellow, red, brown and stark black shadows. In the distance, several miles away between two hills I could make out some more regular shapes of white and a few green trees – Bethlehem, my home, occupied by the Philistines! A great sadness filled my heart and a great longing for my father's house, to have family around me once more, not to be an outlaw in this lonely wilderness.

"It would be good to be home," said Elika, "to have done with fighting."

Well, there was nothing to be done about it and at least I had my two best friends with me.

"Joab has given us the hottest part of the day," said Shammah, cheerfully. "I knew he didn't like us."

Apart from the heat, it was an easy duty. In front we could follow the course of the ravine, winding down towards the Salt Sea. If anyone approached from that direction we would see them a mile or more away. To our right we could see down into the ravine, almost a sheer drop. We could see the sentry-post below. Behind us, we could just see the entrance to the cave, a black triangle against the red-brown rock. The ravine opened out a little in front of the cave and there were tents pitched on the sloping ground, for several hundred men had now come to join David. In the heat of the day everyone was keeping out of the sun, in the cave or in their tents.

We decided to keep watch by turns; one stood guard while the others rested. We used our spears and cloaks to rig up some shade from the sun. However, it was dry and dusty work, for gusts of wind from the East stirred up little clouds of dust that filled our mouths, our nostrils and our eyes.

It was also boring, for nothing was moving on the hills or in the valleys; there was nothing to do and little to talk about. However, we had learned that war generally means days of boredom interspersed by short periods of frantic action and sheer terror.

At last the sun began to near the western horizon.

Suddenly, on the hill behind us, came the sound of stones clicking and rattling as someone climbed up. It was still too early for our relief; who could it be? Elika, who happened to be the one on watch, walked back to the edge of the hill.

"It's David," he hissed at us, urgently. "Get up; it's David himself."

A Jar of Water

Shammah and I struggled to our feet and the three of us stood straight and tall, with our spears held upright at our sides.

"Stand easy, men," said David as he breasted the hilltop. "Shammah, Elika and Elhanan, my old comrades. How goes it?"

"Nothing to report, Sir," said Elika. "Nothing moving anywhere."

David glanced round, then stared away in the direction of Bethlehem.

"I like to come up here every day," he said, "just to look at home - your home as well, Elhanan," he said to me. "I remember your father's house, by the town square. Do you miss it too?"

"Yes, Sir," I said.

"So close and so out of reach," said David. "Those accursed Philistines."

David and I stood together, reminding ourselves of people and places we had known. Then we talked about the campaigns and battles we had all shared and, sadly, of comrades who had not survived them.

The sun was just touching the horizon when we heard the sounds of men climbing the hill, voices, and the sound of swearing as someone slipped on the loose stones.

"Language, Uriah, language," called David. "Praise to Yahweh, even when you stumble. Praise, don't curse."

"Yes, Sir. I'm sorry," said Uriah, scrambling up the last few paces.

There were six men in this group, for they would have to stay on watch all night. We handed over the watch to them and started down the hill, David accompanying us. We walked wearily into the camp and over to the entrance to the cave. Here a trickle of water came out of the rock, filling a pool that had been carved out at some time long ago, by unknown

Found in Translation

hands. The water filled the pool and overflowed, quickly disappearing into the dry and stony ground. It was this water that made it possible to camp here. It was a good spring but only just enough for the three or four hundred men now assembled in Adullam.

We scooped up water in our hands and drank thirstily.

"Remember the first time we drank together?" said David.

"We do indeed, Sir," said Shammah. "We hope we will soon be able to drink together after victory over the Philistines."

"Perhaps, Shammah, perhaps," said David. Then he gave a deep sigh. "It's good water but not so good as the well in Bethlehem, eh, Elhanan?"

"No, Sir," I said, a little surprised. I had never thought of the Bethlehem water as being special. If anything, this spring gave clearer water.

"If there's one thing I could wish for," said David, "I would like a drink from the well near the gate of Bethlehem." Then he made a gesture as if pushing the wish away from him and turned away. "Good night to you all," he said and walked into the cave.

We looked at each other and Shammah said, "I think we know what we have to do."

"He didn't mean us to go to Bethlehem," said Elika.

"That's why we have to go," said Shammah.

. . . .

We made good time to Bethlehem, in spite of the darkness; after all, it was my home country and I was very familiar with the tracks through the valleys. Our most difficult part had been getting past our own sentries. They were naturally suspicious that we might be returning to King Saul after spying out David's camp. Shammah told them that we

A Jar of Water

had been sent out to scout the Philistine positions around Bethlehem. They knew us, of course, and they knew I came from Bethlehem, so it was quite natural that we should be sent on such a mission; so they let us pass. But I was very uncomfortable at having to lie to our comrades.

We left our spears behind as being too clumsy for the sort of work we were about, but we had our swords and shields, our slings with a few round stones in our pouches, and a jar for the water. By the time we approached the town it was around midnight and the Moon, just past full, was half-way up the sky. Keeping low to the ground, we crawled to within a hundred paces of the town wall. By lying down we could see the buildings of Bethlehem clearly silhouetted against the lighter sky. It was a trick we had learned from Jonathan on an earlier campaign.

The wall round Bethlehem wasn't a proper fortification; it was only meant to keep wild animals out and domestic animals in. The gates were gateways, with wooden hurdles that could be dragged across at night and tied in place.

We waited and watched, remembering the age-old military axiom 'time spent in reconnaissance is never wasted'. There was no sign of any Philistine patrols or pickets outside the town. We were close to the southern gateway and we could see two sentries there. The Philistine warriors wear very distinctive helmets with a circular crest of horsehair. The silhouette is very different from our own round 'pot' helmets, so we could be sure those sentries were Philistines and not Israelites. Presently, we saw another Philistine walking around just inside the wall. He came up to the sentries and we heard a low murmur of voices as they exchanged the watchword. This third man spent a few moments talking to the sentries, then walked back on his patrol round the wall.

As far as we could see, almost all the houses were in darkness but there were still one or two lights. We could hear the sound of singing.

"Philistine drinking party," whispered Shammah.

I touched Shammah and Elika on the shoulder and led the way to the left, moving round the town until I found a good place to lie among some boulders. As we settled ourselves, we saw the patrolling sentry pass along the wall once more. I spoke to the others in as quiet a voice as I could manage.

"We're about halfway between the North and South gateways," I said. "The wall is low enough here for us to climb over. The well is near the North gate."

"Only two of us should go," said Shammah. "Elika, will you stay here with your sling ready?"

Elika nodded, "You should take off your helmets," he whispered. He was quite right; if we could recognise Philistine helmets in the dark, they could recognise ours. Without them, we should be mistaken for off-duty Philistines. So Shammah and I removed our helmets and laid them delicately on the ground.

We waited until the sentry passed by again and was out of sight to our left; then Shammah and I made our way up to the wall. It was only chest height, and we scrambled over easily and noiselessly. "But it won't be so easy with a jar full of water," I thought. As usual in times of danger, my mouth was dry and I could feel my heart beating in my chest. I led the way up a narrow alley between two houses until we could see into the town square. It was empty, but we saw that there had been a huge fire in the centre – the embers were still glowing red. The singing was coming from a house to our right. Across the square was my father's house. How I longed to go across and walk in the door! To see my family again! So close but so far away.

A Jar of Water

There was no possibility of moving stealthily through the middle of the town. We straightened up and walked boldly out into the square, turned left and walked up to the well. I put down the jar, picked up the bucket on its rope and dropped it into the well. Of course, the sentries at the North gateway heard that and turned. One of them shouted a challenge. Fortunately we've all picked up a few words of the Philistine tongue and Shammah called back a greeting.

"Good party?" called the sentry.

"Good!" replied Shammah, somehow managing to slur the single word so that he sounded drunk.

The sentry laughed and turned away.

By that time I had hauled up the bucket and filled the jar with water. We both drank a little from the bucket. Then we turned and headed back to the square. Suddenly a door opened – the door of the house where the singing had been coming from – and half-a-dozen men came out! They were clearly drunk; they were still singing and they were leaning on each other for support.

Boldly, Shammah waved at them and called out his greeting; they shouted back. One of them called, "Have a drink with me!"

That was the most dangerous moment! If we refused, they might get suspicious; if we went closer to them, they would see that we were Israelites. Fortunately for us, one of the men finally succumbed to the drink and collapsed face-down on the ground. A second man began to be sick against the wall of the house. The others turned to help, and Shammah and I walked quickly into the alley and back towards the wall. We crouched in the alley, waiting for the sentry to pass again, then started to climb the wall. Shammah went first, I passed the water jar to him and started to climb over. A shout came from our left!

I looked that way. It was the sentry. We must have made a noise. He was standing only a few yards away with his spear levelled. There was a whistling sound, an odd metallic clunking, a sort of grunt from the sentry, and he fell full length on the ground. Elika is a deadly shot with his sling!

I scrambled over the wall and ran with Shammah to where Elika was waiting. All three of us ran down the hill and behind us we heard first one shout, then a whole chorus of shouts of alarm.

We paused at the foot of the hill and looked back. There were the lights of torches bobbing along the wall and at least one was outside the wall close to where Elika had waited for us.

"They're after us," said Shammah, grimly, "Lead the way, Elhanan."

I led off up a steep ravine and over the ridge, then down to the track that would lead us back to Adullam. I was worried about the water. It was sloshing about in the jar, and I had already spilt some of it. We stopped here for some time, listening for sounds of pursuit and to catch our breath. The last thing we wanted was to lead the Philistines to our camp. We heard nothing, so we set off along the track, taking turns to carry the water.

The Moon had long passed the zenith and was dropping behind the hills to the West. The sky over the hills to the East began to grow lighter. Soon we could see the track and the hills clearly. We stopped again at a place where we could see several hundred paces of the track behind us. We waited here for a long time until we were sure there was no pursuit.

The sun was well up over the hills before we climbed wearily back up the ravine to the cave of Adullam - and found we were in trouble. Joab was standing with the sentries and six men at his back.

"Where have you been?" he asked us angrily.

Shammah replied, "We've been into Bethlehem, to fetch some water for Commander David." I held up the jar.

A Jar of Water

Joab had been looking angry. He now looked angry, suspicious and puzzled. "What are you talking about?"

"David said he was longing for a drink of water from the well in Bethlehem," explained Shammah, "so we went and fetched him one."

"But the Philistines have occupied Bethlehem."

"That's why we had to go at night," said Elika.

"Come with me," said Joab, turning on his heel and leading the way up to the cave. We fell in behind him and his men fell in behind us. Several of them were grinning at the obvious discomfort of their chief.

David was waiting at the entrance of the cave. He looked grave rather than angry.

"Here are the absentees, David," said Joab.

Shammah decided to take the initiative before David could speak. "We have been to Bethlehem," he said, "and brought you water from the well."

I held up the water jar.

Conflicting emotions passed across David's face: bewilderment, astonishment, uncertainty, distress. He took the jar and looked into it, poured out a drop of water onto his cupped hand.

"But why...?" he began.

"You wanted it, so we fetched it," said Shammah.

"But I never ... I never meant ... I didn't order you ..." It was the first time I had seen David lost for words.

"You were longing for some, so we brought you some," said Elika.

"You could have got yourselves killed," said David quietly. He almost sounded reproachful.

That was true and, after the excitement of the night, I suddenly realised what a mad thing we had done. I felt drained, exhausted.

113

"Drink, David, Commander of the armies of Israel," said Joab, in a strange, faraway sort of voice.

"I cannot drink this," said David, and his voice also sounded strange. "It would be like drinking the blood of these men who risked their lives." He lifted the jar high so that everyone could see it. "See, Men of Israel, this is water from the well in Bethlehem, brought here by these men because of the foolish whim of your Commander! See, O Yahweh, God of Hosts, is not this the blood of these men who went into deadly danger? Far be it from me to drink it. Let it be an offering to you, O God of Israel!"

He turned over the jar – and the water poured out over the dry soil and drained into the ground.

The Song

> *One interpretation of the 'Song of Songs' is that it is a collection of love poems that tell a story. But what story? Is it the story of King Solomon's love for his Queen, Pharaoh's daughter? Unlikely; Solomon's marriage was the normal way of sealing a political alliance (I Kings 3:1) and there is no indication that it was a love-match. Solomon did not live with his bride; he built her a separate palace (I Kings 7:8b). So perhaps the original story went something like this...*

The wheat harvest was over – and a good harvest it was that year. The grain had been threshed, winnowed and stored away in each family's silos. The poor had gleaned and reaped along the edges of the fields. Offerings had been set aside in baskets to be taken up to the Temple in Jerusalem. The King's District Officer had received the required tithe of the grain, olives, figs, honey and grapes. Now the entire town met on the threshing floor outside the North Gate to enjoy the Feast of First Fruits.

Eliab the Levite had accepted the loaves baked with flour from the new grain and waved them as an offering to Yahweh. He had poured out new wine. He had slaughtered the lambs and they had been roasted - the best of the meat to be a wave offering to Yahweh, the rest to be shared amongst the townspeople as a fellowship offering. All afternoon the feasting and drinking had continued and now, as the sun approached the western horizon, Sheba sang a psalm to the accompaniment of his lyre. Then he tapped out a rhythm on his tambourine and dancing began.

First the young men stepped out in a formal, processional dance. Then the young women and older girls took their turn at a graceful, intertwining dance around and between the fires.

"Asahel, who is that girl?" said Seth, pointing.

"That's Abigail, the daughter of Joram," replied his friend.

"No, the one behind her," said Seth.

"I don't know," Asahel shrugged his shoulders.

"She's beautiful. I must know who she is."

"She's OK," said Asahel, casually, "though I prefer Abigail myself." He stared for a moment and then said, "She's not bad at all. I wonder why we haven't seen her before. Her father must keep her in strict seclusion."

The two young men continued to watch as the dancers flowed round the fires, swaying and pirouetting, arms outstretched, long dresses swirling. Seth's eyes followed the movements of the girl behind Abigail. He had no interest in the other dancers, no matter how graceful their movements or how fair their faces. New and unfamiliar emotions were rising in his chest.

But the fires were beginning to die down, the sun was setting, light was fading, twilight was brief. Seth watched the girl as the dance broke up, and she disappeared among the crowd on the other side of the fires. He strained his eyes but could not see the faces of those she went to. He walked round, threading his way through the crowd, and caught a glimpse of her speaking to an older man - presumably her father. He did not recognise him. Several women were pressing round, perhaps to congratulate the father on his daughter's dancing. One of these women glanced at Seth, then looked more keenly. Seth was embarrassed; he had been caught staring at a girl. It was the height of disrespect. He dropped his gaze, turned away in confusion and made his way slowly back to his own parents.

Full darkness came and the moon was rising. The party was breaking up. Families were exchanging blessings and making their way home. Seth found his parents and his sister, Miriam, and followed them back to the family home.

The Song

Seth found it hard to settle to sleep. Novel thoughts and feelings were circling in his brain. He could picture the girl, her face illuminated in the firelight, her graceful figure bending and swaying in the firelight, her slender neck; even her sandalled feet seemed beautiful. And there was that strange feeling in his stomach, a strange, hot longing in his head and a feeling of strength in his arms – he wanted to take that girl and hug her to himself. He turned from side to side on his mattress. He could hear his father snoring in the next room. At last he rose and stepped quietly to the doorway, drew aside the curtain and went out into the courtyard. The moon was setting over the western roof of the house, and the sky in the east was already lightening, forecasting the sunrise. The air felt fresh and cool on his face and he drew in deep lungfuls. He stretched and yawned, turned and went back to his bed, settled down and immediately fell asleep.

He was awakened by the boom of his Father's voice.

"Isn't that boy awake yet? Miriam, go and stir up your brother."

Seth hastily sat up and began to pull on his tunic.

"I'm up!" he called, just as Miriam appeared in the doorway.

Soon they were breaking their fast together, after Father had given thanks.

"Remember what happened to the sluggard, Seth," said Father in his severe voice. "A little too much sleep – and poverty came upon him like a bandit."

"But you couldn't sleep last night, could you Seth?" said Miriam mischievously. "I heard you gadding about before sunrise."

Seth felt his cheeks grow hot, but Mother said sharply, "You must not have slept yourself, young lady, if you heard Seth."

"Not slept?" said Father. "Why, yesterday tired us all out, I suppose. I hope you are ready for a good day's work, boy."

"Yes, Father," said Seth, automatically.

Miriam, however, was not ready to be suppressed. "What kept you awake, Seth?" she said, still in that mischievous tone.

Seth looked at her. She smiled back at him. There was something about her expression. It was the one she used to wear when, as children, they had played together and shared secrets from their parents. Did she suspect?

"Well," said Father, "what kept you awake? Your sister seems very anxious to know."

Seth looked at Father. He had spoken sternly but his face had a neutral expression. Seth looked at his Mother. There was just the beginning of a smile at the corner of her lips. Seth took a deep breath before he spoke.

"I have seen the girl I want to marry."

Mother's face broke into a real beaming smile. Miriam clapped her hands in delight. "I knew!" she cried. "I saw you!"

"Saw what?" demanded Father, but did not wait for an answer. "What nonsense is this? You know perfectly well that your mother and I have been talking to Jotham and his wife about their eldest daughter. She is an excellent match for you."

"Oh Father!" said Seth. "But she is short and dumpy."

"Ooooh!" cried Miriam. "Don't you dare tell her so."

"She has a good figure for child-bearing," said Mother. "Just the woman to give you a son for the family inheritance."

"So who is this girl?" said Father. "What is her family?"

"She is the most beautiful girl in the world," said Seth.

"No doubt," said Father in a sarcastic voice, "but she has a name, I trust."

"I don't know her name," Seth had to admit. "I saw her last night in the dance."

The Song

Father snorted with disgust, but Miriam clapped her hands in delight. "Love at first sight!" she exclaimed. "It's so romantic."

"Be quiet, Miriam," said Mother, sharply. "Seth, how can you want to marry a girl you've only seen in the dance – and in firelight, at that?"

"She was so graceful. And she danced so beautifully."

"A boyish fancy," said Father, then added sternly, "I want to hear no more of it."

"Perhaps," said Mother, "if you could find out her family, and her name, your Father might..."

But Father had returned to his breakfast, and every line of his face and body said that, as far as he was concerned, the matter was closed.

. . . .

"Take a bushel of wheat and another of barley down to Reuel the potter," said Father, "in payment for that new cooking pot and water jar of your mother's."

"Yes, Father."

Seth decided to take Hannah, the most cooperative of the donkeys. He filled two baskets with the grain and, with the help of one of the day-hands, roped them on the donkey, carefully adjusting them so that the weight was evenly balanced on either side of her back. He walked out of the courtyard, with Hannah patiently following, headed for the Fountain Gate and soon arrived at the house of the potter. Reuel was in his yard, working at his wheel but, on seeing Seth, he at once greeted him, brushing the clay from his hands.

"Peace to you, young Seth."

"Peace to you, sir. I have brought the grain in payment."

"Excellent," said Reuel. "Your Father is prompt to pay his debts - not like some I could name. I hope you take after him."

"I do my best, sir."

They unloaded the two baskets and Seth helped carry them into Reuel's store room. Seth led Hannah back out of the yard. The Fountain Gate took its name from a small pool of water, good water, fed by a spring, just inside the town walls. Indeed the wall had been deliberately built around this spring, and the people had long ago built a low, circular stone wall to enclose and protect the pool. Seth decided to water Hannah before returning home. There was a woman already drawing water, so he waited at a respectful distance for her to finish and move away.

The woman filled her jar and straightened up, hoisting the jar onto her shoulder. The graceful movement was unmistakeable. It was the girl! Seth let out an audible gasp of surprise. The girl turned towards him, and he caught a glimpse of a lovely face before she hastily turned away and walked, balancing her water jar with practised ease, towards a large house nearby.

Seth did not move. He simply watched as she reached the house and passed through a doorway. But as she entered, she glanced back – and her glance lingered on Seth much longer than was necessary.

She disappeared. Seth stood for a few moments, shook himself and led Hannah towards the animal trough that was fed by the overflow of water from the pool. Hannah quickly satisfied her thirst, but Seth stared long and hard at the house which the girl had entered. It was a large house; it must indeed have been one of the largest houses in the town. He could see that the doorway led into a yard around which the house had been built, with rooms being added as required by a growing family, or by increasing wealth. On one side, a second storey had been added. He could see two latticed windows to this upper room. The ground floor walls were all blank and windowless, as was usual for security. As he watched, he saw a

The Song

movement at one of the lattices. Was it possible that the girl was looking out at him? Or was it someone wondering suspiciously who this stranger was, watching the house so closely?

Seth left Hannah by the trough and walked back into Reuel's yard. It might be the height of rudeness, but he had to take this chance to learn who she was.

Reuel, however, answered his question readily enough. "That house belongs to Hophni the merchant."

"Thank you," said Seth. That was all he needed to know, for everyone had heard of Hophni. He was a landowner of course – everyone except the poorest men owned some land. He was also a dealer in spices. When he was younger, so the story went, he had himself journeyed far to the East to bring back spices to the city of Jerusalem. He had grown rich and used his wealth to buy a large estate. Now he was older and it was his sons who made the long journeys to buy and sell. Where they went was kept secret, and no-one in the town had ever tried to discover the source of their spice.

Seth returned to where Hannah patiently waited by the water trough and made his way home. He had little hope that a man of Hophni's status would welcome him as a son-in-law. Perhaps he should simply forget the daughter. But she was not easy to forget. So, at supper time that evening, he told his parents that the girl he had seen was the daughter of Hophni.

"He would never look at our family," was Mother's immediate reaction.

"Ohhhh! She is beautiful!" was Miriam's response. "I would love to be one of her bridesmaids."

Seth looked anxiously at Father. There was no expression of instant rejection on Father's face. He looked thoughtful.

"It would be a good match for our family," he said. "Better than we should expect. I have little hope, but I will consider approaching Hophni."

. . . .

The next few days were difficult. Hophni's daughter was never far from Seth's thoughts. He remembered her graceful movements in the dance. He dwelt on her face and figure as he had seen them so briefly at the Fountain Gate. He threw himself into his work in the family fields, in the vineyard and with the animals but, even as he worked, his thoughts would stray.

At last came a morning when Father said to him, "Make sure your hands and face and feet are well washed, your hair well combed and you wear your best tunic. Be ready to come with me to the house of Hophni."

They walked together to the house by the Fountain Gate. Seth's mind was a heady mixture of hope and fear. He felt sick with anticipation and longing. Father led him into the courtyard of the house, where a servant greeted them and presently ushered them into the presence of Hophni himself.

"Welcome to my house," said Hophni but did not rise to greet them.

"Peace be to this house," responded Father as he and Seth took the seats that Hophni indicated to them.

Seth saw that his hoped-for father-in-law was a good many years older than his own Father. His beard and hair were streaked with grey. He was a portly man, but his dark skin and the wrinkles at the corners of his eyes showed that he had once led an outdoor life, and the big hands folded on his lap were roughened from hard work. He appeared to be what he in fact was: a man who had worked hard for his wealth and now enjoyed a modest retirement on the fruits of his labours.

"So this is the young man who wishes to steal from me the delight of my eyes and the support of my old age," said Hophni, sternly. "Stand up, boy, and let me look at you."

The Song

Seth scrambled to his feet and stood in embarrassment as Hophni studied him carefully.

"Come nearer," said Hophni with a gesture. Clearly he was a man accustomed to give orders and have them obeyed, so Seth did so. Hophni reached up to feel his shoulder and arm, and to examine his hand.

"You are strong, I see, and your Father has accustomed you to hard work. That is good," said Hophni. He looked carefully at Seth's face. "And I believe that women would consider you handsome." He gestured to Seth to sit down once more.

The servant reappeared with a tray on which were three goblets and a jug. He poured out wine and offered it to Hophni and his guests. Seth sipped his wine cautiously. It was good wine, he realised, as would be expected for a well-to-do household, and it had a very familiar taste...

"Good wine, boy?" said Hophni.

"Why yes, sir," stammered Seth. He looked sideways at Father who was sipping his wine with casual enjoyment. "It is very like my Father's wine."

For the first time Hophni smiled. In fact he gave a short, pleased laugh. "It is your Father's wine. It is because your Father's vineyard produces the best wine south of Jerusalem that we are talking together now. A marriage is not just a matter of love, my boy, although your Father tells me that you believe it is, as all young people do. It is a business arrangement. I see great opportunity in the alliance of your family with mine."

"Thank you, sir," said Seth, because he did not quite know what to say but felt it would be rude to say nothing.

"Your Father tells me that you are somewhat of a scholar also?"

"Somewhat, sir," replied Seth. "Baruch tells me that with some years of apprenticeship and if I applied myself

123

consistently, I would make a passable scribe." Baruch was the only scribe in the town, an important figure who drew up legal contracts and made visits to Jerusalem where he mixed with the Temple scribes and lawyers. He taught the town boys to read, and those with aptitude and interest he taught to write, although these were very few in number.

"That is high praise from Baruch," said Hophni, "but do you wish to become a scribe?"

"No, sir. I had thought only of maintaining my Father's estate."

Hophni nodded and looked pleased. "That is good, but some skill in reading and writing is needed for a man of business. My own sons have no head for figures, and I scarcely trust them with either my merchandise or my money. Can you add up an account twice and get the same total each time?"

"I can, sir."

"Good." Hophni rapped on the table and when the servant appeared said, "Call my daughter."

There was a short pause before the girl entered. She went to stand beside her father and waited modestly, with her eyes cast down and her hands folded in front of her. Seth, out of well-trained courtesy, once more rose to his feet while the two fathers remained seated, as was their prerogative.

"My daughter," said Hophni in a voice much more kind and gentle than he had been using to Seth, "this is the young man who wishes to steal you away from me."

"Yes, father," said the girl quietly, but without looking up.

"Walk with him. Talk with him. Let me know your honest opinion."

"Yes, father," said the girl again. She turned and left the room and Seth followed her. His cheeks felt hot, and he could feel his heart thudding in his chest. Behind him he heard Hophni say, "I am a man of business, but I will not use my daughter as a business asset."

The Song

The two young people came out into the open air of the courtyard. The girl stopped and turned to face him. He looked down at her and saw a lovely face, dark eyes with finely-pencilled brows, perfect skin of pale bronze, high cheekbones and scarlet lips, the whole supported by a slender neck. She wore a sky-blue gown caught in at the waist by a girdle which had gold threads in it. Clearly, she had a good figure under her gown.

She looked up at him and saw a tall young man, with broad shoulders and neck. He was handsome, although scarcely bearded, but there was strength in the line of his jaw and mouth. He was looking down at her with delight in his eyes and a broad smile. Powerful and novel feelings came sweeping over her. She felt her cheeks redden and she dropped her gaze. Just before she did so, she smiled and Seth saw two perfect lines of white teeth.

"Please," he said in a voice that was not as steady or as strong as he would have wished, "I have not yet been told your name."

"My name is Tabitha, sir" she replied, and her voice seemed gentle and musical to him.

"That is a lovely name," he managed to say, then added with more confidence, "You are well-named, for I saw you dance and you truly are a gazelle."

She looked up at him again and smiled; and again he saw those perfect teeth. Suddenly she turned away from him with a cry of, "My loaves!"

She dashed across to the corner of the courtyard, where Seth saw two ovens from which, he now realised, the delicious smell of baking bread had been filling his nostrils, but he had been too taken with Tabitha to notice.

She snatched up a cloth, bent down and pulled a tray of loaves out of one oven and a second tray from the other.

"Not burnt," she said in relieved tones, "but they so easily might have been." She looked back at Seth with a smile. "That would not have been a good sign for a prospective husband."

"I am glad that you see me as a prospective husband," said Seth.

"There have been others," she said lightly, "but you are the first that my father has welcomed."

"I hope you might learn to welcome me, Tabitha."

She blushed and dropped her eyes again. Then she picked up a platter and offered it to him.

"Honey cakes, freshly baked," she said shyly.

"Baked by you, or perhaps your mother," said Seth, looking around him.

Tabitha's expression changed to one of sadness. "My mother died three years ago."

"I am so sorry," said Seth in shame. "I had no idea." He paused then added, "I see why your father says that you are the support of his old age. I also see why you are the delight of his eyes."

Tabitha smiled and held up the platter once more. "Will you try one of my honey cakes, sir?"

"My name is Seth," he said, choosing a cake and biting into it carefully. "It is delicious," he said a moment later.

"My father says that I am a passable cook, sir."

"Please call me Seth."

"Would that be proper, since we have only met today?"

"I wish you would."

"As you wish – Seth."

. . . .

Much later, as Seth and Father walked home together, Father said, "I am surprised, but Hophni does seem to look favourably on this match. It was the wine that pleased him. My

The Song

father's father knew well what he was doing when he planted our vineyard."

Seth nodded in reply. He did not trust himself to speak. His heart was full of delight - full of hope, but mixed with fear, for there was much still to be agreed before a match could be made.

. . . .

"Well, my princess, what do you think of that young man?"

"He seems strong, but I think he is gentle," Tabitha replied cautiously. Then her feelings got the better of her. "He has gorgeous eyes - eyes like doves. They are so deep. They sparkle like the mountain streams. They are mounted in his face like jewels."

"I am pleased that he pleases you," said Hophni.

Tabitha caught his hands in hers. "But father, how can I leave you on your own - with no companion?"

"I have a house full of servants!" exclaimed Hophni. "And Keturah the housekeeper will take care of me. When your brothers decide they are ready to settle down and marry, I will have two daughters-in-law." He sighed. "But they will never replace my princess. Perhaps when you are married, you and your husband will take the trouble to walk a little way to visit your aged father."

"Of course I will, father."

. . . .

Tabitha did not sleep well that night. Her heart and mind were too full of longed-for thoughts and feelings. She had talked with other girls about boys. She had felt both happiness and jealousy when her closest friend Naomi had been married.

She had had her own private dreams. Now it was happening to her! A young man wanted her to be his wife! She was happy! Yet she was anxious. Suppose their fathers could not agree on a marriage contract. Was Seth as wonderful as he seemed? Would he be good to her? Men could be deceitful. Her mother had warned her of that, years ago. It would be good if her mother were still alive to advise her. She needed someone to talk to. She must visit Naomi in the morning. Was it nearly morning? The room was still dark. She rose from her bed and went to the lattice window. The sky was still black and the stars bright. She looked down at the pool where she had first seen Seth. How romantic it would be if he were to be there, looking up at her window...

. . . .

For Seth the days now seemed to drag. Father met several times with Hophni and they had asked Baruch the scribe to begin drawing up the marriage contract. Mother and Miriam had visited Tabitha. Miriam was overjoyed that Tabitha had asked her to be one of the bridesmaids. Father had spoken to Joram the artisan about extending the family house. Joram and his young men had begun work on building the extra rooms with a small, private courtyard. Hophni's sons had returned from their latest mercantile journey. Seth was relieved to find that, after a cautious start, they had become good friends. He had asked Asahel to be his best man at the wedding. Invitations to be ready to come to the wedding feast had gone out by word of mouth to all their relatives and friends. Hophni's sons had left to go to Egypt, and the wedding would take place when they returned.

After that, there seemed to be nothing for Seth to do except wait. He carried on with his work on the family estate, but he spent a good deal of time day-dreaming, even though

The Song

Father rebuked him: "He who works his land will have abundant food; he who chases fantasies lacks judgement. The sooner we get this wedding over and done with the better."

. . . .

"So tell me, how soon is the wedding to be?"

Tabitha and Naomi were walking back from the fields in a group of women who had been taking the midday meal out to their menfolk.

"Father has not said," replied Tabitha. "I hope that my brothers will return soon from Egypt. Then the wedding can be held as soon as father gives the word. Keturah has been hinting that it will be next month; she has been making arrangements to have the food for the feast ready whenever father wishes."

"We will finish your dress before the next Sabbath," said Naomi, for she had been helping Abishag the seamstress with that most important item.

"Tell me truly, Naomi," said Tabitha, "what is it like to be married?"

"Very good, Tabitha, if you are married to a good man – and Seth is a good man. I am sure of it."

And the two girls bent their heads together and talked as young women do about men and marriage. At the last, Naomi said, with all the wisdom of ten months of married life, "And you must make sure that Seth understands that you are the head of the house. The man may be the head of the marriage, but the wife is in charge of the house."

"Coooo...eeee! Tabitha! Naomi!"

They were passing one of the town's vineyards and, looking round, the two girls saw Miriam standing at the edge of the rows of vines. Like them, she carried a basket and a water jar. They waited as Miriam hurried over to them. The three girls exchanged hugs.

"Tabitha, you look so beautiful!" exclaimed Miriam. "No wonder Seth can't wait for the wedding."

"Has he said so much?" asked Tabitha, not sure whether to be delighted or embarrassed.

"No, he won't say anything to me," said Miriam, making a face, "but he only thinks about you. You can see it in his face. Father says he has become quite useless at his work."

Naomi gave a little gasp. "There he is!"

The other two looked round. Naomi was pointing towards the row of vines where three young men, Seth among them, had appeared, working steadily away at their pruning. The day was hot and they had rolled down the tops of their tunics to the waist.

Tabitha stared, her lips slightly parted. Strange feelings, longings, swept over her. This sturdily-built young man wanted to marry her – her, of all women!

"He is handsome," said Naomi critically, "and broad shouldered. I can see why you like him."

Tabitha's lips moved, but she spoke so softly that her friends did not hear her: "Like an apple tree in the forest is my love. How I long to sit in his shade and taste his sweetness."

"Ooh! There's Johanan!" said Miriam in an excited voice. "I wish he would look at me!"

A fourth young man had come into sight among the vines. Without a thought for the proprieties, Miriam waved vigorously. One of the men looked up, saw the girls, said something to his companions and they all turned and stared. Johanan waved shyly back, and Miriam blew him a kiss.

"Shameless! Shameless!" said a woman's stern voice. Several of the older women had seen what was happening and their faces showed their disapproval.

The Song

"Get about your business," said another woman. And the three girls, knowing how quickly gossip and rumour spreads and that scandalous stories might get back to their fathers or Naomi's husband, turned and hurried off towards the town gate. Comments about the behaviour of young women and the slack discipline of their parents followed them.

. . . .

For all his young life, Seth had been an excellent sleeper. Not so now. Often he rose and wandered out into the courtyard to look at the stars. Then came the night of the full moon. The courtyard was brilliantly lit with its soft light. Seth drew on his cloak and wandered out into the street. He headed towards the Fountain Gate. It was madness, of course. It was the height of impropriety. But his longing to see Tabitha again was so intense.

Suddenly, there were two men walking towards him. He stopped, his heart pounding. They were the watchmen of course. There was little danger and almost no crime in the town but the precaution of keeping the watch at night was maintained, and all young men were required to take their turn.

"Who goes?" came a gruff challenge and, a moment later, "Why, it's young Seth."

Seth was relieved to recognise one of the watchmen as a neighbour.

"I am Seth," he confirmed.

"What are you doing out so late?" said the other watchman, suspiciously.

"Taking the air – and the moonlight," replied Seth. "I couldn't sleep," he added, feeling that more explanation was needed.

"It's a grand night to be out," said the gruff voice, "for those who have to be out. And easier to do our job."

"I'll bid you goodnight," said Seth.

"Goodnight to you," said the watchmen and moved on down the street.

Seth wondered whether to go home. He turned back, hesitated; his desire was too strong, and he headed again for the Fountain Gate. There was the gate and the pool and the house. He stood in the moonlight and looked up at the lattice window behind which, he now knew, his beloved was sleeping. He stood there, sick with longing. How long he stood there he did not know. Then he realised that the full moon was much lower in the sky, almost touching, as it seemed, the roof of Hophni's house. He had better return home. It occurred to him that he was thirsty, so he went over to the pool and picked up the bucket. He paused. This was the bucket she used to draw water. Her hands had touched it. On an impulse, he raised the bucket to his lips and kissed it.

"That was foolish," he thought. He lowered the bucket into the pool, drew it up and scooped up water with his hand to his mouth. He put down the bucket, wiped his lips with the back of his hand and turned for a last look up at the lattice. Was that a little gasp he heard? Was that a movement he saw? That whole wall of the house was now in shadow. It must have been some trick of the moonlight. He waited but there was no sound or movement. He turned and began to walk towards home.

. . . .

Tabitha had found it difficult to get to sleep. The full moon shone straight through her lattice window. Still, it made a good atmosphere for romancing. What would it really be like to be married? How would it be to be alone with Seth – husband and wife? Slowly the moon rose to its zenith before beginning its descent to the western horizon. As it descended,

The Song

it no longer shone on her window, and she fell at last into a shallow sleep. Much later she awoke with a start. What was that sound? She heard a distinct splash. Someone at the pool? At night? She rose from her bed and walked cautiously to the window. There was someone at the pool: a man. Who could it be? She leaned closer to the lattice. The man stooped to drink, then looked straight up at her window. She started back with a little gasp, putting her hand to her mouth. It was Seth! No doubt about it; the moon still shone on the pool, full on his face as he looked up at her window. He had come by night to look up at her window! How romantic! And how risky!

A thought came to her - so dangerous that she was surprised by it. She would go to him. She pulled on her sandals and her cloak. She moved quickly, for she knew if she stopped to think, her mind would prevent her. It was an outrageous thing, quite improper. If her father caught her she would be whipped at the very least. She was not a dancer for nothing; she moved swiftly but silently out of her room, down the stairway and into the courtyard. She unbarred the door and opened it slowly, so that it did not squeak.

She was too late! He had gone. Disappointment flooded over her; it was followed by determination. He could not have gone far. She had never been out of the house at night, but she was sure there was no danger for a woman in the streets of the town. In any case, the moon was still lighting the streets as if it was day. She hurried away.

There was someone ahead of her. "Seth," she called quietly. The person turned round. No, it was two people.

"Who goes?" said a gruff voice.

It was the watchmen. She walked quickly up to them.

"What are you doing here, missie?" said the gruff voice in a tone of surprise.

Tabitha lifted her head proudly. She was no 'missie'. She was the daughter of one of the wealthiest men in town, and she had no need to be ashamed before two humble watchmen.

"I am looking for Seth, the one my heart loves," she said, and the younger of the watchmen sniggered at those words. "He has been this way. Have you seen him?"

"He has passed us just now," said the gruff-voiced one, pointing down the street. "But, miss, you should not be out in the streets at this hour. Let us escort you back to your house."

"Thank you, sir, but I will go on. Please stand aside."

"Of course, miss." The two watchmen separated and she passed between them, walking quickly. Behind her she heard the beginnings of an argument, before she turned a corner – and there was Seth. He was standing still, looking towards her. Perhaps he had heard the watchmen's voices. She ran to him and caught his arm.

"Tabitha?" It was a cry of astonishment. It was a question.

"Oh Seth, I am so glad to find you. You came to watch my window, and I wanted to run to you."

"Tabitha," said Seth seriously, "you should not be out here and neither should I. If your father should hear of this..."

"Oh, but I have so longed to see you again, to talk to you. You are the one my heart loves. I want to cling to you. I want you to hold me. I want to take you to my mother's room..."

"Tabitha," said Seth again. He felt he was in danger of losing control. The moon, now low in the sky, shone directly down the street. She stood there in the moonlight, her face lit up, her eyes like deep pools, smiling up at him, her lips slightly parted. When he had seen her before, her hair had been decently covered. Now it was loose and dropped in black waves to her shoulders. Her cloak had fallen open; she was wearing only the most delicate of gowns.

"You are beautiful, my darling," he said. "Your hair is – is like a flock of goats on the mountainside. Your mouth is

The Song

lovely; your neck is like a tower of ivory. Your two breasts are like two fawns - twin fawns, my gazelle."

"Oh Seth," she murmured, dropping her eyes. She leaned against him. "Oh! If only you were to me like a brother!" she added vehemently. "Then I would kiss you, here in the street, and no-one would despise me. I would lead you and bring you to my mother's house. I would give you spiced wine to drink, the nectar of my pomegranates."

"Truly you have stolen my heart, my sister," breathed Seth in her ear. "With one glance from your eyes, you have stolen my heart. But," he said, drawing back and taking her delicate hands in his, "you are a garden locked up, my sister, and we should not arouse or awaken love until the time is right."

He led her back to Hophni's house, left her at the door and hurried home, fearful now that it was close to sunrise and that his Father might discover what had taken place.

. . . .

"The King is on his way here. He will stay in our town tonight." Asahel came breathlessly into the courtyard.

"Eh? What's that? Remember your manners, boy!" said Father.

"Sorry, sir," said Asahel. "Peace be to you and your house, sir."

"Peace be to you, young man," said Father. "Now give me your message."

"The King is coming. His forerunners have arrived to say that he will stay in the town tonight. The Elders will meet him at the Sheep Gate, and every house has to be ready to give hospitality to him and his servants and bodyguards."

"I thank you for your message," said Father. "Be on your way and remember your manners."

Asahel disappeared, and Father turned to Seth. "Go and tell your Mother while I select a tender young goat from the flock."

Mother, predictably, threw up her hands in dismay at the news. "We have nothing fit for a King!" she exclaimed. "Miriam, we must bake more bread - a great deal more bread. Soldiers have such large appetites. And we must bake cakes – honey cakes – and fig cakes – and we need milk. And Father must bring out his finest wine. Seth, make sure all the water jars are full so that our guests may wash their hands and their feet."

The afternoon passed quickly in business and preparation. Seth found himself sweeping the yard, clearing out rubbish and generally doing jobs that he would normally have expected to be done by the womenfolk. Soon there was a delicious smell of baking bread, joined later by the smell of roasting meat. Indeed, it now seemed as if the whole town had been turned into one great bakery and kitchen.

Asahel came with another message: the Elders requested Father to accommodate four of the King's bodyguards. The King himself would spend the night at the house of Hophni, as that was the largest and finest house in the town. Father at once gave Seth a skin of his best wine to take to Hophni for the King's supper.

"And may I then go down to the Sheep Gate to see the King arrive?" asked Seth.

"I suppose you may," said Father, grudgingly. "Make sure you show due respect."

Seth and Asahel hurried towards the Fountain Gate, pausing only at those houses where Asahel had to deliver a message regarding accommodation.

Seth banged on the door of Hophni's house and, forgetting Father's last words, opened it and walked straight in. The courtyard was a scene of domestic busyness, even more so

The Song

than his own house, for there were more servants to be busy. A male servant came towards him, frowning at his discourtesy, but at once Tabitha, from a group of women busy around the ovens, saw him and came running to greet him.

"Peace to this house," said Seth, remembering his manners with an effort. He held out the skin of wine. "My Father sends this wine to you. It is our finest vintage to set before the King."

"I thank you in the name of my father," said Tabitha, taking the wineskin and handing it straight to the servant. "But..."

"My friend is too hasty," said Asahel. "I have been sent by the Elders with a request that your father provides hospitality for the King himself tonight."

"Go, call my father," said Tabitha to the servant. "I am sure my father will be most pleased that his house is considered worthy of this honour," she added to the two young men.

Seth smiled at Tabitha. Tabitha smiled back. Asahel coughed and smiled at no one in particular. There was an embarrassed silence.

"What's this, what's this!" said Hophni's voice. "Have you young people all forgotten the courtesies? Do you not know that it is considered bad fortune for a betrothed couple to meet before their wedding day?"

Tabitha, blushed and dropped her eyes, looking suitably contrite. "I am sorry, father." She turned and rejoined the women around the ovens. Seth thought, "If he only knew."

"Peace to you, sir," said Asahel formally. "The Elders of the town send their greetings and request that you provide hospitality for the King himself and his attendants this night."

Hophni had been looking stern, but now his face broke into a warm smile. "I will be most pleased. Tell the Elders that it will be an honour to welcome the King to my humble house.

And thank your Father for his most excellent gift of wine," he added to Seth.

The two young men bowed hastily and turned to leave, for it seemed to both of them that, once Hophni's pleasure had had time to abate, he might deliver a lecture on manners and courtesy and how the young men of today paid little respect to the wisdom of their fathers.

They walked across town to the Sheep Gate, where already a crowd was gathering. At one side of the gateway, the Elders of the town were gathered as a respectful welcoming party for the King. Asahel went over to inform them that all their requests for hospitality had been agreed by the recipients. "Not that anyone would dare to refuse," he said quietly to Seth. "It's not often the King visits our little place."

"Not since we were boys," agreed Seth, just as if he were looking back on years and years of adulthood.

More men were arriving, and also boys and girls; most of the womenfolk were still busy with their baking and cooking. It was going to be hard to find a good place to get a good view of the King. So Seth and Asahel joined a group of young men and older boys who had decided to go outside the town walls. They spread themselves along both sides of the road and waited, with varying degrees of patience and impatience. The road wound away between the fields before disappearing into a shallow valley through the southern hills. The heat of the day was past and the sun was already low in the western sky when they saw a man come running up the road. He carried a shield and spear, and on the shield was the King's badge.

The man hardly glanced at the young men and boys waiting on each side of the road. He ran straight between them and through the gateway of the town.

"He must be a forerunner," said Seth. "The King himself must be close now."

The Song

"Look!" Asahel pointed along the road. A drift of dust could just be seen, like a slender column of smoke, rising up from the valley through which the road ran. Eagerly the young men stared at that distant dust. Soon they could see figures moving on the road - at first no more than tiny stick figures; then marching men, the lowering sun glinting on polished metal; at last a column of warriors, marching two-by-two. Dust spurted up each time their sandaled feet hit the road. They carried long spears of polished wood with bronze heads; swords were belted at their sides. They wore helmets and muscled breastplates, also of bronze. They carried round shields of wood, bound with bronze and decorated with silver, on which sunlight sparkled. They tramped up the road between the lines of waiting men - thirty warriors in all the pride and vigour of young manhood. They passed through the gateway and into the town.

And now the watchers broke into spontaneous cheers, for here came the chariot of the King, drawn by two horses - not mere donkeys but real horses. The wooden framework of the chariot was overlaid with silver. Standing beside the driver was the King himself: a tall man, armed with breastplate and a helmet with a long plume of horses' hair. He held a bow in his hand and balanced easily with the irregular pitching of the chariot as it rolled over the stones and hollows of the roadway. He raised his right hand in acknowledgement of the cheers, and his chariot passed between his subjects and entered the town. At once there came a burst of cheering from the citizens waiting inside the gate.

There was more to come: first a group of attendants, richly attired; two older, grey-bearded ones riding on donkeys; the others on foot; then three wagons drawn by oxen. The first one had a raised cover, as if for carrying people as well as goods, and indeed it did for, as it passed, Seth and Asahel could see two young, veiled women peeping cautiously out through the drapes at the rear of the wagon. "Serving maids," said Asahel with a sigh. "How I would love to be a king."

At the end of the procession marched a rearguard of thirty more warriors, armed like the vanguard. As soon as they had passed, the young men surged around to follow them into the town. Seth saw that the King had dismounted and was being formally greeted by the Elders. Then the gathering began to break up. Two of the Elders escorted the King towards the Fountain gate and Hophni's house. The attendants and soldiers were guided towards their billets for the night. The crowd dispersed - those who had hospitality responsibilities hurrying to their homes; others moving off slowly, talking animatedly, reluctant to go home, for in a monotonous country life, the arrival of the King and his procession was indeed an event of great excitement.

When Seth eventually arrived home he saw that the four soldiers who had been billeted on them were already there. Their equipment, spears and shields were neatly stacked against one wall of the courtyard, and the four men were just refastening their sandals after washing their feet.

"Hullo Seth, my old playmate," called one of the soldiers.

Seth looked, stared, smiled broadly in recognition and hurried forward.

"Caleb, it's good to see you." The two young men hugged each other's shoulders.

"You two know each other?" said one of the other soldiers.

Caleb took Seth by the arm and pulled him forward to introduce him.

"This is Seth. We've known each other since... oh, as long as I can remember – until I left home and got into bad company."

"Well, mates, you see what he thinks of us," said one of the others.

The Song

"I don't think you look like bad company," said Seth. "Bodyguards to the King - what could be better than that?"

"You haven't seen them when they've had a few drinks," said Caleb.

Father called them in to the meal, and soon they were seated and enjoying a rather better supper than Seth was accustomed to. But even he was surprised at the quantities which the soldiers ate eagerly.

"Does the King starve you?" he asked, earning a frown from his Father for gross discourtesy.

"No," said Caleb, "but he works us hard."

Caleb, like Seth, had been born and raised in the town, but Caleb was the third son in his family. When his older brothers got married, the family estate proved to be too small to support the extending family. So Caleb had had little choice but to leave home to try to make his own way in the world. Seth had heard that he had gone to Jerusalem and become a soldier, but that had been several years ago, so the two young men had a great deal of catching up to do. Seth listened eagerly as his friend described a life that seemed so much more adventurous that he had ever dreamed possible.

. . . .

Hophni banged at the door, pushed it open and walked into the courtyard. Seth looked up, startled; how could such a dignified elder as Hophni so forget the courtesies? And what had happened to make Hophni look as he did? His face was grey under his tan; surely those were tear streaks on his cheeks. What could possibly make a man such as Hophni cry? A cold chill spread over Seth from his heart to his head. Tabitha. It must be Tabitha. Was she sick?

"Call your Father," said Hophni, and there was a tremor and a hoarseness in his voice. "I must speak with him – and with you."

"Come inside, sir," said Seth, and he could hear the anxiety in his own voice. He gestured to Hophni to precede him into the house, at the same time calling, "Father! Father!"

They entered the family room, and almost at once Father appeared saying, "What? What? Have you lost all manners, boy?" Then, seeing Hophni, he exclaimed, "My friend, what has happened?"

Hophni sat down without waiting to be invited; or rather he flopped down, as if his legs were suddenly too weak to sustain him.

"She has gone!" he gasped out in a desperate tone. "He has taken her!"

"What? Who?" said Father, and "Tabitha?" said Seth simultaneously.

"The King," said Hophni. "She danced for him – yesterday evening – you know she is a beautiful dancer – I let her dance for him, fool that I am! This morning he commanded that she go with him – and he took her!"

"You let him take her?!" Seth's voice rose to a scream.

"He is the King!" said Hophni and buried his face in his hands.

"Seth," said Father. "You cannot refuse a man who has sixty armed soldiers at his back."

But Seth was no longer listening. He ran out into the street. He headed for the Jerusalem gate and ran full tilt.

There had been a crowd by the gate, watching the King's departure, but they were now dispersing to their work, gossiping over the excitement of the royal visit. Seth pushed his way past and ran through the gateway. The road that ran northwards was empty. Seth ran to the brow of the hill and stopped. The road curved downwards into the valley, then up

The Song

again until it disappeared into the pass. Seth, staring hard, thought he saw a faint drift of dust but, almost at once, a breath of wind dispersed it and there was nothing! The King was gone! And Tabitha was gone!

Seth stood staring into the distance. He felt as if his heart had been torn in two.

. . . .

How long he stood there he did not know. The sun was high in the sky when at last he turned and walked slowly back home.

Hophni was still sitting with Father when Seth reached home. Hophni seemed more composed, but his face showed the pain he was feeling.

Father was speaking gravely. "Only from Yahweh does a man get justice. It is as the prophet Samuel foresaw when Israel first asked for a king: 'You will become his slaves.' So Samuel warned our fathers, and now it has come upon us."

"I am sorry for you, young man," said Hophni to Seth. "It would have been a good match and would have consoled my old age. Now I am alone..."

"Not alone, my friend, not alone," said Father.

"Is there nothing we can do?" said Seth.

Father shrugged his shoulders. "He is the King. What can we do?"

"Can we not follow the King to his palace, petition him to release Tabitha, plead with him?"

"I told him she was betrothed," said Hophni despairingly. "It made no difference."

Presently, Hophni pulled himself together sufficiently to take his leave. As soon as he had gone, Seth turned to his Father.

"Father, I must go to Jerusalem."

"What can you do there?"

"I don't know!" said Seth desperately. "I must do something. I must get her back!"

"It cannot be done. Stay here and I will go back to Jotham to see if he is still willing to allow his daughter..."

"I do not want to marry that girl!"

"My son..."

"It's all very well for you, Father. You've never been in love!"

"Seth," said Father in a much more gentle tone than he had been using, "it is true that my marriage to your Mother was arranged by our parents, but after we were married, we fell in love. If I were to lose her, I would be losing half my heart."

Seth said nothing.

"A wife of noble character who can find?" said Father quietly, as if speaking to himself. "She is worth far more than rubies. Well, Seth," he continued, raising his voice, "if you love this girl – and she seems a worthy character – then do whatever you must to win her back. And you have my blessing."

Seth looked at his Father in astonishment. Suddenly his feelings overcame him. He stepped over to his Father and put his arms around his shoulders. His father reached up and embraced him, and they hugged each other, Father and son...

. . . .

The King's procession marched on its way to Jerusalem: the soldiers at front and rear, the King in his chariot, his attendants and advisers, and the three wagons, bumping and rolling over the rough, stony surface of the roadway.

Tabitha sat in the covered wagon. She sat frozen in shock, her mind too numb to think, unable to grasp what had happened. As the wagon jolted over the bumps her body

The Song

swayed automatically, making no attempt to keep her balanced. Her eyes stared unseeing at the ox-hide canopy of the wagon.

The two veiled serving-girls sat opposite her. They spoke to her, but she did not answer. They asked her her name and told her theirs. It is doubtful if Tabitha even took in that she was being spoken to. One of them tried to speak reassuringly, telling her that life was good in the palace harem. Presently she gave it up, and the journey continued in silence.

The procession stopped about the middle of the day while the soldiers rested and ate. The two girls brought out bread, olive oil and cheese, and wine mixed with water. Tabitha paid no attention to what she was offered.

They went on - sometimes downhill, sometimes climbing steeply. The sun, which had shone on the right side of the wagon when they set off, now lit up the canopy on the left. At last there came a change. The wagon was moving over a smoother surface than the rough roadway. A shadow fell over the wagon and almost immediately passed away. Men's voices were calling out greetings and salutations. There were more shadows, alternating with patches of sunlight. The wagon stopped. A man came to hold the heads of the horses. Another man unlaced the canopy at the rear. One of the serving-girls climbed out and turned to take Tabitha by the arm, while the second girl took her other arm. There was no help for it. Tabitha half-climbed, was half-pulled down, to a pavement of broad stone slabs. The girls, continuing to hold Tabitha's arms, firmly but not cruelly, led her up a broad flight of stone steps and through a wide and high doorway. She was led through a series of corridors, deeper into the building. They came to a doorway where two soldiers armed with swords stood on guard. One of the soldiers opened the door and Tabitha was led through.

"This is the harem," said one of the girls.

Found in Translation

. . . .

"Baruch," said Seth, "I wish that you would take me to Jerusalem."

Baruch, short and slightly built but with a full, dark beard, looked up from his writing desk.

"Young Seth, isn't it?" he said.

"Yes, sir," said Seth. "Peace be to you and your household."

"And peace to you," said Baruch. "Why should I take you to Jerusalem?"

"You said once that, if Father was willing, you would make me your apprentice and teach me to be a scribe."

"I did. But I thought that you were determined to work on your father's land and not learn the demanding but rewarding trade of a scribe."

"May I not change my mind, sir?"

"Seth," said Baruch sternly. "Do not play games with me. You want to go to Jerusalem because your betrothed has been taken there by the King, and you want me to take you to Jerusalem in the hope that you will see her again."

Seth hesitated, then, "You speak the truth, sir," he said.

"Good. Then let us understand each other. I know that your heart aches from what has happened, and I would help you if I could. But I can do nothing for you."

Seth opened his mouth, but Baruch held up one hand as he continued.

"When I next go to Jerusalem, it will be to deliver this scroll which I am copying." He indicated his writing-desk on which two scrolls were lying, partly unrolled. One was already filled with writing, the other little more than half-filled. "I will go to the Temple of Yahweh and hand this copy and the original to the scribes there. I may spend a few days in talk with the scribes and the priests, discussing certain matters of

The Song

the Law. I will be given another scroll to copy, and I shall return home. I have no business in the palace, where your girl will now be in the harem. Nor is there any way I can help you to gain entry to the palace."

"Take me to Jerusalem as your servant," said Seth.

"My servant?"

"All I wish is for you to take me to Jerusalem. Show me the way; show me where the King's palace is. That is all I ask of you, Baruch."

Baruch chuckled. "Me with a servant? My friends in Jerusalem will think that I have suddenly become wealthy."

"Please – sir."

"Well," said Baruch, "I like the thought of arriving in Jerusalem with a servant – unpaid, of course." He looked sharply at Seth.

Seth felt a first spark of hope. "Of course, sir."

"It can do no harm, I suppose," said Baruch, speaking as much to himself as to Seth. He looked the younger man in the eye. "If it teaches you that your cause is hopeless, it will perhaps do some good ... Very well. I will take you to Jerusalem."

. . . .

Tabitha felt as if she had been in a deep sleep and was moving into a nightmare. She looked around. She was standing in a large, dimly-lit room in which couches, stools and tables were scattered. Everywhere there were girls - lounging on the couches, seated on stools, standing in twos and threes. They were wearing a good deal less clothing than she - less clothing than she had ever dared imagine - and their long hair was loose and flowed free in curling tresses around their shoulders and down their backs. There was a buzz of chatter in girlish voices as Tabitha and her escort entered the room, but it ceased at once and every face was turned towards the newcomers. Then one woman rose and walked towards them. She halted and stood, tall and straight-backed, a few paces in front of Tabitha, and looked her up and down with an expression of some distaste.

"Well?" she said at last.

"Please, my lady," said the girl who held Tabitha's right arm, "this is Tabitha. The King saw her dance last night and commanded that she be brought into his harem."

The tall woman made a sound through her nose that Tabitha had never heard before. It did not sound pleasant. "If the King wishes it, then it shall be done," she said, wrinkling her nose as if she had smelt a bad smell. "Take her and bathe and dress her. Then bring her to me."

"Yes, my lady."

The two girls led Tabitha across the room, through another doorway, along a passage and into yet another room - a room of which Tabitha had never seen the like. The floor was covered with smooth tiles. The walls were plastered and covered with painted trees: stately cedars, slender palms, fig, olive and pomegranate trees, vines growing up the walls, spreading and twisting everywhere, huge bunches of grapes hanging from their delicate branches - all painted with a realism that astonished Tabitha. In the middle of the room was a pool of water. Sweet fragrances rose from it.

At once Tabitha felt herself being undressed by the two girls. She was still too dazed and too surprised to resist. She allowed the girls to do as they pleased and, having undressed her, they proceeded to disrobe themselves. They led her to the steps that led down into the pool, and at last Tabitha gave a little squeak of fear and resisted. But they held her arms firmly and pulled her down the steps. To Tabitha's further astonishment, the water was warm. In a moment the three girls

The Song

were seated on the smooth tiling of the pool with only their heads above water.

Tabitha at last began to relax. The water was so warm and somehow comforting; the scents from the pool were sweet and invigorating. She moved her arms and legs cautiously. The water was supporting her body like the softest of beds. The two girls were smiling at her, and she realised that she was smiling back.

"That's better," said one of the girls.

"This is one of our great pleasures," said the other. "It is so good to be able to wash the dust of travelling off oneself."

How long they enjoyed soaking away the travel stains Tabitha could not have said, but at last the two girls led her out of the pool, brought from a ledge along one wall soft towels of finest cotton, and they began to dry themselves. Tabitha, even in her well-to-do father's house, had never known such a luxurious feeling as she dabbed at herself.

"You are beautiful," said one of the girls. "No wonder the King desires you."

Tabitha now noticed, for the first time, how pale-skinned her two companions were. She looked at her own hands and arms, which were dark brown – and presumably her face was also.

"I have been darkened by the sun," she said, "while you have been veiled against its heat."

"It will pass in time. Some of us were as dark as you when we first came here."

They took Tabitha to the next room where all three dressed in beautiful, light, but skimpy clothing. Tabitha felt underdressed, but at least she was no worse off than her companions.

"Please tell me your names."

Found in Translation

"I am Rebecca," said one girl, who had very dark hair, "this is Deborah." Deborah was a redhead and taller than her companion.

"You are both beautiful also," said Tabitha sincerely. "I hope we can be friends." She held out her hands.

"We try to be friends here," said Rebecca, "for who else will befriend us?" She took one of Tabitha's hands in hers and squeezed it. "Your hands are used to hard work," she said, turning Tabitha's hand palm up and examining it closely, "but soon your skin will soften and be as gentle as ours to the touch."

"One thing we must warn you of now," said Deborah. "None of us can ever be friends with the Lady Tamar. She is the Chief Concubine. Her eyes are sharp and her tongue is sharper. She has an ash rod which she does not hesitate to use on any girl who does not hasten to do her bidding."

Deborah and Rebecca led Tabitha back to the room of couches and presented her to the Lady Tamar.

"That is better," said Tamar, looking Tabitha up and down carefully, "almost presentable. So you are a dancer. Let us see." She clapped her hands. "You there! Music for dancing!"

At one side of the room a group of three or four girls had been playing their musical instruments in a quiet, restful melody. Now one of them struck up a lively rhythm on her tambourine, while a second girl played the tune on her flute.

"Dance then!" snapped Tamar. "What is your name? Tabitha? Dance, Tabitha. I wish to see you dance!"

Hesitantly Tabitha tried to step out to the music. She did not know the tune or what dance she was supposed to be dancing. She pirouetted clumsily and heard titters from the watching girls. But then the rhythm of the tambourine began to enter her blood. She rose onto her toes and circled a space in the middle of the room. Suddenly she realised that she felt light as a feather – this harem clothing weighed nothing

The Song

compared with the heavy dresses of linen and wool that she had always worn at home. She stretched out her arms, rippling her fingers. She danced, her body swaying, around and between the couches. She scarcely noticed the faces of the girls following her movements with admiration. For a few precious moments she was completely lost in the pleasure of the dance. Instinctively she knew when the tune would end. As the tambourine rattled out the final climax, she came smoothly to a halt in front of the Lady Tamar and curtsied deeply.

There was instant and hearty applause and cries of admiration from the girls. Even Tamar's expression had softened.

"Well," she said, "I see why you caught the eye of the King. With proper training and hard work I see no reason why you should not become a passable dancer."

"Thank you, my lady," said Tabitha.

Tamar inclined her head sharply, straightened up and stalked (one could hardly say walked) out of the room.

"Oh! That was wonderful!" exclaimed Rebecca. "One day you will be the King's favourite."

"Perhaps you will be the one to put Tamar's nose out of joint," said Deborah.

"Come over here," said Rebecca. Taking Tabitha's hand she pulled her over to one of the low tables and made her sit down. There were little pots scattered across the table, little brushes and wooden spatulas, and a round metal plate, highly polished, apparently of silver. Now, under Rebecca's instruction, Tabitha began to learn the art of cosmetics and make-up, of colouring the cheeks and lips and eyes, and painting the nails. And these things were like a revelation to her.

"Now you are even more beautiful, if that were possible," said Rebecca. "See for yourself." She picked up the metal plate and held it in front of Tabitha's face.

Tabitha gave a little gasp of astonishment. She had a mirror at home. Her brothers had brought it home from one of their trading journeys, and father had allowed her to keep it with a stern warning against vanity. "Your mother never needed such a thing," he had said. "I was all the reflection she needed." That mirror had been of polished bronze. Tabitha had seen her face, but dimly, and she knew that the bronze gave an unnatural yellow colour to her skin. This mirror was indeed of silver, polished so that it gave back an almost perfect reflection. Tabitha gazed long and hard, not so much at her make-up but at the wonder of seeing her own face looking back at her.

"Truly this is a wondrous place," she said to Rebecca.

Later, there was a meal and later still came the time to sleep. The girls slept six to a room and the bed was softer by far than her own. But when she lay down, memory flooded back to her, so that she could not believe how she could forget her home, her father, her beloved Seth. She could not believe how easily she was being seduced by the luxuries of the harem. Then came overwhelming sorrow and bitterness of soul, and she wept for all she had lost.

"Stop that blubbing, and let us sleep," came a voice from one of the other beds.

Tabitha only wept harder. Then suddenly an arm came around her shoulders, and she felt the comforting weight of a friend on her and Rebecca's gentle voice whispering, "Oh it is so hard, my Tabitha. We have all known this sorrow. All we can do is be kind to each other."

Tabitha felt her sobs subsiding. She clasped her new friend's hand. At last, mercifully, they slept, with their arms around each other.

. . . .

The Song

"Jerusalem, city of David, established on Mount Zion, the glory of Yahweh rises upon you." Baruch, with a broad sweep of his hand, gave the impression that he was claiming ownership of the panorama that came into view as they crested the hill.

Baruch was riding his donkey while Seth walked beside him. Seth halted to breathe himself after the last climb, brushed back his hair and blinked through the sweat that dropped from his forehead. He was looking across a valley of irregular shape at the higher ground beyond. A spur of rock pointed out towards him - a spur which was crowned with walls and, within the walls, tall buildings of stone that gleamed white in the bright sun.

"And that," continued Baruch, "the building on the highest point of the city," (he pointed) "that is the temple, the temple of Yahweh, built by King Solomon."

Seth looked and felt a little disappointed. The temple was not so big or so impressive as he had expected. Perhaps it was because they were still so far away. But somewhere in that city was his beloved. At that thought his spirits rose again.

They continued down into the valley, then up again, following a winding course as the road picked out the easiest slopes. The city on its spur of rock was now on their right. The road turned towards a gate with a high tower over it. Now that they were close up, the wall certainly looked taller and more formidable than from across the valley. They began to meet other travellers, coming from or heading towards the gateway - some on foot, some on donkeys, or leading a train of donkeys. A cart drawn by two oxen filled the road from side to side and they had to squeeze up against the rock face while it passed. Now they were passing through the gateway itself, under a high stone arch, between two heavy wooden doors. There were two soldiers here, occasionally stopping a traveller to ask his business, but they paid no attention to Baruch and Seth.

Found in Translation

Baruch led the way through streets that, although paved, were narrower than Seth was used to. The buildings were higher and closer together, and Seth felt shut in, as if the air was thicker and harder to breathe. There were far more people as well. They came to a place where the street broadened out and a market was being held. Here it was more crowded than ever, and noisier as people haggled over bread and meat, fruit and vegetables, pottery and metalwork. The smell was not pleasant and almost overpowering. And where, Seth wondered, was the King's palace with its harem where Tabitha would now be held?

They struggled through the crowds and came to a quieter street. There was a high wall in front of them. Baruch dismounted and tied his donkey to a hitching post and handed Seth the bag of scrolls to carry. They passed through a narrow gateway and came into a wide courtyard.

Baruch halted with another of his broad flourishes: "The temple of Yahweh!" he exclaimed.

Seth looked and tried to make sense of what he saw. There was a long, high building, of several stories, with each upper story set back from the one beneath, giving the appearance of a giant staircase. The white stones were so carefully tooled that they fitted together perfectly, so that you could scarcely see the crack between two stones. There was a pillar of bronze at the end of the building to his right. There was a huge bowl of bronze standing on what looked like small bronze bulls. A queue of men, many of them leading young rams, or carrying bird cages or sheaves of wheat, wound round the courtyard and disappeared behind the bronze bowl. From behind the bowl smoke was rising. There was a smell of blood and roasting meat.

"I was glad when they said to me, 'Let us go to the house of Yahweh,'" said Baruch, in a loud voice, "and now our feet are standing in the very gate. Lift up your eyes to the One who

The Song

is in heaven; our eyes look to Yahweh our God. Those who trust in Yahweh are like Mount Zion; they cannot be shaken."

Seth looked. This was the house of Yahweh! In that building was the Holy Place and the Holy of Holies where Yahweh spoke to the High Priest from above the Ark of the Covenant.

"Yahweh," he thought, "I do look to you. Give me success in rescuing my beloved. I will fear you and walk in your ways all the days of my life."

Baruch turned left into a long, low building against the temple wall. It was well-lit by natural light, and Seth saw a row of writing desks, each with its scribe working away at a scroll in front of him. A man who had been looking over the shoulder of one of these scribes straightened up and came towards them.

"Shalom, Zeriah," said Baruch. "I bring you a completed scroll." He took the bag from Seth and, handling it with reverence, he handed it over to this man.

"Shalom, Baruch," said Zeriah, "and thanks for your labours. I have few here who can be trusted like you to copy without errors." He turned and glared at the scribe whom he had been supervising. "And have you brought an apprentice with you?" He looked at Seth.

"Servant," said Baruch hastily. "Yet he does write with a fair hand and with few mistakes. I hope I may yet find him worthy to be apprenticed."

"I will have your scroll checked although I know there will be no errors," said Zeriah, "and I have another scroll which I would like you to copy. It is very old and decaying. It needs the attention of a learned and careful scribe. Go to the house of the scribes and refresh yourself after your journey. I will talk to you after the evening meal."

Baruch bowed and Seth followed suit. They walked back out of the temple, across the street and entered a small

155

Found in Translation

courtyard building, apparently the 'house of the scribes'. Baruch was as well known here as he was to Zeriah, and one servant hurried to prepare a room while a second went to attend to Baruch's donkey.

"But where is the King's palace?" demanded Seth, whose impatience now got the better of his manners.

"Patience, Seth, patience," said Baruch, then sighed, "Patience comes with the wisdom of years, and you are yet young. I will show you the palace."

It turned out that they were already close to the palace. A narrow street behind the house of the scribes suddenly broadened out into a square and there on the right were the palace walls with an imposing flight of steps leading up to a pillared entrance. Seth started forward but Baruch caught his arm.

"Patience," he said. "Let me talk."

They walked slowly up the steps. Two soldiers at the top barred their way.

"What is your business here, father?" said one of them respectfully to Baruch.

"Can a scribe explain his business to a simple soldier?" countered Baruch.

"No, father," said the soldier. "I will call my captain." He turned and walked through a doorway at one side of the entrance. Almost at once he returned with a man whose higher status was shown by the breastplate he wore.

"Well?" said this man, without showing any sign of respect.

"As you can see, I am a scribe," said Baruch, "and I seek an audience with the King."

"Do you have a message for the King?" asked the captain, suspiciously.

"Perhaps I do," said Baruch, "but it is not a message in writing. It concerns a matter of a personal nature."

The Song

"I cannot allow you entry at this time of day," said the captain. "If you have a petition for the King, return here tomorrow at the third hour."

"Very well," said Baruch, turning to go down the steps. Seth hesitated, then followed.

"You were not thinking of fighting your way in, I hope," said Baruch, as they walked back towards the temple. "That would have had most unfortunate results."

They returned to the house of the scribes, where they were served a meal and where Baruch enjoyed a long and technical discussion with Zeriah. Seth excused himself after a short time and went out into the street where he paced up and down in his impatience. To have come so far, to be so close, and now to be forced to wait before anything could be done!

. . . .

Before the third hour next morning the impatient Seth and the calmer Baruch returned to the square in front of the palace and were dismayed to find a crowd of petitioners already waiting. At the third hour the palace doors were opened; they were allowed in and were directed to a large, long, high-ceilinged room. There was a good deal of jostling for position until some attendants marshalled the petitioners into two queues, one on each side of the room. One of the attendants picked out a man from the queue opposite Seth and Baruch and ushered him through a door at the end of the room.

There was a wait and then the attendant returned, selected another man from the queue opposite and led him through the inner door.

"I fear we have been placed in the wrong queue," said Baruch.

So it proved. How the attendants sorted and selected the petitioners was not clear, but it was certain that the group on the opposite side of the room was being favoured. There was a certain amount of grumbling and protest from the less favoured group, but the attendants were unmoved.

"Five days I have waited here," said a man standing near Seth.

"And I have waited seven," said another. "They say you have to attend for ten days before you are even noticed."

"Through patience a ruler can be persuaded," said Baruch philosophically.

"I do not think our King has heard that proverb," said the first man.

The attendants continued to select men – single men, men in twos, or men in threes – to enter the inner room. Sometimes there was only a short wait before the next was called. Sometimes the wait seemed everlasting. Seth fretted, folded his arms, unfolded them, paced around, until Baruch chided him for impatience - at which Seth came close to losing his temper and seizing one of the attendants to demand admission to the King.

At last the chief attendant came back from the inner door and announced, "It is now midday, and the King will hear no more petitions this day. If you return tomorrow at the third hour, the King may be pleased to hear you."

There was a moment of silence, followed immediately by an outburst of grumbling. The attendants quickly began to usher people out of the waiting room, out of the palace entrance and down the steps.

Seth managed to contain himself until they were once more in the square. Then he turned and brandished his fists impotently towards the palace.

"What sort of King is this, that keeps his people waiting and waiting and then turns them away without a hearing? And do not tell me to be patient" (for Baruch had opened his

The Song

mouth as if to speak) "I have no more patience! I must do, not wait!"

Baruch nodded. "The kingdom is in a sad state," he agreed. "I must return to the writing-house, but you ..."

"I will go my own way for now, Baruch. I must walk off my anger."

They separated, Baruch turning towards the temple while Seth walked in the opposite direction, staring up at the blank wall of the palace. He came to the corner of the palace wall, where he could make out the head and shoulders of a guard standing at his post at the top of the wall. In any case, he could already see that the walls were too smoothly finished to climb without a ladder or rope.

He turned up the narrow street at the side of the palace and saw two more soldiers on guard at another doorway. He walked towards them cautiously and, as he did so, the doors they were guarding opened and a half-a-dozen men walked out, soldiers by their dress, but off-duty, since they carried no weapons. Prudently, Seth stepped aside as they walked towards him, for they had the air of men who did not give way to anyone.

"Seth! What are you doing here, my friend?" One of the soldiers was looking directly at Seth and smiling; it was Caleb. The two friends clasped each other's hands and Seth felt his spirit lifted by a new hope.

"Come and share a glass of wine with me," said Caleb, and the two of them followed the other soldiers through the streets to the market, where they found a shop that opened onto the street, with an awning over small tables and stools and a bar at the back.

"Wine not as good as your Father's," said Caleb, bringing two pottery cups from the bar, "but welcome after six hours on guard duty."

Found in Translation

They settled onto stools and Caleb said, "Tell me all the news. Why are you here in Jerusalem?"

Seth took a deep breath and began to tell Seth the whole story. "So now," he finished, "I need to petition the King to release Tabitha to me."

Caleb shook his head. "It cannot be done," he said, "not unless you are wealthy or you have a friend in the palace who can speak to the King for you."

"But I do have a friend – I have you!"

Caleb laughed derisively. "I am a nobody! I mean someone like the Secretary, or the Army Commander, or the Priest-Counsellor - someone who has the ear of the King."

Seth's spirit fell again with disappointment.

"Then I must rescue her somehow. Will you help me?"

Caleb frowned with thought, "I can get you into the palace, but what then? The harem is guarded by armed eunuchs."

"Eunuchs?" Seth had never heard the word before. Caleb explained the meaning of the word in blunt soldier's language. Seth blushed when he understood.

"You would never get into the harem, or if you did, you would never get out of the palace alive."

Caleb studied Seth's face carefully, "Do you really mean to attempt this thing?"

"I must," said Seth, simply.

Caleb picked up his cup and drained it. "Finish your wine," he said. "I will show you something"

Caleb led the way back to the palace and along the side wall, exchanging greetings with the two sentries who stood on guard. The palace seemed to Seth to be enormous and the wall here as unclimbable as at the front. Then they came to a place where the wall abruptly dropped lower, although still about twice man-height. Seth was surprised to see green-leafed branches and palm fronds above the wall.

The Song

"The palace gardens," explained Caleb.

Caleb led Seth on and soon turned another corner. Seth realised that they must now be walking past the rear of the palace.

At last Caleb stopped, looked up and down the alley, saw that it was deserted, and pointed up at the wall. "The garden of the harem," he said.

Seth looked at the wall and was disappointed. The wall was still made of smoothly jointed stones, still unclimbable.

"Look here," said Caleb.

Seth looked where his friend pointed and saw that there had once been a narrow gateway in the wall. It had been closed up, but with stones that were smaller and less well-fitted than the wall itself.

"If you can still climb as we used to when we were boys, you can get up here," said Caleb, indicating some cracks that were wide enough to make hand- or footholds. "And see this." He put his fingers into two of the cracks, on either side of one of the stones, about chest height, and worked it out of the wall. Seth bent eagerly to peer through, but was disappointed to see only leaves. He straightened up and reached experimentally for two higher cracks and felt for a toehold.

"Not now!" hissed Caleb. "We are too likely to be seen. You must come back at dusk. You can climb to the top of the wall from here, and the branches of that tree will shield you from anyone in the harem unless they come right up to the wall."

"So I must wait and hope that Tabitha comes close to the wall," said Seth, disappointed.

"Not so," said his friend with a broad smile. "Wait for one of the girls to come close. Give her a whistle, like this," (he demonstrated, softly) "then ask her to bring Tabitha here."

"You have done this before?" said Seth.

161

"We all do it," said Caleb, "but not too often. It is our greatest secret. Why should the King have all the best-looking girls? And the girls like to see us young men. The King is getting old."

Seth could not speak; he simply grasped his friend's hand once again.

"Come on," said Caleb. "We have stayed here too long already."

They continued to walk along the wall to the next corner, turned right again and walked back to the square in front of the palace.

"We may not be able to meet again," said Caleb, "so I will say farewell and wish you good fortune."

"Farewell, Caleb, and may the blessing of Yahweh go with you," said Seth, sincerely.

. . . .

The sun was setting as Seth made his way back to the rear wall of the palace. He had spent the afternoon and evening in a fever of impatience. He had returned to the house of the scribes for the evening meal but had eaten little. Baruch had looked at him closely but had refrained from questioning him. Now he looked carefully up at the wall and picked out likely hand- and footholds. He started to climb. It was easier than he had expected, and this reminded him that Caleb had told him that others had climbed here before him. Soon he was able to reach out and grasp a sturdy branch and haul himself up until he could see over the wall. He could have climbed onto the top of the wall itself but judged it would be safer not to do so.

Looking down into the garden he saw mostly foliage. There was a belt of shrubs as well as trees along the wall. He could see figures moving about but could make out no details. He hung where he was for some time.

The Song

At last he saw a girl approaching the wall. He whistled softly as Caleb had instructed him and she came closer. Seth nearly fell from his perch with astonishment. Caleb had not thought to tell, or warn, him how little the harem girls wore. Seth had never seen, never imagined, anything like this vision of feminine beauty. The girl looked round cautiously as she pushed her way carefully between the bushes until she stood under the tree and looked up. She saw Seth and smiled. Automatically, Seth smiled back. Her expression changed to one of puzzlement.

"You are new, are you not?" she said, softly.

"Y-y-yes. Very new," Seth managed to stammer out.

"It is good to see a new face," she said reassuringly.

"Do you know Tabitha?" said Seth. "I need to talk with her."

The girl looked disappointed. "Don't you want to talk with me?"

"I'm sorry. I must see Tabitha."

"Tabitha, Tabitha," said the girl thoughtfully. "I do not believe we have anyone of that name."

"She has only just been brought here."

"Oh! Of course! The dancer. I know now why you wish to see her," said the girl archly.

"She is my betrothed."

"Oh, I understand. I am sorry for you. I will send her here." The girl turned to make her way out of the bushes, but just before she disappeared she turned and blew him a kiss.

Seth grasped his branch and wondered how long he could continue hanging there. It seemed a long time before a girl came through the bushes. Like the first she was scantily clad, and it was only when she looked up, recognised Seth and smiled that he recognised Tabitha.

"Seth, is it really you?"

"Of course it is me!" said Seth desperately, for his arms were ready to give way.

She looked up at him with a sad smile. "Oh Seth. I am so sorry."

Suddenly Seth remembered the loose stone that Caleb had showed him.

"Wait there," he said to Tabitha and began to climb down the wall. Quickly he found the loose stone and worked it out of the wall. He put his hand through the gap and Tabitha grasped it in both of hers.

"My darling!" said Seth. "My dove, my flawless one."

"Oh my love!"

They stood thus for a very long time.

At last Seth's mind began to work again. He looked up at the wall. How to get Tabitha over it?

"Tabitha," he said, "are you able to climb this tree that overhangs the wall?"

There was a pause before Tabitha replied, "Why, I believe I can. Shall I do it now?"

Seth's brain was now working quickly. "Not now. The city gates will be shut and we cannot leave before sunrise. Can you come here when the sky begins to lighten – while it is still dark?"

"I can."

"Have you your dress? You cannot walk the streets like that."

"No. They took away my clothes. But there are long cloaks here, with hoods. I will bring one of those."

"Come then, just before first light. I will be here to help you over the wall."

"I will. Do not fail me, Seth."

"I will not, my love."

The Song

He felt her kiss his hand, then she was gone. Seth replaced the stone and walked slowly away, his heart pounding with excitement.

. . . .

It was, no doubt, the excitement that enabled Seth to keep awake that long night. He felt as if he had lived a lifetime before he thought it was time to put his plan into operation. He picked up his own cloak and crept out of the sleeping quarters in the house of the scribes. Fortunately, it seemed that Baruch and the other scribes were all good sleepers. Once outside he made his way to a well that he had noticed earlier. He unfastened the rope from the bucket. It was a most serious crime to steal a well rope - people and animals might be going thirsty as a result. But Seth needed a rope, and he would have done anything short of murder to obtain one.

Soon he was outside the harem garden once more and, in spite of the darkness, swiftly climbing the wall. This time he straddled the wall and looped the rope over the strong branch of the tree which overhung the alley. Then he gave a soft whistle.

"Is that you, Seth?" Tabitha's voice came from the foot of the tree.

"Yes. Can you climb up now?"

Seth heard the rustling and scraping as Tabitha scrambled into the branches. She reached out her hand, and he grasped it and hauled her up until she could sit on the wall.

"There is a rope here, over this branch. Can you climb down it?"

For answer, Tabitha grasped the rope, swung herself off the wall and dropped to the ground. Seth followed her. He pulled down the rope and coiled it. It would never do to give away Caleb's secret viewing place.

Found in Translation

Tabitha threw her arms round his neck and kissed him. He hugged her and realised that she still only had on the skimpy harem garments. He pulled away in embarrassment.

"Have you brought a cloak?"

"I have it here." She stooped and picked a bundle up from the ground.

"Put it on," he said, pulling his own cloak round his shoulders. "We must not be recognised."

Seth took Tabitha's hand and led the way through the streets until they were close to the city gate by which he and Baruch had entered.

"Now we must wait until the gates are opened at sunrise," he said.

He drew Tabitha into a narrow alleyway, and they sat down with their backs against the wall. Instinctively he put an arm around her shoulders, and she clasped his free hand in both of hers. Overhead, the sky was beginning to show the first signs of approaching dawn.

Gradually the sky grew lighter and bluer, while the stars grew fainter. They could not see the eastern horizon, but presently the sound of a trumpet rang out through the fresh morning air.

"Come on." Seth rose to his feet and pulled Tabitha to hers. They adjusted their cloaks, Tabitha pulling her hood over her long, loose hair. They left the rope there and stepped cautiously out into the street. Seth took her hand and led the way until they could see the now open city gate and the sentries guarding it.

Seth paused. Was it better to walk out straight away? Or would that look suspicious to the guards? Perhaps it would be better to wait until there were more people about. Almost at once a man leading half-a-dozen mules came in through the gateway. A gang of men with spades and picks went out. They were followed by other workmen and two men who looked

The Song

like merchants, for each was riding a mule and leading another, heavily laden. Soon there was a steady stream of men and baggage animals passing in and out of the gateway.

Seth made up his mind and stepped out towards the gate. The two guards paid them no attention for they were looking out through the gateway. Seth walked on boldly and was close to the guards when they stepped apart and he saw that the gateway was blocked by an ox-drawn wagon. There was no choice but to halt and step out of the way as the wagon moved, with painful slowness, through the gateway, the two guards, one on each side, shouting directions and warnings to the driver.

For a few tense moments it seemed as if the wagon would become stuck. It did indeed scrape along one of the wooden gates. At last it was clear and Seth stepped forward.

There was a shout from behind. "Wait! Stop those two. Close the gates, by the King's order!"

Tabitha gave a little gasp of fear. There was no chance to run. The two guards closed in on Seth and Tabitha. They looked back and saw three or four soldiers, an officer in the lead, hurrying towards the gate. The officer strode straight up to Tabitha and pulled open her cloak. She gave another gasp of shock and shame.

"Ha!" said the officer. "It seems we have caught our runaway. You two will come with me." He looked at the guards. "Close the gates! Did you not hear the order? You will be told when they can be reopened."

The guards hurried to push the gates shut, in spite of shouted protests from those who were still trying to enter and leave the city. The officer ignored these protests, turned and marched back towards the palace. Two of his men lined up beside Seth and Tabitha, ushering them after their leader, while a third soldier brought up the rear.

Seth felt an overwhelming despair. What would happen to them now? Tabitha gripped his hand and huddled close beside him as if expecting him even now to protect her. But what could he do now?

In no time they were back at the square in front of the palace. Seth caught a glimpse of Baruch's startled and anxious face amongst the people who were already collecting there in hopes of petitioning the King. Then they were being hustled up the steps and through the entrance. An exclamation of dismay caused Seth to look one of the guards in the face – it was Caleb. The prisoners were urged on, and they found themselves in a small room with the three soldiers guarding them. They waited – and waited.

At last the officer returned with a man dressed like one of the King's attendants that Seth had seen – was it only yesterday? And with them was a furious Lady Tamar. She went up to Tabitha, jerked her hood back, put a hand under her chin, stared into her face and snapped out, "Yes! This is the girl."

The attendant snapped his fingers and pointed at the door. In a moment the runaways were being hustled out of the room, along a corridor and into a much larger room, with a high ceiling and full of people. Seth suddenly realised that it was the throne room. At the far end of the room was a dais with six steps and on each step were two lions, carved from ivory. Seated there on his throne was the King himself. Seth made a move forward – surely their only chance was to plead with the King for mercy. But he was promptly grabbed by the arms and held back.

Once again they were forced to wait. The King was conducting business with his officials and counsellors. A man was called to the dais to read from a scroll. Another man hurried out of the room on some errand for the King. The King talked with a man in a resplendent soldier's dress and

The Song

another man who was dressed like a priest. He dictated a letter to a scribe and an officer was ordered to deliver the letter. The attendant who had taken charge of Seth and Tabitha moved forward and whispered to another attendant. This man looked at the prisoners and indicated that their attendant should move forward. He moved on to speak to yet another attendant and so by degrees came closer to the King on his throne. At last he was at the foot of the steps, bowing and speaking to the King.

The King looked at Seth and Tabitha and beckoned. The soldiers urged them forward. A voice behind Seth said, "Kneel to the King!" and at the same moment he felt a kick on the back of his leg and a pressure on his shoulders that brought him down to a kneeling position.

The hearing that followed was short. The attendant explained that the girl who had escaped from the harem had been recaptured together with her accomplice. Lady Tamar confirmed that Tabitha was the girl who had escaped. The officer explained how he had captured Seth and Tabitha at the Valley Gate.

The attendant looked at Seth and said, "Have you anything to say before the King gives his ruling?"

Seth struggled to speak because his mouth and throat were so dry. "My lord King," he managed at last, "this woman which you took into your harem is my betrothed. Soon we were to be married, and I love her dearly."

"Why did you not petition the King to release her?" asked the attendant.

"I waited all yesterday morning but was not invited to make my petition to the King."

"That is no excuse. You should have waited on the King's pleasure today, and tomorrow, and the next day."

The attendant looked up at the King and Seth looked also, but there was nothing in the King's face to give him hope.

The King spoke, "Lady Tamar, you will take this girl in your charge and have her soundly whipped. The young man will be executed at once."

Tabitha sobbed aloud. Seth could scarcely take in the meaning of the King's words.

A sudden commotion at the back of the throne room made the King look up with a frown while the courtiers looked around with astonishment. Three men pushed their way to the front and boldly faced the King. Several attendants protested angrily at this unprecedented intrusion, while soldiers moved to seize the newcomers. Seth looked up and saw that one of the men was a soldier – his friend Caleb – beside him was Baruch – and a third man who looked like –

"My lord King," said Caleb, "forgive my audacity, but let me present to you the Father of the prisoner."

Seth's spirit seemed to leap with a new hope. Then he despaired again. Surely his Father had simply come to witness his son's execution.

But the King said, "Let him speak."

"My Lord King," said Father (and Seth understood for the first time the strength of his Father's voice, the strength of his spirit) "your forefather King David ordered the death of Uriah the Hittite in battle in order that he might enjoy Uriah's wife. Will you be like your forefather and execute my son?"

There was complete silence as everyone waited for the King to speak. At last he said, "Will you be like Nathan the prophet, who was sent by Yahweh to rebuke my forefather?"

"I am no prophet, nor the son of a prophet," replied Father. "I am a peasant, and I work the land that was assigned to my family by lot when Joshua led Israel into Canaan. But I remember the words that the prophet Samuel spoke in the days when he judged Israel and all the people asked him to give them a king. Samuel said, 'A king will take your sons to run before his chariots, to plough his ground and reap his harvest. He will take a tenth of your grain and your wine and your flocks. He will take the best of your fields, your vineyards and olive groves for his officials and attendants. He will take your daughters to be perfumers and cooks and bakers in his household.' Now O King, have the words of Samuel come true this day?"

There was a long silence.

The King spoke: "Give the young man his betrothed and let them both return to the house of his Father" (for the first time he looked Seth in the eyes) "and may Yahweh bless you with grain and wine and olive oil, with flocks and herds and with many sons and daughters."

Found in Translation

Gentled Horses

Matthew 11:27
A western story exploring what Jesus meant by being 'gentle'

Steve settled himself in the saddle and gripped with his knees.

"Let her go, Matt."

Matt swung open the gate and the buckskin colt sprang into the corral – and instantly began trying to get rid of the strange *thing* on his back. He bucked, he galloped round the corral, he kicked, he jumped – all four legs off the ground together – he rushed at the corral fence full tilt, pulling up a fraction of a second from disaster. But the *thing* stayed just where it was; the strange, constricting *thing* stayed firmly round his chest, and the weight of the hateful man-creature still bore down on his back. Steve was the best breaker-in of horses in the whole of Wyoming Territory, and no horse was going to get him off its back until he, Steve, was ready to get off.

The foreman of Powder Creek Ranch strolled up to the corral with that easy, long-legged stride that looked so casual, but covered the ground so quickly that many a man had to trot to keep up. He leaned on the top rail of the corral fence and watched Steve on the colt.

"How many today, Matt?" he asked.

"That's number four," replied Matt.

The foreman looked at a piece of paper in his hand, "Still twenty-three tuh go."

"Steve and Ike are doin' O.K." said Matt, "and Shorty."

"Where is Shorty?"

Found in Translation

"He's out with that big black colt that gave us so much trouble yesterday."

The buckskin colt was clearly tiring. There were long pauses between his rushes and his jumps. Steve brought him to a halt alongside the corral fence. He swung down and ran his hand down the horse's flank and then down his neck. He tickled and patted the horse's nose. The dust kicked up from the ground in the corral began to drift slowly to earth.

"I reckon he's ready for Shorty now," was Steve's judgement.

"Stranger coming," remarked Matt, "fello' in a black coat and hat."

Steve looked in the direction indicated, but the foreman said, without raising his eyes, "It's the bishop o' Wyoming Territory."

"Oh, yes," said Matt. "I guess you saw him coming way off and thought yu'd see how long it took us before we noticed him."

"Colonel Taylor said he'd be coming, 'bout the end of the month." Colonel Taylor was the owner of Powder Creek.

"So we're goin' to get religion tonight?" said Steve.

"You're goin' tuh be *offered* religion," said the foreman, "Whether yu' take it or not is up tuh you."

The black-coated bishop rode up to the group of cowboys and reined in his horse. It would be better perhaps to say that his coat and hat *had* been black, for both were now liberally coated with the white dust of Wyoming.

"Good mawning, seh," said the foreman, in his polite southern drawl.

"Good morning," said the bishop, looking down at the cowboys, who were as liberally coated with dust as he was himself, and round at the corrals and horses. "What's going forward?"

174

Gentled Horses

"Hawss-breaking," said the foremen. "Step down and see for yu'self." For the bishop had courteously remained in the saddle, rather than dismount uninvited.

"Gladly," said the bishop, swinging down from his saddle and throwing the reins over his horse's head, letting them trail, so that the horse stood quietly. "I've never seen horses being broken-in. Are they to be cow horses?"

"No, seh. These hawsses are to be cavalry remounts. The Colonel has a contract to provide a hundred remounts tuh the United States army this spring."

"Have you bred these horses here on the ranch?"

"They breed themselves, seh. The hawsses run free on the range a'most all year and we have rounded up the two-year-olds." The foremen pointed to a corral some distance away where about a score of horses were standing quietly. "That's the balance of the broncos we have not yet broken-in to the saddle."

"Broncos?" said the bishop. "They seem to be quiet enough; not at all wild."

"If you would care to try to put yore laig across the back of one of those mustangs, seh," said the foreman, "you would soon find him wild enough to satisfy yu'."

"I'll take your word for it," said the bishop, with a laugh in his voice.

"Then, in the next corral, Ike has a colt on the lunge-rein."

"Lunge-rein? What's that?"

The foremen led the bishop over to another, smaller, corral where Ike had a colt walking round him in a circle of perhaps twenty yards radius. The bishop saw that the horse was bridled and that it had a rope attached to its bridle by which Ike was controlling him. The foremen explained that the rope was the 'lunge-rein'.

Found in Translation

"We lunge the hawsses tuh get them used to men and to the bridle and rope, and to obedience. Yu' see that Ike is teaching the hawss to stop and to start to his orders."

"Then back hyeh," continued the foreman, "Steve and Matt are useding the hawsses to the saddle and cinch, and to having a man on their backs. Then we hand the horses over to Shorty to gentle them."

"Gentle?" said the Bishop. "I've never heard that word used of horse training before."

"Here comes Shorty now," said Steve.

A horse with an almost black coat and a jet-black mane and tail was coming in at a canter. As they watched, the horse slowed to a walk and approached them sedately, stopping alongside the bishop's horse. A young cowboy swung down from the saddle, patted and smoothed the horse's neck, tickled and petted him on the nose, while making soothing and encouraging noises. The horse nuzzled the young rider; then the two horses put their heads together and greeted each other by some horsey means that was not obvious to the little group of humans.

"How's he comin', Shorty?" asked the foreman.

"He's a good horse," said Shorty, giving the animal's neck another pat. "Give him a while longer for his bones to get strong and he'll be a hard-working horse, won't you, Blackie?"

The horse might have disagreed if he had fully understood, but he nuzzled Shorty's arm trustingly.

"So how do you gentle a horse, Shorty?" asked the bishop.

"This hyeh's the bishop o' Wyoming Territory," explained the foreman.

Shorty looked puzzled, as if the question had never occurred to him before. He took off his hat, revealing an untidy mop of blonde hair, and looked at the ground, then at the horse, twisting the hat nervously in his hands.

176

Gentled Horses

"Why, you have to make friends with him - and you have to be careful not to startle him - and you have to make sure he knows who's boss. A horse is always honest, so you have to be honest to him." Shorty's voice was mild, but his face had a strained look, as he struggled to put his thoughts into words.

"Shorty knows real well how to gentle a hawss," said the foreman, "even if the words don't come so easy to him."

"Gentle," repeated the bishop thoughtfully. "This is a hard country, from what I've seen of it. It breeds tough men and I thought it would breed tough horses."

"Oh, he's tough enough, aren't you, Blackie?" said Shorty, "And he'll get tougher yet."

"So a gentle horse," persisted the bishop, "is not a *soft* horse?"

"No, sir!" said Shorty, with more energy in his voice than he had yet shown. "A gentle horse is a riding horse - a working horse. He has to be strong and smart."

"So when the Lord said that He was 'gentle', he didn't mean that he was soft," said the bishop. "He meant he was like a gentled horse, a working horse, strong and smart."

The cowboys looked puzzled, but the bishop, with an air of excitement, pulled a book out of the pocket of his frock coat. The book was thick, the leather binding was worn with long use and the pages were stained from frequent reading. The bishop turned the pages quickly.

"Here it is," he said, "the Gospel according to Saint Matthew, chapter 11, verse 29. Jesus said, 'Take my yoke upon you, and learn of me; for I am gentle and lowly in heart: and ye shall find rest unto your souls.'"

There was a moment's silence, then a voice, a clear military voice, broke in on their thoughts. "Bishop, I am glad to see you. Come on up to the house. Don't let these men keep you standing here in the dust." It was Colonel Taylor.

"They haven't been keeping me," replied the bishop. "It is I that have been keeping them from their work with my questions." Then, seeing the Colonel's puzzled look, he explained, "They have been teaching me how to gentle horses."

The Colonel looked round at his men and at the horses in the several corrals. "All going well?" he said to the foremen.

"Very well, seh, and the bishop has been giving us a sermon in one verse and one sentence."

The Cruise of a Lifetime

> *The Christian life has been likened to many things: to a race (Phil 3:12), to a fight or struggle (Ephesians 6:12), to an ordeal by fire (I Cor 3:12-15), to being living stones in a temple (I Peter 2:5) and to a pilgrimage or journey (I Peter 2:11). One sort of journey that is very popular today, especially for retired people like myself, is the ocean cruise on a luxury liner. Imagine that you are trying to make a telephone booking for a cruise. The conversation might go something like this...*

Pre-recorded voice: "Thank you for calling Gold Star Bookings. Please note that this call may be recorded for quality assurance and training purposes. Please hold and you will be connected to one of our booking agents as soon as possible."

Short pause while a ghostly orchestra plays the first movement of Beethoven's 5th symphony: "Di di di DAA! Di di di DAA!"

"Hullo, Gold Star Bookings, Kathy speaking. How may I help you?"

You: "Well, er, I'm thinking about a cruise on an ocean-going liner."

"Why, you're in luck, Sir. By calling today you qualify for a ten per cent reduction on the list price for a ten-day cruise on the world's largest, newest, luxury liner."

"That sounds good."

"This ship has first class cabins for over four hundred passengers, with every facility and every comfort."

"Yes, I want a comfortable cabin. What sort of recreational facilities are there?"

"There's a swimming pool, sauna, squash court and sundeck."

"What about entertainment on the voyage?"

"They have a live stage show every evening, cinema, TV in every cabin, orchestra, cabaret for the parents and a disco for the youngsters."

"I'm not bringing any children. And I would want some peace and quiet as well."

"Don't worry, Sir. There's a ship's library, reading room and writing room."

"What's the food like?"

"This liner offers you a full English breakfast, three-course lunch and three-course dinner – with a full waitress service at every meal."

"And wine with the dinner?"

"According to the brochure, they have the finest wine cellar of any cruise liner."

"That suits me. Er, where exactly will this cruise take us to?"

Kathy sounds surprised. "Well, Sir, back here of course. It's a pleasure cruise."

"Doesn't the ship stop anywhere? Doesn't it visit any foreign ports?"

Kathy now sounds as if she is politely explaining something perfectly obvious to a dimwit. "It's not about visiting foreign ports, Sir. This is an ocean-going pleasure cruise. The important thing is to have a great time on the voyage."

"But we don't actually get anywhere?"

"No, Sir, just back where you started. But you will have had a brilliant cruise - time to relax, unwind, enjoy yourself, be pampered."

"What happens if the weather's bad?"

"There's plenty of entertainment under cover."

"You see, I've never been on a cruise before and I'm a bit nervous about going to sea."

The Cruise of a Lifetime

"This ship is so big that you'll hardly know you're at sea."

"But what's the point of going on a cruise if you don't know you're at sea?"

"If you book an outside cabin," says Kathy, patiently, "you will have a porthole looking out on the sea. If you have an inside cabin, then there are promenade decks for walking and taking in the sea air. And, if it should unfortunately rain, there are promenade decks that are closed in against the weather."

"But supposing there's a storm?"

"Look, Sir," (Kathy is clearly about to lose her professional cool. She decides to get technical) "this liner displaces 66 000 tons and the engines have 55 000 horsepower. If there is a storm, the ship will just drive straight through it."

You are beginning to lose confidence in Kathy. She sounds just a bit too clever. "What if we *should* happen to sink. I can't swim."

"This ship's hull has a double bottom and the whole ship is divided into 16 watertight compartments. She *can't* sink."

You feel reassured by this but you have one last question. "What is the name of this ship?"

"What is her name? Just a moment, Sir, while I check. Oh yes, here it is. She's called Titanic."

Found in Translation

Found in Translation

An interstellar expedition discovers an old song on a new world

"Space – the Final Frontier. Who first said that?" I wondered. I was sitting in one of the observation domes of the star cruiser *Swiftsure* as she closed in on the star Susephe. We were passing one of the outer planets of the star, a gas giant, three times the size of Jupiter. It was a spectacular, beautiful sight, filling one sixth of my field of view, with its broad bands of clouds, in different shades of pink, yellow and orange. By swivelling my seat I could see, in the opposite direction, the blackness of deep space, speckled with brilliant starlight. "Look how the floor of heaven is thick inlaid with patens of bright gold." Shakespeare had said that and nobody seems to have expressed it better in the last, oh, seven hundred or so years.

"Space-dreaming again, Roger?" The cheerful voice of Tina Miller interrupted my reverie. She plonked herself into the chair next to me.

"It *is* breathtaking," she said, settling herself comfortably, brushing back a lock of auburn hair and gazing up at the giant planet.

"So are the stars," I said, reluctantly making polite conversation. I felt a little miffed at having my privacy invaded, but the observation domes were free for anyone and we were probably the only two people on the *Swiftsure* with time on our hands - the crew being fully involved in manoeuvring the cruiser and the rest of the scientific staff being committed to making their planetary and stellar observations.

"Haven't you seen enough stars while we were in deep space?" Tina swung her chair round to follow my gaze. "This is where the interesting stuff starts – if we find a planet with intelligent life."

"It goes on forever," I said. "Well, not forever, but thirteen billion years at least."

"It's vast," she agreed, "and maybe it just happened, or maybe something made it. But how you can believe that that *Something* takes a personal interest in our benighted little Earth and insignificant lifeforms like us – that beats me."

"You said it yourself," I pointed out. "The interesting stuff happens on insignificant little planets where maybe, just maybe, you find intelligent life."

. . . .

Personal Log of Roger Carpenter, expedition philologist, star cruiser *Swiftsure*, in orbit around Susephe Three, star date: 2365/18/21.

The chief problem with meeting an intelligent, alien lifeform for the first time is that of communication. The 'Universal Translator', beloved of writers of science fiction, is simply that: fiction. Although computers have greatly improved the recording and analysis of alien speech patterns, every inter-stellar expedition for the last hundred years has included a philologist, an expert in the science and structure of languages. On Susephe Three, the situation was eased by the fact that the inhabitants were humanoid, had similar lungs, voice box and mouth to ours, and similar vocalisations; that is, both races tended to use the same sounds when speaking. On the other hand, the Susephe Three natives use a variety of languages, and I have first had to spend time trying to identify the most widely used one.

At last I am beginning to make progress. I have managed to identify a number of concrete nouns, such as a word that means 'house' or 'dwelling place' and another that is used to mean a 'vehicle for personal transport'. I have been able to identify, with some uncertainty, a number of words used for items of clothing and others referring to different types of food. As the food items are as alien as the inhabitants; a translation of these words is not appropriate. The next step is to try and identify some verbs and the syntax structure of simple sentences.

The task is not made easier by the fact that Captain Blackwood has kept our starship, the *Swiftsure*, in high orbit and has not allowed anyone to land even covertly on the planet, let alone to interact directly with the inhabitants.

The native race of Susephe Three is technologically quite advanced, particularly in electronics, and that means that there are extensive radio and television broadcasts which we are able to monitor. These are providing me with the raw material I need to translate their language. They are also experimenting, in a primitive way, with space flight and have a large number of scientific and communication satellites in orbit. One of Captain Blackwood's concerns is that we might be detected by their fairly sophisticated radar systems and the *Swiftsure* is therefore being maintained in 'stealth' mode. This does not make our scientific investigations any easier. In particular, Tina Miller, our anthropologist, has been harassing me to make better progress with translation because her anthropological studies are being hampered by our inability to understand their language.

. . . .

"Listen to this," said Tina, coming into my cabin without knocking.

"I'm working," I objected.

"This is work," she said, leaning across my desk and plugging a memory module into my computer. She told the computer to read and play her memory module. It did so and a tune started to come out of the speakers. Then a group of voices started to sing. It was obviously a recording she had made of a Susephan radio broadcast. It was a pleasant, catchy tune, and I found myself humming along to it.

"So what?" I said as the song drew to a close.

"This is a very popular song," explained Tina. "There are several versions of it being played on Susephan broadcasts by different singers. There's one radio channel that uses it as a theme tune. All the radio and TV channels that broadcast any music play this piece; some of them play it several times a day."

"So, it's popular. So what?"

"It must be telling us something about their culture. A song as popular as this must be saying something important to the Susephan race. If you can translate the words it may give me a key to understanding them better."

"If it's a pop song, won't it just come and go?"

"This has been 'going' for weeks," insisted Tina. "It was included in the first broadcast we picked up from the planet."

"It'll probably just be a love song."

"What do you mean, *just* a love song?" demanded Tina. "Love songs are important in almost every culture. In any case, I want to find out about love in this culture. What does it mean to them? What are their customs and rituals? We don't even know yet whether they mate for life. We don't know if they're monogamous. We don't even know which sex is dominant."

"No doubt about which sex is dominant for Earthlings," I grumbled. "All right, I'll give it some time, but don't expect results soon."

"I'll come and see how you're getting on tomorrow," said Tina, sweetly, and blew me a kiss as she went out of the cabin.

Found in Translation

For three days Tina pestered me, hampering rather than helping my work. Fortunately, I was beginning to make progress, and on the fourth day was able to show her the paper with my first thoughts about her popular song. (Yes, I know I should be using the computer, but I still find pencil and paper the best way. You can see your mistakes and false starts and crossings-out, which the computer deletes, and that's often helpful.)

"As far as I can see," I said, handing her the paper, "it starts something like this..."

```
If/maybe/perhaps I sing ... ... ... and/but do not have X
I am ... ... ...
... ... ... if I have ?
I am ... ... ...
X is ? X is ?
It is not ... ... ...
Etc for several lines
X ... ...
... ...
It will ...
And/but now ... ? Numeral
And/but ... ... is X
```

"I guess this word X is the theme word or concept of the song," I said. "It's certainly the most frequent."

"It *is* a love song," said Tina triumphantly. "I bet X is their word for love."

"No it's not," I retorted. "I'm pretty sure I've identified their word for love, and it's completely different. The two words don't even appear to have a common root."

Tina looked disappointed; then she brightened again. "Perhaps it means homosexual love."

"I didn't know your mind worked that way."

She made a sound which, if she had been a man, I would have described as a snort of impatience.

"Several historical Earth cultures have encouraged homosexual love," she said, "and they have regarded love between males and females as necessary but inferior."

"If you say so."

"I *do* say so."

"So you think this is a song about love between two males, or two females?"

"It's possible."

"Does that seem to be consistent with their culture?"

Tina frowned, "It's too early to say but, no, not as far as I can see yet." She picked up my handwritten notes. "Keep up the good work, darling."

"I need those notes," I said, pulling them out of her hand.

She looked disappointed but managed a smile and a friendly wave as she went out.

. . . .

Once you have a few verbs and begin to grasp the syntax of a language, understanding starts to become easy. The Susephan language was actually fairly simple, for they made very little use of inflection, but they had a large vocabulary. Concrete nouns are one thing; it's much more difficult to grasp the meaning of nouns used for abstract concepts. Still, I was getting somewhere, and suddenly Tina's song began to get quite exciting. I managed to keep her at arm's length for a few days until I felt strong enough to face her again. Then I surprised her, pleasantly I hope, by actually inviting her into my cabin.

"Here is where I've got to," I said, showing her my latest page of notes.

"Ooh," she almost cooed, "you have made progress, you lovely man."

She pored over my scribbles, jottings and crossings-out, which now read:

Found in Translation

> If I sing in a Susephan/ human language, or a ? language
> But do not have X
> I am an empty jar or a hollow (?)cymbal
> If I have the wisdom of the wise, or the knowledge of the (?)ancients
> But do not have X
> I am nothing.
> X is patient, X is kind
> X does not boast, X is not ?
> X does not become angry
> X does not remember (?)insults
> X protects, X ?
> X hopes, X perseveres
> X does not fail
> Knowledge fails
> Wisdom fails
> Knowledge is only a mirror
> Wisdom is only a reflection
> X brings perfection
> And now there are three things that can be trusted:
> X, ? and Hope
> But the greatest of these is X.

"Hmm," she said at last. "X doesn't *quite* sound like erotic love. But," she added in a puzzled tone, "the song does begin to sound vaguely familiar."

"So it should," I agreed. "Look at this. Computer, bring up the Bible, Twenty-fourth Century Translation."

"Check," responded the computer.

"Turn to I Corinthians, chapter 13."

"Check."

Found in Translation

The words flashed up on the screen and I gestured to Tina to sit down and study the passage. She looked at the screen, looked down at my notes, then back again at the screen. Her face was a study in conflicting emotions, of which puzzlement and astonishment were the predominant ones.

"But," she said at last, "the song looks very similar to this Bible passage."

"Not just similar," I said, "allowing for the problems of translation and the difference in culture, the two passages are expressing identical concepts."

So X does mean 'love'," she said.

"Yes, but not 'erotic love'," I explained. "The translators of the old English versions of the Bible used the word 'charity', but the original Greek uses the word 'agape' – which means 'God's love' or 'Christian love'."

Tina looked at me. A little frown of puzzlement creased her forehead.

"You're really claiming that this passage from Earth's Bible and the lyrics of this Susephan song are the same?"

I nodded.

"But how can that be? We're over four hundred light years from Earth."

"And there is no record of any previous Earth expedition to Susephe and certainly no evidence of any expedition from Susephe to Earth; they simply don't have the technology for that."

"So how could two entirely separate civilisations have written the same passage?"

I shrugged my shoulders.

"Why don't you work it out for yourself?" I said.

Found in Translation

Three Days in Jerusalem

A Roman Officer investigates the Resurrection of Jesus with the help of 21st Century technology

Assignment

"I'm sending you to Jerusalem, Rufus," said the Tribune Caecilius. 'They've reported a crime which the Legate wants solved ASAP."

"Don't they have their own investigating officers?" I said. The prospect of travelling from Antioch down to Jerusalem did not please me.

"Yes, but they don't have anyone with your experience."

"What sort of crime?"

"Tomb-robbing."

I shrugged my shoulders. "Happens all the time," I said.

"Not in Jerusalem, it doesn't," said the Tribune. "Don't you know about the Jews?"

I shrugged my shoulders again. "Not much. They're practically atheists, aren't they? They only believe in their own god, not in anyone else's."

"They're religious fanatics. A lot of them would rather die than recognise another god. They have very strict rules about what they call *holiness*. Contact with a dead body, or a grave, makes them *unclean* until they've been through a ritual purification. So they don't rob graves."

"The Egyptians put curses on the tombs of their kings, but it doesn't stop people robbing them."

"Be that as it may," said the Tribune impatiently, "Legate Vitellius wants this thing cleared up. He said to send my best man and that's you."

"Yes, sir," I said. Legate Vitellius was the Governor of Syria. Clearly I was not going to be able to wriggle out of this one. "Can I take Julius Ursus?"

"Your Optio? Of course. You'd better take a Scene of Crime Officer as well."

"Yes, sir."

"Carry on, Prefect. The sooner you get this sorted, the sooner we'll get some peace and quiet here."

. . . .

Perhaps I should introduce myself: Marcus Julius Rufus. You can tell from my 'three names' that I'm a Roman citizen. My grandfather was made a citizen as a reward for military service under the great Julius Caesar. I've served thirty-five years in the army myself and my present substantive rank is Camp Prefect of the Legion VI Ferrata (you might translate that last word as 'ironclad' or 'ironsides'). Functionally, I serve under the Legate of Syria, Lucius Vitellius, as a supervising police officer and get my orders through the Tribune Caecilius. I reckon I'm a good police officer and, unfortunately, my superiors do too. That means I get all the sticky assignments. At my age of fifty-four years, I could do with an easier life.

Day One

"Do *you* know anything about the Jews, Ursus?" I was driving the police Audax 4x4 down the coast road, which was dusty in spite of running on the Plain of Sharon alongside the Mediterranean Sea, through Galilee, past Caesarea, through Antipatris and up to Jerusalem.

"Not much, boss," replied Ursus. "They worship one god and refuse to recognise any other. They have strict food laws –

Three Days in Jerusalem

they never touch pork. Every seven days they have a holy day, they call it the *Sabbath*, when they do not work. Their god has only one temple, in Jerusalem. If they can't get there for the Sabbath, they meet together in their towns and villages."

"When Pompey the Great conquered Judea and captured Jerusalem," said Lucilius Crescens, the SCO, from the back seat, "he entered their temple and found they had no image of their god."

"No statue of their god?" I queried, surprised.

"It's against their laws, sir," said Crescens. "Pompey found an empty chamber at the heart of the temple."

"What's the name of this Jewish god?" I asked.

"He doesn't have a name," said Crescens, "or at least, he has a name that is so holy, the Jews won't tell anyone what it is. They call him the LORD." I could hear the capital letters as Crescens spoke this last word.

"Doesn't Tiberius Caesar have anything to say about that?" I said. "*Lord* is one of his titles."

"I think our Emperor wants to keep the peace in the East, so he tolerates Jewish eccentricities," said Crescens.

"We'll have to be careful with them," said Ursus. "They don't like contact with foreigners."

I glanced sideways at Ursus. He was indeed a great bear of a man - over six feet tall and broad shouldered with massive hands and feet. The idea of Ursus being careful with anyone, or anything, was difficult to picture. That was why I had made him my Optio (you might translate that word as 'sergeant') years ago, because he looked unstoppable. With Ursus at my side, I never had to argue or fight. One look at him and people became co-operative.

. . . .

Found in Translation

Before long we were approaching Jerusalem from the north. The fields and hillsides near the road were crowded with tents.

"Jews come from all over the Empire to celebrate the Festival of Passover in Jerusalem," said Crescens. "The city can't hold them all, so they camp out all round the city."

We began to pass vehicles - vans, cars, trucks - parked off the road. There were soldiers searching them but we weren't stopped until we reached a check point close to one of the city gates. The soldiers manning the checkpoint were in desert camouflage uniforms and wore the badges of an Auxiliary cohort.

"The garrison of Judea has five infantry cohorts and a unit of light tanks," said Ursus, "all Auxiliaries - no Legionary troops."

My Prefect's identity card drew a respectful salute from the sentry who inspected it. However, it did not stop his back-up aiming their machine-gun at our vehicle and, "No vehicles allowed in the city, sir," he said apologetically. "If you could just park over there, please. We'll keep an eye on your vehicle."

"What? No vehicles at all?" I queried.

"No, sir. Governor's orders. Streets too narrow and too many pedestrians."

Reluctantly, I parked the Audax on a hard-standing as indicated by the guard. In front of us, a row of wooden posts stretched along the roadside - about twenty of them. They were rough-hewn, with nail holes and dark stains on the wood. There were dark stains on the ground in front of them as well.

"Looks like they have a lot of crucifixions here," said Ursus.

"Judea is full of terrorists," said Crescens. "A lot of Jews just won't accept Roman rule." He walked over and started examining the posts closely. "These three have been used

Three Days in Jerusalem

recently," he said, indicating the first three posts. "The others haven't been used for weeks."

"How do you know?" I asked.

Crescens pointed to the dark stains at the foot of the first three posts. "There's not more than ten days' dust covering these bloodstains. And there are still some footmarks: military boots. The dust at the foot of the other posts has been building up for several weeks."

"Good work," I said. I hadn't had any choice of SCO but it looked as though the Tribune had found me one who was sharp.

We shouldered our kitbags, turned and trudged up to and through the city gate, turning left to the Tower of Antonia, the base of the cohort in garrison at Jerusalem. It was a narrow street, with the city wall to our left and the high wall of the Tower in front of us. As we neared the Tower, we could see, stretching off to the right, another wall with a much more imposing building beyond it. Crescens said that that was the temple of the Jewish god.

"You've certainly done your homework," I said.

"I was here once before, about five years ago, helping investigate a murder."

We climbed a steep stairway up to the gate of the Antonia Tower, showed our ID to the guards and presently we were ushered into the office of Petronius Justus, the Prefect of Cohort I Sebastena, the cohort in garrison.

"Glad you could come, Julius" he said, and I got the feeling that he didn't quite mean that. He looked uncomfortable - much more uncomfortable than a man with five hundred soldiers at his command ought to look. "We need to have this business cleared up quickly."

I put my recorder on the desk and switched it on. Petronius frowned. "Is that really necessary?"

Found in Translation

"I've been ordered to carry out an official investigation," I said. "You're about to brief me, so the investigation starts now. So, yes, it is necessary."

"Haven't you already been briefed?" Petronius sounded surprised now.

"All I've been told is that it's a case of tomb robbing. And I've no idea why you need outside help to clear it up. Tomb robbing is pretty routine stuff. What makes this case so special?"

Petronius cleared his throat, "It's unusual because no goods were stolen," he said. "It was the body that was removed from the tomb."

Ursus grunted with surprise. I was surprised myself.

Crescens said, "I thought the Jews would never touch a dead body if they could avoid it, let alone steal one."

"You're quite right," agreed Petronius. "The Jews think that contact with a dead body makes them impure, unholy. They have to go through a ritual of purification after handling a corpse."

"So they must have needed a strong motive to steal a body," I said. "Don't you know who would have such a motive?"

"The thieves would have to go to the Jewish temple here to be purified," said Crescens. "Why don't you just pull in anyone who comes for purification?"

"I have arranged for the Temple Police to do that," said Petronius impatiently. "Let me tell you the story from the beginning."

I settled myself more comfortably in my chair and wondered if Petronius was going to offer us coffee.

"Ten days ago," began the Prefect, "the Jewish priests and their religious Council brought to the Governor a man they had arrested and wanted to be executed. They charged this man with blasphemy against their religion and also charged him with treason against the Emperor. Apparently he claimed to be what the Jews call a *Messiah*, which meant he was also claiming to be king of the Jews.

"Now there have been quite a few of these messiahs from time to time. Sometimes they manage to collect a group of terrorists or bandits. They hide out in the hills. It doesn't usually come to much. Either they just fade away or we track them down and crucify them.

"This particular messiah was called Jesus. He was from Nazareth in Galilee, outside Pilate's jurisdiction, but Herod's agents were keeping an eye on him."

"Herod is the, er, *Tetrarch* of Galilee?" I asked tentatively.

"Yes. He likes to be called 'king', but officially he's just a tetrarch. He certainly doesn't want any rival kings around. Pilate and Herod don't usually get on with each other, but we liaise with Herod's military.

"So we knew about this Jesus. He became active in Galilee about two years ago. He wasn't a bandit leader. He was very popular. Everywhere he went he gathered a crowd to hear him speak. He had a gang of sorts but they never carried weapons, as far as Herod's agents could tell. He was actually telling the Jews that they had to get on with other people. 'Love your neighbour' was one of his sayings. And by that he included the Samaritans. Samaritans and Jews hate each other's guts. They usually try to avoid each other.

"Of course, I told Pilate we thought this man was harmless, so he decided to let him go. But the High Priest kept pressing the Governor. It was the time of the Jewish holy day called *Passover*. Jews from all over the world come to Jerusalem for this festival: from Egypt, Greece, Rome itself, and Galilee. They camp all around the city. A lot of them are still here, waiting for another holy day called *Pentecost*. This man Jesus had ridden into Jerusalem on a donkey, and the High Priest said that that was a claim to be the messiah. What sort of king rides on a donkey, I ask you! But that's what the Jews believe. This Jesus had a lot of support from Galileans who had come to Jerusalem for Passover. My agents watched him come into the city. There was a lot of shouting and singing, and waving palm branches and cloaks, but it all seemed quite friendly and cheerful. Nothing sinister or threatening, nothing ugly about the mood of the crowd. Still, the High Priest insisted that there was a real danger that this Jesus would declare himself king and messiah and the people would follow him; so Pilate began to get worried."

Up to this point Petronius had been speaking in a deadpan voice, as one does when delivering a formal report, but now his voice became more thoughtful, almost puzzled.

"Jesus had done one thing. There's a sort of market in the Temple courtyard. The Jews buy animals and birds for sacrifice there and change their money into Jewish coinage. Jesus cleared the money-changers and traders out of the courtyard. He said the courtyard was too holy for business like that. No-one was hurt, but if this Jesus could do that and have the crowd support him against the Temple authorities, then I can see that the High Priest *would* be worried about losing control to this Jesus.

"Still, Pilate tried. He even offered them a choice; he would release a prisoner, either this Jesus or a man called Barabbas. And they chose Barabbas."

The Prefect swore quietly under his breath. He was looking angry now. "This Barabbas was a *real* terrorist," he said, "and a murderer. I really wanted to see *him* hanging on a cross. There *will* be trouble now he's on the loose again. Anyway, in the end Pilate gave in and signed the warrant for Jesus' crucifixion. What's one religious fanatic more or less? Judea's full of them.

"So we crucified Jesus and a couple of Barabbas' men with him. He died the same day..."

"That was quick wasn't it?" I interrupted. "Men usually take days to die from crucifixion."

"He'd been flogged before he was crucified but, yes, you're right; he did die quickly. Came over dark when he died as well; definitely a bit spooky. The priests wanted them all off the crosses and buried before their holy day, so my men broke the legs of the two bandits and they died quickly after that. Then a Jew called Joseph of Arimathea went to Pilate and asked to be allowed to bury Jesus. Pilate released the body to him and he, Joseph that is, put it in a tomb, and we thought that was the end of it."

Petronius paused a moment to take a breath before continuing.

"Next day however, the High Priest was back talking to Pilate. He must have been pretty worried because it was a holy day, what the Jews call a Sabbath, and they usually want no contact at all with us *foreigners*." (He said the word with a sneer) "They say it makes them impure. The High Priest said that Jesus had told his followers that he would rise from the dead after he had been put to death." Petronius spoke this last sentence slowly and clearly. He obviously was at last coming to the key point and I was already beginning to see where this was leading. "The High Priest asked Pilate to put a guard over the tomb of Jesus in case his gang stole the body and claimed he had risen from the dead. Pilate was sick and tired of the whole business by then. The Temple has its own Police Force, so Pilate told the High Priest that if he wanted to guard the tomb with them, that was his affair. So the priests set a guard on the tomb."

"Not a very efficient guard," I said drily.

"No. The next day they were reporting that the tomb had been raided and Jesus' body had been stolen."

"Was there a fight?" asked Ursus. It was the sort of thing he was interested in.

"No. The guards reported that they had fallen asleep."

Ursus gave a snort of disgust.

"Sound sleepers, these guards," I said.

Petronius was now looking uncomfortable again. "It was three days before the priests told us what had happened. By then there was a rumour in the city that this man Jesus *had* risen from the dead. I put a guard on the tomb straight away but we still have no idea what happened to the body. And so," he said, smiling at me as if he was telling me I'd won the lottery, "we would like you to find out what really happened."

I sat for a moment while my brain got into gear. "Have you rounded up these followers of Jesus?"

Petronius looked embarrassed. I almost felt sorry for him. He seemed to be experiencing a lot of bad emotions during this briefing. "They've gone to ground. We think some of them have gone back to Galilee. They're nobodies really. No criminal records. They could just go back to their homes and blend in with the crowd. I can give you some leads - places where you might get information." He slid a thick document wallet across the desk. "This is our file of information on Jesus and his gang."

I opened the wallet. As I had hoped, there were photographs of Jesus - two official photographs, full face and profile, taken while he was under arrest. It showed the fairly ordinary face of a man in his early thirties, dark-skinned, with black hair and beard. He looked tired, which was understandable, but relaxed. And his eyes - even in the photograph there was an extraordinary depth to them.

"I'll need to interview these Temple Police guards," I said to Petronius, "and this Joseph of Arimathea and your officer who oversaw the crucifixion, and the Governor and the High Priest; see if they can explain this messiah business to me."

"We'll need to go to the tomb," put in Crescens.

"We'll start there," I agreed. "While you're setting up these interviews for me," I said to Petronius.

"Centurion Helvius oversaw the crucifixions," said Petronius. "He should be down at the tomb now; his century is providing the guard there."

I switched off my recorder and stood up.

"You'll probably need this." Petronius passed across an A-to-Z street map of Jerusalem. "And this is Joseph of Arimathea's address." He scribbled on a slip of paper and handed it to me.

"We'll need an office," I said, "and living quarters."

"We can accommodate you here in the Antonia," said Petronius. "I'll see if I can set up your interviews with the Governor and the High Priest." He picked up the telephone.

. . . .

"What do you make of it so far?" I asked the others as we walked out of the city to the site of the tomb, which Petronius had thoughtfully marked on the map.

"Open and shut case, boss," said Ursus. "The followers of this man Jesus stole the body so they could pretend he had risen from the dead."

"But what about these sleeping guards?" said Crescens.

"They must be in on the plot," said Ursus. "For all we know this Jesus had been recruiting a secret organisation here in Judea as well as in Galilee."

We walked past the crucifixion posts and came to the area of the tombs. There was a low, rocky cliff-face with a number of doorways cut into it. It was obvious which tomb was the one we were looking for, because it was taped off and there were several guards - Roman soldiers from the Sebastena cohort. The Centurion, a tall man with two scars on his right forearm, inspected my ID.

"You're Centurion Helvius, who supervised the crucifixion of this man?" I asked.

"That's right, Prefect."

I pulled out my recorder. "Tell me about it."

"It seemed fairly routine at first," said Helvius. "I was ordered to crucify the man Jesus and two bandits that we had in the cells. We nailed them up on the first three posts by the city wall." He pointed back towards the city gate. "We usually crucify people there because it's a busy highway, so there are plenty of passers-by to see what happens if you set yourself up against Rome."

"You said, 'routine at first'," I said. "In what way did it become not routine?"

"When I look back, there were a lot of odd things about it," said Helvius, and I thought he sounded uncomfortable - guilty, almost. "I'd heard the reports about this man Jesus, and he didn't seem to be inciting anyone to violence or terrorism or rebellion. I could understand the priests being annoyed - he certainly attacked *them* verbally - but I didn't see why it concerned the Governor. Then Pilate ordered him to be flogged. No reason for that, that I could see - except to satisfy the priests. Still, orders are orders, so my men carried out the flogging." The Centurion was beginning to sound as though he was talking to himself, not to me, as if he were going over things in his mind and trying to justify himself. "Then, while I went to report that we'd flogged Jesus, my men decided to have a bit of fun with him. They'd heard the accusation that he claimed to be King of the Jews, so they dressed him up like a mock king. They found an old scarlet military cloak, and they gave him a stick for a sceptre, and someone made a sort of coronet out of thorn twigs. Most of my cohort are recruited from Samaria," said Helvius, apologetically. "Samaritans and Jews hate each others' guts. When I found out what was happening, I stopped it, but..."

Three Days in Jerusalem

He paused and looked at me as if expecting me to say something.

"Soldiers are soldiers," I said, keeping my tone as neutral as possible. "What happened next?"

"Well, Pilate finally agreed to crucify Jesus. I was given the job with my century. We got the two bandits up from the cells and took all three of them out to death row. They were carrying their own cross-beams as usual but Jesus was so weak after the flogging he soon collapsed. I had to pressgang a man from the crowd to carry his cross-beam.

"We crucified the three men in the usual way. The two bandits screamed and cursed when we hammered the nails in, but you get used to that. Jesus didn't, although you could see he was in just as much pain. But he said something. He said, 'Father forgive them; they don't know what they are doing.'"

"What did he mean by that?"

"Apparently he used to call god, that's the Jewish god, his father. So he was praying to his god to forgive us for crucifying him."

"That sounds unusual. Anyone else would have cursed you for what you were doing."

"As the bandits did. By this time it was about nine o'clock. Nothing much happened for a while, except some of the priests came along with their supporters. I suppose they wanted to make sure we really had crucified Jesus. They didn't want Pilate to let him go secretly. They jeered at Jesus. He's supposed to have healed a lot of sick people, miraculously, in Galilee, so they challenged him to do another miracle and come down from the cross. I shut them up after a bit." Again there was that air of guilt about Centurion Helvius.

"About midday, it started to get dark. It was uncanny. There didn't seem to be any clouds in the sky; it was just as if the sun was going out. Jesus called out something. I couldn't understand it – it was in Hebrew. But there was a little group of women and a young man nearby. The man told me Jesus was calling out to his god."

"It didn't do him much good?" I said.

"I'm not so sure. A bit later, Jesus shouted out something really loud, almost triumphantly. The young man said that Jesus had shouted, 'It is completed!'"

"Are you sure he didn't say, 'It's all over'?" I asked, with a hint of sarcasm in my voice that I didn't really mean to put there.

"It didn't *sound* like a cry of despair."

"I understand that Jesus died unusually quickly."

"Yes. He died right after shouting out. And then it started to get light again. Then I received orders to break the legs of the crucified men so that they would die quickly. Apparently the Jews didn't want the men to hang on the crosses over their holy day, which began at sunset. So my men broke the legs of the two bandits, but Jesus was already dead. One of my men stabbed him with a spear, just to make sure."

"Didn't it surprise you that Jesus died so quickly?" I asked.

"It did – and yet it didn't," replied Helvius. "There was something about Jesus ... I wouldn't be surprised if he did work miracles."

Roman Centurions are usually hard-headed, cynical men, so it surprised me to hear Helvius say this.

"Then a messenger came telling me to report to the Governor," continued Helvius. "When I got to the palace, Pilate asked me if Jesus was dead, and I confirmed that he was. There was a Jew there named Joseph. I'd noticed him at the crosses, standing by himself. Pilate told me to hand the body of Jesus over to Joseph for burial. So we walked back to death row. Joseph had brought some men of his own, and my soldiers helped them take Jesus' body down from the cross, and they carried it off to these tombs."

"Are you sure Jesus was dead?" I asked. Had Jesus really died so quickly, I wondered, or had a live man been placed in that tomb?

Helvius looked offended at the question. "Of course he was dead. I know the difference between a live man and a dead one, as I'm sure you do yourself, Prefect. He wasn't breathing, his eyes were fixed and there was no response when one of my men stuck a spear into his side. Anyway, when we took him down from the cross, the body had gone cold and begun to stiffen. He was dead all right."

"Hmmm, what do you make of all this, Centurion?"

Helvius looked uneasy once more. "I guess Jesus' followers stole the body. I'd like to have words with those *** useless Temple Police, though."

"You 'guess'," I prompted him.

"Who else would want to take the body?" Helvius' expression changed again. "Jesus was innocent," he declared, defiantly, "and I'm sorry to have had to put him to death."

"You were following orders. It was the Governor's decision; it was his responsibility."

"Some orders you wonder if you should follow." Helvius looked around cautiously and lowered his voice, not wanting to be overheard; apparently he had forgotten about my recorder. "I think, *think* mind you, that maybe Jesus *was* the son of the Jewish god. After all, if Emperor Tiberius can be the son of the god Augustus, why shouldn't a king of the Jews be the son of the god of the Jews?"

He was referring to Augustus who had been Emperor before Tiberius and had been officially declared a god after his death. Helvius' words sort of made sense, if you believe in that sort of thing.

"Thank you, Centurion," I said aloud. "You've been very helpful. I may want to talk to you again."

"You know where to find me, Prefect," said Helvius and straightened up smartly.

I looked round. Ursus was standing a few yards away looking bored. Crescens, I was glad to see, had his camera out and was taking photographs.

"Let's have a closer look at this tomb," I said.

The doorway of the tomb, I saw, had been roughly hewn out of the living rock. Just to one side of it, a huge round, flat stone stood on edge, leaning against the rock.

"That was used to close the entrance," explained Helvius. "The Temple guards put a seal between it and the rock wall, so they could tell if it was moved. You can still see what's left of the beeswax."

Crescens took some more photographs.

"How many men would it take to move that stone?" I asked.

"Two," said Ursus.

"Three or four," said Crescens.

"You try and move it, Ursus," I said.

Ursus flexed his arms, bent down and put a shoulder to the stone. At first, nothing happened. Ursus stepped back, flexed his arms again, bent down slightly lower and heaved. This time he rolled the stone a good foot. It made a scraping noise against the rock.

"Those guards must have been very sound asleep," I said, "if they weren't woken up by that."

"Can we go inside?" asked Crescens.

"Help yourselves," said Helvius.

Crescens stooped a little and disappeared into the dark entrance. Ursus said, "I'll wait outside, if you don't mind, Boss?"

Ursus was clearly far too big to pass easily into the tomb, so I nodded to him. "Talk to these soldiers," I said.

Three Days in Jerusalem

I went in to the tomb myself, stooping, like Crescens, to get through the low doorway. We both paused while our eyes grew accustomed to the darkness. There was an oil lamp burning in a niche in the right hand wall, but most of the light was coming through the narrow doorway.

The tomb was simply a small cave hollowed out of the rock. There were several niches in the walls, like the one that the lamp was standing in. Against the left hand wall, a long slab of rock had been left in place to form a sort of table or platform. On this platform were two pieces of what looked like cloth.

"This is great!" said Crescens. "I've always wanted to get a look inside one of these tombs."

He clicked and flashed away with his camera.

"Do you understand this place?" I asked him.

"Yes, it's a Jewish burial practice - very unusual," he explained. "The body is brought in and laid out on this platform. Then it's left to for the flesh to decay until there are only bones left. That takes about two years. Then the tomb is reopened, the bones are collected into an *ossuary*, a stone box, and placed permanently in one of these niches. It's a family tomb, you see. You could have several generations buried here. The cave can be enlarged if necessary." He looked around carefully. "This must be a new tomb, though; there are no ossuaries in any of the niches. Unless they've been removed as well."

"We'll have to find out," I said. "So the body of Jesus would have been laid here. What are these cloths?"

Crescens bent down and looked at the material. He pulled out a torch and a magnifying glass.

"It's linen," he said. "Good quality, too. These look like bloodstains. I'd say this large piece was used to wrap the body and this smaller piece was wrapped round the head."

"Do you realise what you're saying?" I asked him.

"What do you mean?" said Crescens, in a puzzled voice.

"You're telling me that the grave robbers came and stole a body and they unwrapped it before they took it away."

"Ye-e-s, I see what you mean, sir. And they've laid out the cloths as if they were still wrapped round a body. Now why would they do that?"

"And why would they waste time doing it? They must have been nervous about the guards waking up."

"They wanted to make it seem as if the body had 'risen' and passed through the cloth," said Crescens, slowly.

I looked around once more. There didn't seem to be anything else interesting in the tomb but Crescens might still find something. That was what he was trained to do. At the moment he was taking out some evidence bags and pulling on his gloves.

"I'll send these cloths off to the forensic lab in Antioch," he said, "and I'll try and get some blood samples from those crosses."

"I'll leave you to it," I said. "Ursus and I will go and look up this Joseph of Arimathea."

I went out of the tomb, blinking in the daylight. Ursus was talking to a couple of the soldiers. I beckoned him to follow and we walked up to the city wall.

"There ought to be another gate here," I said, looking at the map. One of the first things you learn as a police officer is the need to make yourself thoroughly familiar with your territory, especially the back ways and side alleys. "Did you find out anything?" I asked Ursus.

"Nothing new. It was their century that crucified Jesus of Nazareth, and they saw the body taken away for burial. The next thing they heard was five days later when the cohort was ordered to maintain a twenty-four hour guard on the empty tomb. After five days of it, they're bored silly."

We found the gate easily enough, for the city walls here formed a re-entrant, and the gate was in the corner. Jerusalem was a typical unplanned city - mostly narrow streets with no pattern to them, small open spaces filled with stallholders, buildings varying from tenements to grand city mansions, public fountains with women drawing water, multiple smells (mostly unpleasant), noise, jostle and bustle. The city being built on hills, there were steep streets, stairways cut out of the rock and stone-built viaducts. Although, as the sentry had advised us, there were no motor vehicles, there were plenty of donkeys and asses.

In due course we found ourselves at the address that Petronius had written on the slip of paper and Ursus knocked at the door. In spite of all the high-tech support represented by Crescens with his camera and his forensic lab, we were back to the familiar, timeless pattern of police work: knocking on doors, looking for people to 'help us with our enquiries'.

The door was opened cautiously by a young man. I flashed my ID card at him.

"Police Officers. We would like to talk to Joseph of Arimathea."

The young man hesitated, then opened the door wide enough for me to enter - not wide enough for Ursus, however, and he pushed the door hard. As soon as we were in, the man shut the door quickly.

"Wait here," he said and went through a doorway to the right.

We were in a narrow atrium, lit by natural light from a window in the ceiling, with a mosaic in the floor and patterned wall hangings. Joseph of Arimathea was obviously a well-to-do man.

The young man reappeared. "Master Joseph will see you."

He ushered us into a room comfortably furnished as a sitting room. An elderly man was rising from his armchair. He looked at least seventy, maybe more. His hair was completely grey, almost silver, as was his full beard. Even his eyebrows were the same silver grey. By contrast his eyes were dark. He was a short man but sturdily built, not fat, and he was straight-backed. His long gown was good quality cloth, matching the furnishings of his house.

"Peace to you," he said, in a Jewish greeting that I hadn't heard before.

"Thank you for seeing us, Father Joseph." (The 'Father' slipped out automatically. It seemed natural to call a patriarchal figure like this 'Father'.) "We're making enquiries about the disappearance of the body of Jesus of Nazareth. I understand that it was you who buried him."

"Please, sit down," said Joseph. "Would you like some refreshment? A glass of wine, or coffee, perhaps?"

"I am gasping for some coffee," I said. This was the first drink any of us had been offered since we arrived in Jerusalem.

Joseph nodded to his servant, who left the room and returned presently carrying a tray with two enormous mugs of coffee and a small glass of wine. Meantime, Ursus and I had settled ourselves into two soft armchairs. We tasted the coffee thankfully while Joseph sipped his wine.

"Excellent coffee, Father," I said, "and very welcome. The roads here are very dusty."

"Our dry season has started early this year," said Joseph.

I took out my recorder. "This is an official investigation, Father Joseph," I said, "so I have to record this interview."

"Naturally," he replied, unconcerned.

"I understand that you are a member of the Jewish Council that condemned Jesus of Nazareth and accused him before the Governor," I began.

Three Days in Jerusalem

"I am a member of the Council; that is correct," said Joseph, "but I was not present when Jesus was condemned. The council was held in the middle of the night, and I was not called to the meeting. Doubtless the High Priest considered my age and infirmity and felt that I should be left to my sleep." He spoke quietly and evenly, but I detected a note of sarcasm in his last sentence.

"Why did you decide to bury Jesus?"

"I did not agree with the priests' view that Jesus was a blasphemer and a rebel."

"Could you explain that, please? As a Roman I'm finding it difficult to understand exactly why Jesus was condemned by your Council."

"Blasphemy means that Jesus was speaking against our religion and against God. According to our Law, which we believe to be God-given, that could be punishable by death."

"But you didn't think Jesus was a blasphemer?"

"No. I listened carefully to what he taught here in Jerusalem and in the Temple. I did not hear him say anything against our religion. I did hear him say that the most important command was that we should love God with all our hearts, minds, souls and strength. I don't think a man could say that with one breath and then curse God with his next."

I was beginning to realise that the Jews seemed to regard a personal relationship with their god as important, unlike us Romans who have contractual relations with our gods and like to keep our distance.

"So what did you think Jesus was?" I asked.

"He was certainly a *rabbi*, a teacher, and a good one too. He could hold a crowd with his teaching and his stories. I thought he might be a prophet."

"*Prophet?*" the word was new to me.

"God speaks to us through prophets. Among our sacred books there are sixteen that record the words that God spoke through individual prophets."

"I understood that Jesus also claimed to be *Messiah*, whatever that is?"

"Our prophetic books say that one day God will send a man who will be a supreme ruler. He will rule with wisdom and justice. He will lead all other nations to worship the One True God, as we Jews do. That man will be the Messiah, which means one anointed by God."

"I see," I said, although I wasn't at all sure that I did, really. I understood Joseph's words all right, but I was not so sure that I understood what he meant. "Did you think that Jesus was this Messiah?"

"I wasn't sure. Many people have claimed to be the Messiah, and they have all come to a bad end. Jesus did ride into Jerusalem on a donkey. That was a fulfilment of a messianic prophecy - a king who comes in peace not war. I am sure his followers thought he was going to proclaim himself Messiah. But, if he had been the Messiah, God would not have allowed him to be executed."

"I can see that, if Jesus claimed to be a supreme ruler, that could be seen as rebellion against the Emperor," I said, "but why would your priests want to prosecute him before the Governor? Why wouldn't they welcome a supreme Jewish ruler?"

"You will have to ask them," said Joseph, drily, "but Jesus did speak out against some of the practices of our priests. Have you heard that he cleared the money-changers and traders out of the Temple?"

I remembered that Petronius had described the incident.

"That showed his control over the people. He accused our priests and teachers of being blind spiritual guides."

Three Days in Jerusalem

Joseph was certainly giving me things to think about. I made a mental note to ask the High Priest about some of these issues.

"So why did you bury Jesus?"

"I thought he was a good man. He was teaching the people to obey God out of love. Most of our teachers tell us to obey God out of duty; they make it seem like a burden. I thought our Council was wrong to condemn Jesus. I thought that burying his body would be a very clear way of distancing myself from their decision."

"It was your own tomb?"

"Yes, I only had it constructed recently. It was intended to be my family tomb. Jesus was the first person to be placed there; it was close to where he was executed."

"It was a very kind and respectful action on your part."

"Thank you," said Joseph, with a quiet smile.

"Did you remove the body from the tomb?"

"Of course not." Joseph spread his hands wide in gesture of surprise. "Why should I? I expected the body to remain there to decay and for the bones to be gathered into an ossuary."

"Have you any idea who did take the body?"

Joseph shrugged his shoulders. "I suppose that some of his disciples could have had some crazy idea of trying to convince people that he had risen from the dead. That is the rumour that is going around. But it may have been his family, wanting to take his body back to Galilee for burial. I would have handed the body over to them, of course, if they had come to me and asked. Perhaps they were afraid of being arrested themselves and so did it secretly."

I made another mental note - to make enquiries about Jesus' family. I stood up. "Thank you, Father Joseph, you have been most informative."

"You are very welcome. I hope you are able to find the body and make sure it has a proper burial. I hate the thought of a man's body being treated with disrespect."

. . . .

The sun was already setting as Ursus and I left Joseph's house. We made our way back to the Antonia in the darkening twilight, where we found Crescens in the office that Petronius had allocated to us.

"I've sent the shroud and the other cloth to the forensic lab in Antioch," he reported. "I also managed to get some blood samples from the crosses and the ground around them. And Centurion Helvius gave me a bag of stuff that had been left near the tomb by the Temple guards - just some empty ration packs and a wine bottle, but I've sent them to Antioch as well, just in case there might be something on them."

"Good work," I said, automatically. "So where have we got to?"

"It seems as if the Governor may have executed an innocent man," said Ursus, slowly.

"It sounds to me as if the words 'innocent' and 'guilty' have a flexible meaning around here," I said, "but I guess that's true of the whole Empire right now. It would be easier if we didn't have to take these extraordinary Jewish religious beliefs into account."

"Do you think they *are* extraordinary?" said Crescens.

"Aren't they?" I said, surprised. "A supreme ruler, from the Jews of all people?"

"I expect if you'd told people three hundred years ago that one day Rome would be an empire and the supreme ruler of the world would be a Roman, they would have laughed at you."

"I suppose so." History was not one of my strong points.

Three Days in Jerusalem

"There are a lot of good things about the Jews' religious teaching, when you get to know it," continued Crescens.

"Well, that's by-the-by," I said. "Right now, we have to find these tomb robbers."

The door opened and the Prefect Petronius came in without knocking.

"I've arranged for the Governor to see you first thing in the morning – that means eight o'clock," he said, "and you can go straight from him to the High Priest."

"Just you," he added, looking at Ursus, "they don't want anyone else present."

"Privilege of rank," I said.

"I've told the Captain of the Temple Police to have his four sleeping sentries ready to be interviewed by you at any time after ten o'clock tomorrow," continued Petronius, "and I've got an address for you." He handed me another slip of paper. "It's the place where Jesus stayed for a week before his arrest. It's in Bethany, about two miles East of Jerusalem. One or two of Jesus' followers might be holed-up there."

"Very good," I said, "but are they likely to do a runner before we get to them?"

"Not now," Petronius reassured me. "I've got men watching the place. They'll pull in anyone who tries to leave." He looked at Ursus and Crescens. "I've arranged quarters for you in the Non-Commissioned Officers' Mess." Ursus inclined his head in acknowledgement. I was satisfied that it was appropriate for their rank. "And I'd be very pleased if you take a room in my quarters, Julius. I'll be eating in about half-an-hour, if you would care to join me."

"Thank you very much, I'd be delighted," I replied, not with complete sincerity. "I think we're about finished here for this evening."

. . . .

As I expected, Petronius tried to pump me at dinner about what we'd discovered so far, but I'm too accustomed to dealing with journalists, and Petronius wasn't nearly as expert as they tend to be at getting information out of an unwilling victim.

Day Two

The next morning found me walking up the steps to the Governor's residence. Petronius had explained that this was a palace built by Herod the Great when he had been king of all Judea, Samaria and Galilee. It was certainly an imposing building, with a flight of stone steps and a row of Greek-style columns before the main entrance. In front of the palace was a rectangular open space, neatly paved, that could have held a crowd of perhaps five hundred people. I noticed that the soldiers here wore the insignia of Cohort I Ituraeorum. Pilate, it seemed, had brought extra troops into the city to cover this period of Jewish festivals.

A soldier escorted me to Pilate's secretary and the secretary showed me into a huge office. It had a broad window opening to the West, with a view over the city wall. There were rich wall hangings, and the floor was a mosaic with the image of a garden: trees, shrubs, flowers and a spring of water. The Governor was seated at a large desk, much larger than he needed for his papers; its size was clearly also meant to impress, and it was of solid oak, highly polished.

Pilate, however, immediately stood up, came round the desk and shook hands, although he didn't exactly smile. I met his gaze firmly. It was a moot point which of us was the senior. Pilate's rank was Prefect, the same as mine. He was the Governor of a small province and he had a force of several

Three Days in Jerusalem

cohorts, each of which was commanded by an officer with the same rank – Prefect. Rome tends to re-cycle a small number of rank titles. He was also of the Equestrian Order (the middle class between Senators and plain Citizens), probably by birth. On the other hand I had been a Centurion for sixteen of my thirty-five years' service. I had worked my way up to become Chief Centurion of my Legion, VI Ferrata, and was now a Camp Prefect, and I could take command of a detachment of cohorts or even the whole legion if necessary. Compared with Pilate, who was in his mid-thirties, I had great prestige, and prestige is very important to us Romans. Also, I had accumulated sufficient wealth to become a member of the Equestrian Order.

Pilate, as I said, was in his mid-thirties, average height and build, with a definite sense of arrogance in his face and bearing.

"I am glad to meet you, Prefect," he said, formally. "I need to have this business sorted out quickly so that I can make my reports to the Governor of Syria and to Rome."

'And I bet you want to come out of it squeaky-clean,' was my thought, but I only said, "I will do my best, but I am having some difficulty with the religious aspects of this case."

"Everyone has trouble with the Jews' religion," said Pilate. "I've been struggling with it for almost ten years. Won't you sit down? Will you take some refreshment?"

"I've not long had breakfast but coffee is always welcome, if you please."

Pilate nodded to his secretary, who disappeared as we sat down. While we waited for the coffee, Pilate asked me about the latest gossip from Syria.

"One gets very isolated in a troublesome province like Judea," he said.

I answered his questions until the secretary returned with the coffee. Then I took out my recorder. Pilate looked uncomfortable as I switched it on. "This *is* an official investigation," I reminded him, before he could protest. Then I said, "I think it would be helpful if you could give me your side of the story from the beginning, Governor."

"Up until two weeks ago," Pilate began, "I had never heard of Jesus of Nazareth." Something in his voice and face told me that he heartily wished he had still never heard of the man. "Then the Jewish High Priest, Caiaphas, came to me with a warning that there was a potential rebel leader in the city for the Passover. He said that there was a real possibility of this man declaring himself king of the Jews and raising a rebellion. I suppose you know that thousands of Jews, from all over the Empire, come to Jerusalem for the Passover Festival. They crowd the city and the local villages, and they camp all around. A lot of them are still here; they stay on for another festival called Pentecost."

I nodded, remembering the tents we had seen as we approached Jerusalem.

"Caiaphas said that they had managed to infiltrate Jesus' gang and they were hoping to find an opportunity to arrest him quietly, perhaps at night. He said Jesus was so popular that if they, or we, tried to arrest him openly, there was certain to be a riot. Caiaphas suggested that the Jewish Council could try Jesus on a charge of blasphemy and condemn him to death, and asked me if I would be prepared to ratify the death sentence. Of course, I agreed."

"Why 'of course'?" I asked.

"The Jews are fanatical about their religion. They worship one god and refuse to recognise any other gods. They won't even accept that their god equates to our supreme god, Jupiter, Best and Greatest. In order to keep the peace in this province the Emperor Tiberius has graciously allowed the Jews to continue with their religion and not force them to accept the Imperial cult of the deified Augustus.

Three Days in Jerusalem

"When I was appointed Governor," continued Pilate, "I had the strictest instructions from the Emperor to co-operate with the Jewish religious leaders and to keep the peace here. There have been one or two problems, but on the whole I have managed that. Caiaphas and I have a good working relationship. My residence is in Caesarea. I only come here for the major Festivals. I leave one cohort in the Antonia to police the city. They're not allowed into the Temple, so the priests have their own Temple Police to keep order there. Caiaphas is just as eager to keep the peace as I am. All he wants is for his priests to be able to carry out all the Jewish rituals and sacrifices. If Caiaphas said this Jesus was a likely rebel, I was happy to accept that."

"I didn't know Roman soldiers weren't allowed into the Temple," I interrupted.

"Only Jews may enter the Temple. No *Gentiles* (that's what they call all non-Jews) are allowed in. At least, we can go into the outer court, just inside the perimeter wall. There are gateways to the inner courts which we're not allowed to pass. Any Gentile who gets into the forbidden zone is executed – if the Jews don't tear him to pieces first."

"I see," I said.

"After Caiaphas left, I called for a report on Jesus from Petronius. That was when I began to realise that there was no indication that this Jesus was a rebel or a terrorist. He seemed to be a harmless crank, except that he was popular with the crowds. He had a gang of a dozen regular followers, but they didn't carry weapons and they had never done anything violent: no robbery, no murder.

"Then my wife had a nightmare about him. I didn't know she'd even heard of him. But she had a nightmare and, I don't know about you, but I'm never sure about dreams; sometimes they seem to be nonsense, sometimes they seem to be warnings."

Pilate was starting to look even more uncomfortable, so I said, "Yes, you never know with dreams."

"So when, a couple of nights later, I was woken in the middle of the night by a messenger from Caiaphas, saying they'd arrested Jesus and wanted to bring him to me for sentence first thing in the morning, I decided I would hear the evidence myself. The Temple Police brought Jesus along at first light, and Caiaphas came with a few of his priests and council in support. I held the trial at the front of this palace. The priests were purified for their Passover, so they didn't want to enter a Gentile building. I took them by surprise when I asked to hear the evidence against Jesus." For the first time, Pilate gave a slight smile. "They had to think quickly. They made two charges against Jesus: that he opposed payment of taxes to the Emperor and that he claimed to be a Messiah or king, which was treason against the Emperor. I knew the charge about taxes was false, because one of Petronius' agents had heard Jesus say that the Jews *should* pay taxes to the Emperor. I questioned Jesus about claiming to be a king.

"Well, you only had to look at Jesus to see he was an ordinary peasant. He did have personality, though." Pilate managed to look thoughtful and uncomfortable at the same time. "There was something about the way he looked at you - as if he could see right inside your head. There was a sort of openness, a sort of vulnerability, as well. But you could see he was a strong man. I could understand why people would be drawn to him.

"So, I asked him if he claimed to be king of the Jews. At first he wouldn't answer. He didn't say anything. When I pressed him, he said, 'My kingdom is not of this world. If it was, I would raise an army to fight for me.' I began to see what Petronius had meant when he said that Jesus seemed to be a harmless crank.

Three Days in Jerusalem

"I went back to the priests and told them I thought Jesus hadn't done anything for which he should be executed. They were furious. I said I would have Jesus flogged and that would have to satisfy them."

"You flogged a man you thought was innocent?" I remembered that Helvius had had doubts about flogging Jesus, but I was surprised to hear Pilate admit it so openly.

Pilate shrugged his shoulders. "What's one flogging more or less? My orders are to keep the peace here; to do that I have to work with Caiaphas. I have to make sure I keep on good terms with him."

I wasn't convinced. I have had to order a good many floggings in my time as Centurion, but I've never, as far as I know, flogged an innocent man.

"Caiaphas and his priests went on insisting that Jesus deserved a death sentence. By this time the square was beginning to fill up. There is a custom here that the Governor releases one prisoner at the time of Passover, as a goodwill gesture, so I offered the crowd a choice: Jesus or Barabbas. Barabbas was a real terrorist and a murderer, and he didn't care whether he was killing Romans or Jews. I felt sure that the crowd would call for Jesus because he had been so popular. To my surprise, they shouted for me to release Barabbas. In the end, I had to do that.

"Then Caiaphas said to me that there was no doubt that Jesus had claimed to be the King of the Jews and that, if I released him, I would be laying myself open to a charge of disloyalty to the Emperor. After that, I really had no choice. I ordered that Jesus should be crucified."

Pilate stopped speaking. He still looked uncomfortable, but there was also a pleading look in his eye. He was wondering how much of this would go into my report. I could understand his dilemma. I wondered what decision I would have made in his place. What was one man's life, even an innocent man, against a riot or rebellion with hundreds, perhaps thousands, dead?

"And you released Jesus' body to Joseph of Arimathea?" I said.

"Yes. It was the least I could do - give the man a decent burial."

"Yes," I thought to myself, "it was the *least* that you did".

"You didn't put a guard on the tomb?" I said aloud.

"Why should I? It wasn't until the next day that Caiaphas came back with this story that Jesus had claimed he would rise from the dead. By that time I'd had enough. I decided to wash my hands of the whole affair and told Caiaphas to use his own Temple Police if he wanted to guard the tomb. Mind you," Pilate added thoughtfully, "Caiaphas must have thought it was very important. That day he came to me was the last day of the Jewish week. They call it the Sabbath. They have strict rules against doing any sort of work or business on the Sabbath. The only thing they do is go to the Temple or meet in Synagogue, as they call it, for worship. Caiaphas must have been very concerned to come to see a Gentile on the Sabbath."

"I'll ask him about that," I said. "Governor, who do you think stole the body of Jesus?"

"It must have been his gang of followers. Nobody else would have any reason to do it."

"What about this report of the Temple guards falling asleep?"

Pilate made a noise that sounded like 'Pshaw!' "Rubbish!" he said. "The guards must have been in on it. They must be secret followers of Jesus, or they must have been bribed."

"So if Jesus was organising a conspiracy, it must have been deep-rooted to involve the Priests' own police force. And his crucifixion hasn't stopped the conspiracy."

Three Days in Jerusalem

"No. But thankfully there have been no disturbances yet. I'm going to keep extra troops in Jerusalem for the time being. If there's any trouble, I'll stamp on it straight away."

I stood up to take my leave. "Thank you for your time, Governor."

"Not at all," he said. "I hope you can find these grave-robbers."

. . . .

Apparently Caiaphas did not want to be seen meeting a Gentile in the Temple, so I made my way down to his residence. It was close to the Governor's palace, but it was a good deal smaller. The servant who answered my knock showed me into a small ante-room, sparsely furnished. Apparently Gentiles were not entitled to priestly comforts either. Caiaphas kept me waiting for a good quarter of an hour. It's a commonly-used technique; the one who is made to wait is clearly of lesser importance than the one who keeps him waiting. Having had plenty of experience in such matters, I wasn't impressed, just irritated.

When Caiaphas did eventually condescend to appear he turned out to be younger than I had expected. I had presumed that a High Priest would be an older man, like Joseph of Arimathea. Caiaphas was older than Pilate but younger than myself and he seemed to be an active, vigorous man. His hair and beard were black and his manner was haughty.

"Peace to you, Prefect," he said, managing to make it sound as if he was wishing me just the opposite.

"Greetings, High Priest," I responded, and took out my recorder.

"What is that for?" said Caiaphas, and there was a touch of anger in his voice. "I understood that this was to be a confidential discussion."

"It is confidential," I said, firmly, "but it is also an official investigation, and I have to make a complete report to my superiors."

"Very well," he said, crossly. "You wish to talk to me about the body of the blasphemer Jesus, which has been stolen? There is no mystery about it. His disciples stole the body."

"*Disciples?*" I said. "I've not heard that word before."

Caiaphas made an impatient gesture. "This man Jesus was a teacher, a rabbi, or rather he set himself up as one. He had a dozen close followers who were his disciples - students, you might say."

"So he *wasn't* a terrorist or a rebel?"

"Certainly he was a rebel. Once he had used his teaching to gain popularity with the people, he began to claim that he was the Messiah, a king."

"High Priest, I am not a Jew," I said, stating the obvious, "but I have been ordered to carry out this investigation and to complete a report. I'm struggling to understand this whole Messiah business. Perhaps you would be kind enough to explain it to me."

"In the distant past, hundreds of years ago, our national prophets foretold that a Messiah would come from God. The word 'Messiah' means 'the Anointed One'. The Messiah would be king of a restored Israel and would rule over the whole world forever."

"What do you mean by a 'restored Israel'?"

"We Jews are a remnant. Historically there were twelve tribes of Israel but first Assyria, then the Babylonians conquered the land and carried many of our people into exile. In due course, God restored our nation but many of the people had given up the ancient religion of Israel, so most of the tribes disappeared. The tribe of Judah was the largest group to remain faithful to our God, so we came to be known as Jews. When Messiah comes he will restore the original twelve tribes and will call all true Israelites back to this land. As you know, at the moment Jews are scattered all over the world, even to Rome itself."

"I see. And Jesus claimed to be this Messiah?"

"He did, although not openly at first. A week before our Festival of Passover he rode into the city on a donkey. That was a fulfilment of one of the prophecies about the Messiah. Then he cleared the money-changers and sellers of animals for sacrifice out of the Temple. He was clearly challenging our authority as priests."

"So that was why you wanted him executed, for challenging *your* authority?"

Caiaphas looked displeased, but also a little uncomfortable. "Jesus was claiming to be a king, so he was challenging the authority of the Emperor."

"I can understand that the Governor would want to execute someone who claimed to be a King above Caesar, but I don't understand why you would want to do so. If he was going to be a Jewish King, why didn't you support him?"

"And start a rebellion against Rome, against the finest army in the world?" said Caiaphas, putting a tone of sarcasm into the last phrase.

"Surely your Jewish god would fight for a Jewish King," I said. "Our Roman gods help us to win our battles and wars. Or is your Jewish god weaker than our Roman gods?"

"There is only one true God," said Caiaphas firmly. "That is the God we Jews worship, who is the Creator of the whole world. There is no other god with power - only the one true God."

"So why didn't you let Jesus start his rebellion and let your god fight for him and drive us Romans out of Judea?"

"The fact that Jesus was crucified shows that he was a false Messiah. If he had been the true Messiah, God would not have allowed him to die on the cross."

"So you executed Jesus as a test, to see if he was the true Messiah?"

"We knew that Jesus was a false Messiah," said Caiaphas, angrily, "because he was a blasphemer. You are not a Jew; you do not understand these things."

"I am *trying* to understand, High Priest. Could you please explain his blasphemy to me?"

Caiaphas took a moment to calm himself down. "We Jews live by the Law of Moses," he said at last. "This Law was given to Moses directly by God himself, many centuries ago. In his teaching, and by his way of life, Jesus was undermining the Law of Moses."

"Could you give me an example?" I asked.

"The Law lays down strict rules for ritual purity, for holiness. There are strict rules on washing - for example, on washing hands before meals. There are strict rules on avoiding contact with things or people that are ritually unclean. Contact with something impure or unclean makes us unclean, and we have to go through a ritual of purification. Jesus ignored these purity laws and taught his disciples to do the same. He touched lepers and other people whose sickness made them impure. He taught that eating food which we consider to be impure does not make a man unclean. He mixed with prostitutes and tax..." Caiaphas checked himself suddenly and then resumed: "...with other bad characters. He even ate with them. He claimed that they would be included in his kingdom, not judged and cast out by God."

"That doesn't sound like a bad idea: a kingdom that includes everybody."

"I knew you would not understand. God is holy! He is not like the fickle, promiscuous, self-centred gods you Romans

Three Days in Jerusalem

worship. To be acceptable to God, a man has to be holy; he has to be purified - ritually clean."

There was a short silence while I tried to digest what Caiaphas was telling me.

"I have been told that contact with a dead body would make a Jew unclean," I remarked.

"Certainly it would."

"So whoever stole Jesus' body would be unclean and would need to (what was it you said) 'go through a ritual of purification'?"

"Of course."

"So we only have to wait for a group of men to come forward for this ritual... Where does this ritual take place?"

"In the Temple. The men would have to present themselves on the third day and the seventh day after handling the corpse, and a priest would sprinkle the Water of Cleansing on them. The Temple Police have orders to investigate anyone presenting themselves for purification. But remember that Jesus ignored these rituals, so his disciples may do the same."

I nodded and moved onto another point.

"What made you decide to guard Jesus' tomb?"

"One of my colleagues reminded me that Jesus had claimed that if he were to be executed, he would rise to life again after three days. We thought that his disciples might remove the body from the tomb and claim that he *had* risen. So I sent the Captain of our Temple Police to seal the tomb and post a guard over it."

"Not a very effective guard."

"No." Caiaphas was looking uncomfortable again. "They fell asleep. But we were right. Jesus' disciples *did* steal his body."

"What makes you so sure it was Jesus' disciples?"

Caiaphas shrugged his shoulders and spread his hands wide in a gesture of puzzlement. "Who else could it have been?"

"That's what I'm supposed to be finding out," I said, "and so far, they are the only suspects. Well, thank you for your time, High Priest. You have been most helpful."

"It seems to me that your time would be better employed rounding up his disciples and finding where they have concealed the body, rather than questioning me."

"Perhaps, but that is not my decision."

. . . .

I walked slowly back to the Antonia. I could understand Pilate's position, even if I found it hard to agree with. He had executed an innocent man for the sake of political expediency. The Emperor Tiberius did the same in Rome. Caiaphas I was not sure about. Did he really believe all that religious stuff he had poured out? Did he really believe that Jesus had been a blasphemer and a rebel? Or had he simply seen Jesus as a threat to the cosy power-sharing arrangement he had with Pilate? Had Jesus been planning a rebellion? If so, he must have been doing it in great secrecy and showing a great deal more skill than other Jews who had tried to stir up a revolt and been promptly suppressed.

As I entered the Antonia I decided to go and look at this Temple that seemed to be so important in the case. There was an open gateway which gave onto a broad flight of steps leading down to the Temple courtyard. Standing at the top of the steps, I had a perfect view of the Temple.

The main building, the holy place, was smaller than I had expected - much smaller than some Roman and Greek temples that I had seen. However, it was built of a beautiful creamy stone. Each individual block had been perfectly squared off to

Three Days in Jerusalem

fit its neighbour with scarcely a crack showing the join. The faces of the blocks had been expertly tooled to give a smooth finish to the outside of the building. Looking to the left I could see the various courts that led the worshipper up to the sanctuary. At the immediate front of the building I could see a great altar with fires burning while priests were slaughtering sacrificial animals. There was a strong smell of blood, fire, and roasting and burning flesh. A balustrade divided this area from the next one where I could see men watching the sacrifices and other men queuing up with animals waiting to be slaughtered. There was another balustrade and steps down to another court where there were mainly women and some children, but men were bringing up more sacrificial animals, while others were going down after completing their offerings. Then there was another flight of steps down and yet another balustrade. There was a huge courtyard outside this final balustrade, enclosed by high walls, with colonnades lining the walls. This courtyard was crowded with men, women and children. Groups of men were gathered here and there in the shade of the colonnades, and there was a row of market stalls, animal pens and bird cages.

I remembered being told that Jesus had driven out these traders and wondered how he had managed it. He must somehow have got this huge crowd on his side. A man that could unite a crowd behind him like that could certainly be dangerous. And now he was dead and the traders were back in place.

Looking to my immediate left I noticed a group of men at the foot of the stairway. They were all in uniform. Some of them were soldiers from the garrison cohort. I didn't recognise the uniform of the others; they looked like police officers, with blue caps, white shirts with blue epaulettes and blue trousers. Ursus was amongst them, easily identifiable by his height and bulk. After a few moments he looked up and saw me. At once he left the group and climbed up the steps to meet me, bringing one of the white-and-blue-clad men with him. I saw that the badge on his cap was a six-pointed star, apparently made of two triangles, one superimposed on the other.

"Boss, this is Micah, the Captain of the Temple Police," Ursus said by way of introduction.

"Peace to you, Prefect," said the Captain, standing more-or-less to attention.

"Greetings, Captain," I said. "So you're the man with the sleeping guard?"

The Captain looked uncomfortable. "Everyone I've talked to looks uncomfortable," I thought, "except Joseph of Arimathea".

"This is our busiest time of the year," he said apologetically. "There are ten times as many pilgrims here at Passover than at any other time. A lot of them stay on for Pentecost as well. My men are worked off their feet: extra duty, all the daylight hours, not to mention night duty. Some of them are ready to fall asleep in the middle of the day."

"I understand you went yourself to post the guard at Jesus' tomb?"

"That's correct. I inspected the body to make sure it really was Jesus. My men rolled the stone back in front of the doorway, and I put on two seals of beeswax with the Temple seal impressed on them."

A thought occurred to me. "Did that make you ritually impure, inspecting the dead body?"

"Technically, no. I didn't actually touch the body - just looked at his face. But I am going through the purification, just in case."

"I've been told that you are checking out any men who come to the Temple for this ritual of purification after handling a dead body."

"Yes, but so far none of Jesus' known followers have turned up. Of course, if they've gone back to Galilee..." (he

Three Days in Jerusalem

shrugged his shoulders) "and Jesus had a reputation for ignoring the purity rituals, so his followers may do the same."

"So the High Priest told me," I said. "Well, do you have these sleepy guards here now?"

"Certainly, Prefect, I'll bring them here for you." He made a gesture as if he was going to salute me, then changed his mind, turned and went down the steps.

I turned to Ursus. "Let's find some coffee before we start, and we'll need an interview room."

As we walked back into the Antonia, I said, "Have you learned anything useful?"

"Not very much, boss. Everyone I speak to has more or less the same version of events. There is one thing though: the Temple Police didn't want to arrest Jesus."

"Didn't they? Why was that?"

"Jesus was speaking in the courtyard here for several days before he was arrested. Most of the Police seem to have heard him at one time or another and they all seem to have been very impressed with him; they thought he was a brilliant speaker."

"So they didn't think he was a trouble-maker or a rebel or a terrorist?"

"No. They didn't."

"But they *did* arrest Jesus in the end."

Ursus shrugged his huge shoulders. "They were obeying orders. Soldiers always do, when it comes to the crunch."

. . . .

The room was a typical interview room: stone floor, stone walls, completely bare, a table with a notepad, a jug of water and glasses, a few chairs, and a door with a grille.

"The Temple Police are here," said Ursus. "Do you want to see them all together or one at a time?"

"One at a time. We need to see if their stories are consistent." I put my recorder on the table and switched it on.

Ursus opened the door and beckoned with his thick finger. The first man walked in - a tall man but not as bulky as Ursus.

"Name?" I said.

"Joseph, sir," said the man.

"You can sit down," I said. "Tell me what happened at the tomb of Jesus."

"Captain Micah posted us at the tomb, sir, on the morning of the Sabbath day. The Captain came to the tomb himself and inspected the body. We rolled the stone across the entrance and Captain Micah put seals on it. Nothing happened during the day; no one came near the place. Our rations were brought to us. At nightfall we divided the watch between ourselves: one to watch while the others slept. Towards dawn, the last watch, the man on duty fell asleep. That must have been when Jesus' disciples came and opened the tomb and stole the body. As soon as we realised what had happened, we ran back to the Temple and reported to Captain Micah."

He sounded very fluent, as if he had thoroughly rehearsed this speech - which he probably had, knowing he was going to be questioned.

"Were you the one on duty; the one who fell asleep?"

Joseph looked uncomfortable. "No, sir."

"Who was it?"

Joseph looked even more uncomfortable. "Do I have to tell you, sir?"

"One of you four will have to tell me. You'd better persuade the guilty one to own up." I paused to let that sink in, and then asked, "If you were all asleep, how do you know that it was Jesus' disciples that stole the body?"

"Who else could it have been, sir?"

"Who else indeed? But you didn't see them, did you? You can't identify them for me?"

Three Days in Jerusalem

"No, sir."

"Why did you have only one man on guard? Why didn't you have two men, to keep each other awake?"

"There didn't seem to be any need. No one had come near the tomb."

"But they were more likely to come at night."

"I suppose so, sir. But we were dog-tired. We get a lot of extra duties at Passover time. And we'd had a bottle of wine to drink."

"Had you, indeed? Isn't that forbidden while you're on duty?"

"Well, yes, sir. But you know how it is..."

"I know how it is in the Roman Army," I said, sharply. "What sort of wine was it?"

"Sir?"

"Was it a local wine, or Greek, or Italian, or Spanish?"

"Oh... er... local, sir"

"Is the local wine particularly strong, Joseph?"

"Er... I don't think so, sir."

"That stone makes quite a bit of noise when it's rolled. Yet all four of you slept while a dozen men rolled it away from the door of the tomb and made off with the body. It must have been very strong wine if one bottle put the four of you sound asleep."

Joseph didn't answer but went on looking uncomfortable.

"All right. Wait outside, and send in the next man."

The second man was called Joshua. He was quite a bit older, with wrinkles at the corners of his eyes from time spent in the sun. I sat him down and asked him to tell me what had happened at Jesus' tomb.

"Captain Micah posted us at the tomb, sir," he began at once, "on the morning of the Sabbath day - the day after Jesus was crucified. The Captain came to the tomb himself and inspected the body. We rolled the stone across the entrance, and Captain Micah put seals on it. No one came near the place during the day. At nightfall we divided the watch between ourselves: one to watch while the others slept. Towards dawn, the last watch, the man on duty fell asleep. That must have been when Jesus' disciples came and opened the tomb and stole the body. As soon as we realised what had happened we ran back to the Temple and reported to Captain Micah."

"You look like an experienced man to me," I said. "Do you often fall asleep on guard duty?"

Joshua stiffened. "Never, sir," he said proudly. "Never before, anyway," he added uncomfortably.

"So it was not you who had the last watch and fell asleep?"

"No, sir."

"How come you were all sleeping so soundly that you didn't hear the stone being rolled away from the entrance to the tomb?"

"We were all dog-tired. We get a lot of extra duties at Passover, and we'd had a bottle of wine to drink."

"It must have been strong wine."

"I suppose it must have been, sir," he said, sheepishly.

"What was your punishment for sleeping on guard duty?"

"Punishment?" I was pleased to see that he had apparently not been expecting this question.

"I presume you *were* punished for falling asleep on duty."

"Oh yes, sir," he said hurriedly. "Extra duties – extra drill – latrine duties…"

"Really?" I said. "In the Roman Army, a man who falls asleep on guard duty is beaten to death by his own comrades, because he has endangered their lives."

Joshua looked even more uncomfortable, "It wasn't quite like guarding a camp or a fort, I suppose, sir."

"All right. You can go. Send in the next man."

Three Days in Jerusalem

The third man marched smartly into the room. He was well-built and broad-shouldered, although not as impressive as Ursus. His name was Simon.

"Sit down, Simon," I said, "and tell me about falling asleep while guarding Jesus' tomb."

"We all fell asleep, Sir," said Simon, pronouncing the 'Sir' with a capital 'S'. He sat up straight on the chair and squared his shoulders, then began as if reciting a poem. "Captain Micah posted us at the tomb, Sir, on the morning of the Sabbath day. The Captain came to the tomb himself and inspected the body. We rolled the stone across the entrance and Captain Micah put seals on it. Nothing happened during the day; no one came near the place. Our rations were brought to us. At nightfall we divided the watch between ourselves: one to watch while the others slept. Towards dawn, the last watch, the man on duty fell asleep. That must have been when Jesus' disciples came and opened the tomb and stole the body. As soon as we realised what had happened we ran back to the Temple and reported to Captain Micah."

"Were you the one who fell asleep while on watch?"

"Me, Sir? No, Sir."

"What sort of wine did you drink?"

"Wine, Sir? I don't rightly know, Sir. Just a bottle of wine that was brought with our rations."

"How are your ears, Simon?"

Simon looked puzzled.

"Is there anything wrong with your hearing, Simon?" I said, speaking much more quietly than I had been doing.

"No, Sir. I think my hearing is as good as any other man's."

"But you didn't hear the stone being rolled away from the entrance to the tomb?"

"No, Sir. I suppose we didn't."

"No 'suppose' about it, Simon. You all slept through it. How did that come about?"

"We were all dog-tired, Sir. We get a lot of extra duties at Passover; and there was the wine."

"How were you punished for sleeping on guard duty?"

Simon looked taken aback.

"What was your punishment?" I repeated.

"Captain Micah tore us off a strip, Sir. He gave us extra duties. He did talk about a flogging, but nothing came of that."

"I would have given you a flogging, Simon," I said.

"Yes, Sir." Simon went on sitting up straight but his face showed how uncomfortable he was feeling.

"Wait outside, Simon."

"Yes, Sir!" Simon jumped to his feet, snapped to attention, turned and marched out smartly.

"Close the door, Ursus," I said.

Ursus had been sitting in a chair with his arms folded during the interviews. Occasionally he had made a snorting noise which clearly meant 'I don't believe it' and other noises expressing his disgust at the lack of military qualities in these Temple Police.

"What do you think so far?" I asked.

"They're all telling the same story, boss. They must have practised together."

"You're right. They agree with each other almost word-for-word. Be nice if all witnesses did that. So they're all in collusion. If the disciples of Jesus stole his body, these guards must have been in on it. And if Captain Micah didn't punish the guards, *he* must have been in on it as well. You should have another talk with Captain Micah - unofficially, of course. You seemed to be getting on quite well with him in the Temple courtyard."

Three Days in Jerusalem

"He seemed like a good officer," said Ursus. "I can't imagine him letting his men get away with any slackness; and as for sleeping on guard duty..."

"Bring in the last man; and, Ursus, let's try a little bit of intimidation. You stand by the door once he's in."

Ursus called the fourth guard in. It looked as though we'd accidently chosen well. He was the youngest of the four and looked thoroughly frightened. His name was Jonathon. Ursus shut the door firmly and stood with his back to it and his arms folded. Jonathon looked back at him nervously and then looked round the room as if seeking a way of escape.

"Sit down, Jonathon," I said pleasantly.

He did so, perching uncomfortably on the edge of the seat.

"Now Jonathon," I said, "there's no need for you to repeat the story of how you all fell asleep guarding the tomb. We've heard it three times and we know that you've made it up and practised it until you're word perfect. I want you to tell me what really happened."

Jonathon hesitated. He licked his lips and there were patches of sweat in the armpits of his shirt.

"They'll kill me if I tell you," he said, and it was obvious that his mouth was dry. I poured him a glass of water.

"If you *don't* tell me, I will let Ursus kill you."

Jonathon looked round at Ursus, then back at me, then down at the glass of water. He picked it up and drank most of it down in one go.

"Everything was quiet until just before dawn," he said. "I was the only one awake, and I was dozing off. There was a huge round stone closing the entrance to the tomb, and I was leaning back against it. I thought that even if I nodded off, no-one could move the stone without waking me."

"That was a good idea, Jonathon," I said, encouragingly.

"I – I suddenly realised that the stone seemed to be getting warmer. I could feel it on my back. So I stood up and felt it

Found in Translation

with my hands, and it was definitely getting warmer. Then I noticed that there was light all round the stone. When I looked properly, I could see that there was a light inside the tomb, and what I could see was the light coming through the cracks between the stone and the rock face." He shook his head, frowning and looking puzzled. "I just couldn't think what was going on. The light got brighter and I was just thinking about waking the others when suddenly the ground shook and there was a sort of gust of wind. That woke the others up all right. Then the light from the tomb went out."

Jonathon stopped. There was a sort of expression of relief on his face now, as if he was glad to be able to tell his story.

"And then...?" I said.

"I told the others what had happened. They scoffed at me at first. Joseph said I must have fallen asleep and had a nightmare. Then he felt the stone and it was still warm, almost too hot to touch. We argued about it for a few moments; everyone had a feel of the stone. Then Joseph decided we had to check. We broke the seals and rolled the stone to the side. Joseph went in with a torch, and the body was gone."

"But the grave cloths were still there," I said.

"Yes, they were, sir," he said, eagerly.

"So what do you think happened to the body?" I asked.

"I don't know, sir. I really don't know. It's not natural, is it?"

"Your Jewish god is supposed to be very powerful, isn't he? Do you think it was supernatural?"

"I don't know, sir."

"And then you came back and reported to Captain Micah?"

"Yes, sir."

"What did he say?"

"He was furious, sir. First off, he threatened to have us flogged. Then he took us back to the tomb. It was daylight by

Three Days in Jerusalem

that time. When we got near the tomb we saw some women running away from it. The Captain and Joseph went into the tomb again, but everything was just as we had left it. The shroud hadn't been touched. We came back to the Temple, and the Captain went off to report to the priests. In the end one of the senior priests ordered us to say the disciples had stolen the body." Jonathon hesitated, then added, "We were given money, sir."

"A bribe, eh, to keep your mouths shut? A sensible thing to do, under the circumstances."

There was a long silence while I tried to take in what Jonathon had said. I wasn't sure if I quite believed his story, but I was sure he believed it.

"Look, Jonathon," I said, at last, "there's no need to tell your mates that you've told us, if you don't want to. You can tell them you told me the story - the made-up story, that is - and I cross-questioned you about it. Anyway, you can go."

"Thank you, sir." Jonathon scrambled to his feet and dashed through the door as Ursus opened it.

"Send them all away, Ursus," I said. "Go and see if you can find Crescens, and go and talk to that Captain Micah again. Meet in our office about, oh, four o'clock."

. . . .

There was no knock on the door but Petronius came into the office.

"How's it going?" he asked.

I switched off the playback on my recorder and took off the headphones. "Interesting," I said.

Petronius looked for a moment as if he was going to try and question me further. Then he changed his mind.

"I've got a bonus for you," he said.
"Oh?"

Found in Translation

"Jesus' brothers, here from Galilee. They went to the tomb and the guards brought them up here."

I sat up. "I want to talk to them."

"I thought you would. One at a time or all together?"

"All together. Send them in here."

In a few moments four men were crowding into the room. There weren't enough seats for everyone, so I stood up. They were different ages but the family likeness was obvious. They also looked similar, yet not quite similar, to the photographs of Jesus in the file. They were wearing ordinary working clothes: jeans, boots and checked shirts.

"Greetings, brothers of Jesus," I said. "I am sorry that we have to meet under these circumstances."

"Peace to you, sir," said the eldest of the brothers. "I am James, the eldest of us now that Jesus is dead. These are my brothers: Joseph, Judas and Simon. Are you the officer who is going to explain to us what is going on?"

"I am Rufus, the officer from Syria who is trying to find out what is going on. I was hoping you would be able to help me."

"Then it was not you who crucified our brother?"

"I did not; that was the Prefect of Judea, Pontius Pilate. But I have to say to you that it looks as though the Prefect had some reason to condemn your brother. The evidence suggests that he had claimed, or was intending to claim, that he was king of the Jews."

"We knew he would do something stupid like that!" burst out one of the brothers, the one who had been introduced as Judas. "Leaving home, setting himself up as a rabbi, then as a prophet. We could see he was going to come to a sad end."

"May I ask why you have come to Jerusalem?"

"Naturally we came as soon as we could when we heard about Jesus' death," said James. "We came to visit his tomb

Three Days in Jerusalem

and to see if it was possible to take his body home to Nazareth and give it a family burial there."

"And our mother is here," said one of the others. "She came to Jerusalem with Jesus and his disciples. We want to make sure she is all right and take her back home."

I nodded. "I am afraid the body of Jesus is still missing. Everyone seems to think that Jesus' disciples must have taken it, but we now have reason to believe that others may be involved - either as well as the disciples or instead of."

The brothers looked at each other with puzzled, anxious expressions.

"Why would anyone want to steal his body?" asked James at last.

"Perhaps for the reason you want the body. It was given a hasty burial on the day of Jesus' death. Perhaps the disciples wanted to give it a decent burial and didn't want to ask for it openly in case they were arrested. They seem to have been in hiding ever since Jesus was arrested."

"Why the disciples?" said James angrily. "Why not leave it for us, his family?"

"You'll have to ask them, if you can find them. I am told they have gone back to Galilee."

There was another short silence.

"There is another possibility," I said. "Have you heard the rumours that Jesus is alive?"

"Alive? How could that be?" asked James.

"I gather that Jesus claimed that he would rise from the dead."

"That's just the crazy sort of idea he would have!" said Judas.

"It has been suggested to me that the disciples stole Jesus' body so that they would be able to pretend that he *had* risen from death," I said.

James snorted. "Whoever would believe a story like that?"

"So there is no possibility that you might have stolen Jesus' body so that *you* could claim he had risen?"

James snorted again. "Do we look like the sort of fools that would do that?"

"No, I must admit you don't. But I have been told over and over again that you Jews are fanatical about your religion."

"We do believe that there will come a time when God will step openly into the world," said James. "That will be a time of judgement. All the dead will be raised to stand before God's judgement throne. We have to keep ourselves holy and pure, ready for that Day. But for one man to rise from the dead now..." He shook his head. Then he turned to his brothers. "It looks like we've had a wasted journey. The best thing we can do is go back to Nazareth."

"We can find mother and take her back home," said one.

"And when we get back to Galilee we can find those disciples and find out what they've done with our brother's body," said another, angrily.

James turned back to me. "You will let us know what you find out, please, Sir?" he said.

I fished one of my cards out of my pocket and handed it to him. "Certainly I will, and please contact me if you find out anything useful."

"Thank you, sir. Peace to you," said James.

"Farewell to you all," I replied.

. . . .

Crescens reappeared in the office about half-past three. He went straight over to the computer on the side desk and switched it on.

"Where have you been all day?" I demanded. My head was aching from trying to make sense of the interviews that I'd

Three Days in Jerusalem

conducted and I suspected Crescens of deliberately keeping out of the way of possible work.

"Sightseeing, sir," he replied, cheerfully; then, as he heard my growl of anger, he hastily added, "Talking to people, finding out about Jesus."

"And what have you found out that I don't already know?" I said, suspiciously.

"Did you know that he worked miracles?" asked Crescens.

"I know that there have been claims that he worked miracles."

"He healed a crippled man here in Jerusalem, at one of the public pools, called Bethesda. The man was just lying there and Jesus told him to get up and walk - so the man did just that."

"Did you talk to eyewitnesses?"

"One man claimed to have been there and seen it; lots of other people had heard the story."

"I've seen people claiming to be crippled. They live by begging; it's an easier life than working. Maybe Jesus just told this man to stop being a lazy ***."

"Mmm, maybe, sir. Another man told me he'd seen Jesus heal a blind beggar. It was a week before he was crucified. Jesus was coming up to Jerusalem on the Jericho road, and this beggar, name of Bartimaeus, was told about Jesus so he shouted out to him. The people nearby tried to shut him up, but Jesus heard the man and asked what he wanted. The blind man said, "I want to see," and Jesus healed him straight away."

"Hmm, I guess that sounds a little more convincing."

Ursus put his head in at the door, looked around the room and then disappeared again. He was gone for only a few moments, however, before he came back.

"I've ordered coffee, boss," he said.

"I'm glad one of you has my best interests at heart," I said.

"I also learned that Jesus was very popular with the crowds," said Crescens. "Everyone says he was a brilliant speaker and a great story-teller."

"What did he tell stories about?" I asked, curious to know. Jesus had obviously had charisma; that was clear from the people we had spoken to. But what was his actual message?

"His main subject was the Kingdom of God."

"So he did claim to be a king, then?"

"No," said Crescens, slowly, "No-one has said that he claimed to be king. He was trying to explain to people his idea of what the Kingdom of God was like."

"And what was it like?"

"He said things like, 'The Kingdom of God is inside you.'"

"What did he mean by that?"

Crescens shrugged. "That the Kingdom wasn't a country with armies and frontiers, I guess. He said things like, 'The Kingdom is like a tiny seed that you plant and it grows into a huge tree' and 'the Kingdom is like a lamp. If you put it on a stand, it gives light to the whole room; if you cover it up, the room is dark.' Oh, and he said, 'The Kingdom is like a merchant looking out for fine pearls. When he found a particularly magnificent one, he sold everything he had and bought the pearl.'"

"Total commitment, eh? I can see that would make people think."

"Then there was one particular story which upset the priests. It was about a man who planted a vineyard and let it out to tenants. At harvest time, he sent an agent to collect the rent and the tenants refused to pay. The owner sent more agents but the tenants beat them up. Then the owner sent his son, thinking the tenants would respect him, but the tenants murdered the son, hoping to inherit the vineyard for themselves."

"What does all that mean?"

"Apparently the vineyard is a symbol of Judea and the Jewish nation and the owner is their god. The tenants who had to take care of the vineyard were like the Jewish priests. The son might be Jesus."

I began to see the point. "So Jesus *was* making a veiled claim to be the King of the Jews – and to be a son of a god. And riding into Jerusalem on a donkey was a practical claim to be King of the Jews. But you'd have to be a Jew to understand the code. The Governor and his men don't seem to have thought Jesus was claiming to be a King. And the priests did get rid of him. I thought that Caiaphas was a sly ***. But, he was right; when you understand what Jesus was doing and saying, it could be seen as treason against the Emperor."

"Except that the Kingdom of God is inside you," said Crescens, "No armies, no threat."

"I am not sure that Tiberius would see it that way," I said, drily.

Crescens turned back to the computer and started tapping away at the keys. Presently he said, "I've got a preliminary report on the blood."

"Well?"

"The blood on the grave cloths matches blood from the middle one of the three crucifixion posts and the blood that dripped onto the ground at its foot. That tends to confirm that the man who was crucified on the middle post was the man who was placed in the tomb."

"Jesus was crucified on the middle post, according to the Centurion's report," I said, "the other two were the terrorists, part of Barabbas' gang."

Crescens was still looking at the computer screen, "There doesn't seem to be anything interesting in the bag the Centurion gave me – just standard issue ration packs; lots of fingerprints, of course, but they probably belong to the guards. The wine was a local vintage."

The door opened and a servant came in with a tray of coffee and sandwiches which he placed on the desk before leaving as quietly as he had come in. Ursus poured the coffee.

"Did you find out anything more from Captain Micah?" I asked him.

"He said that he had wanted to flog the guards for falling asleep but one of the priests overruled him; so he gave them extra duties instead. But, if you ask me, he wasn't telling the truth. He didn't look at all happy when I questioned him. Then he admitted that they had told him what he called a cock-and-bull story about a light inside the tomb and the stone getting hot."

"Have a cucumber sandwich, sir," said Crescens, offering me the plate.

"Thanks," I said automatically and took a sandwich. Then I told Crescens about the young guard's story of the hot stone and the light from the tomb.

A variety of expressions crossed Crescens' face as I was speaking: interest, surprise, puzzlement, disapproval; finally, a frown of concentration before he responded. "The only thing I can think of," he said slowly, "is that there is another way into the tomb, concealed – or maybe a concealed chamber that we haven't found."

I thought about that as I picked up another cucumber sandwich and swallowed a mouthful of coffee. "You think someone took the body out through a back door?" I said, "That sounds to me like the most sensible suggestion anyone's made yet. Let's go and have another look."

. . . .

"You know, sir," said Crescens as we walked round to the tomb, "the other thing that surprises me is the guards being bribed. I thought the Jews had strict laws against bribery, especially bribing a judge, and the priests are the judges here. So I'm surprised at the judges bribing the guards."

That was something else I hadn't known about Jews. Rome had always run pretty smoothly with a level of, well, let's call them 'gifts' for services rendered. As a Centurion, and like all Centurions, I'd been used to supplementing my stipend by accepting payments from soldiers who wanted to avoid fatigue duties. Bribing a judge was illegal, of course, but that doesn't mean it didn't happen.

There was still a guard of Roman soldiers at the tomb, although no Centurion. As they let us through, Ursus said, "I'll go and have a look round up top," pointing to the top of the low cliff into which the tombs had been dug.

"Fair enough," I said. Ursus was certainly too bulky to be squeezing his way into small caves. Crescens and I went into the tomb. It was just as we had left it. We flashed our torches around. There were certainly no obvious hiding places. We began to examine the walls systematically. Crescens produced a small hammer and began tapping the rock, listening for any sounds of hollowness. A few minutes' work convinced us that the walls were carved out of the living rock. There were a few cracks and splits, presumably natural or left over from the mining work, but none of them showed any signs of yielding when we tried to prise them open. Then we went carefully over the floor and finally the roof, drawing a blank in both cases.

"So much for that bright idea," said Crescens.

"There's certainly no room in here for anyone to conceal themselves, let alone a dead body as well."

"I suppose Jesus was really dead when he was put into the tomb?" suggested Crescens.

"The Centurion who was in charge of the crucifixion said he was; and it was his responsibility to make sure he really was. Centurion Helvius. He said the body had gone cold and begun to go stiff when they took it down from the cross. Does that satisfy the expert SCO?"

Crescens grinned; at least I thought he did in the torchlight. "Yes, Prefect, that's as good as I can expect."

We went outside again, and presently Ursus came scrambling down the rockface.

"Not a thing," he said in answer to my enquiry. "It's pretty rugged up there, but I reckon I poked into all the likely holes. There's no way through into the tomb."

"What about these other tombs?" said Crescens, looking at the other doorways carved out of the rock.

"We'd better check the two on either side," I said. "You look in that one; I'll take the other."

The tomb I went into was similar to the one Jesus' body had been placed in. It looked clean and unused, as I'd expected. We'd been told these were all new tombs. I tapped at the walls, paying particular attention to the wall on the side of Jesus' tomb, but found nothing suspicious. I went out again, just as Crescens was emerging from his tomb. Like me, he had found nothing.

"That rules out the idea of anyone getting into the tomb without being detected," I said. "I wonder if that young guard was telling us the truth about the light and the heat."

"Captain Micah admitted that they had told him the same story," said Ursus, "even though he hadn't believed it."

"I think you'd better come back here in daylight, Crescens," I said, "and see if you can find any evidence for light and heat."

"Right, sir."

The sun was setting and dusk was falling as we walked back to the Antonia.

Day Three

The next morning Ursus and I took the Audax and drove around the city until we reached the Jericho road. Before we left I asked Petronius' secretary to set up another interview for me with the High Priest. After a short distance we turned onto an unmetalled road that led to the village of Bethany and presently stopped in a cloud of dust from our tyres.

We could see that it was a typical peasant village; the road ran curving irregularly over the hill and on either side were scattered, single-storey houses - quite unplanned and un-Roman. Men and women stopped going about their business and turned to stare at us curiously. A crowd of children appeared from nowhere - the boys coming up to our vehicle to peer in the windows, the girls hanging back more cautiously.

Ursus opened the rear door of the Audax and brought out a football that I hadn't known he'd put in the vehicle. He bounced it on the ground, then tossed it into the air and kept it there by heading it repeatedly. The boys gathered round him with expressions of respect and awe.

"Greeting," I called to the men. "I'm looking for the house of Simon the Leper."

"Peace to you," said one of the men, and pointed. "Simon's house is up there."

"Thank you," I said and looked back at Ursus, but he had begun to organise the boys into two teams. He looked up at me with a questioning expression and I waved for him to carry on. After all, it always pays to keep in with the locals and I could question Simon easily enough on my own. I walked up to the house that had been indicated and knocked at the door. There seemed to be a long wait before I heard footsteps and the door was opened by a youngish man.

"Simon the Leper?" I asked.

"Who wants to know?" he replied, cautiously.

I held up my ID.

"Have you come to arrest us?" he said.

"Have you done anything for which you should be arrested?" I countered.

"No," he replied, "but then, neither had Jesus. You'd better come in."

I followed him down a short, narrow passageway and out into a small courtyard. He led me to the left and in at a curtained doorway. I found myself in a fair-sized room, plainly but adequately furnished. A second man rose to his feet as I entered, and two women also rose hurriedly and disappeared through a doorway to the right.

"This is Simon," said the first man.

"Peace to you," said Simon.

"Greeting," I said, automatically.

"This is the Prefect, er ... I'm sorry, how should we call you?"

"Prefect Rufus will do."

"I am James, the son of Alpheus," said the first man.

I recognised the name from the file. "You're one of Jesus' twelve disciples."

"Yes, I am, although we are only eleven now since the traitor, Judas, hanged himself."

"I was told you'd all gone back to Galilee."

"Most of us have," said James, "but we thought it would be safer if we went in small groups; so I am still here."

"Please sit down, Prefect," said Simon. "Will you have some coffee?"

"I don't mind if I do, thank you," I said. "This is a dusty country."

"Once the dry season begins," agreed Simon. He went to the doorway through which the women had gone and said something too quietly for me to catch. I looked round and found a bench to sit on along one wall. It was a plain wooden

Three Days in Jerusalem

bench, with a colourful, folded woollen blanket on it to soften the bare wood. Simon and James also sat down. I studied them carefully. They were of similar ages, early thirties I reckoned, dressed in ordinary working clothes. Both wore woollen shirts; James wore jeans and Simon had denim overalls. Their boots were scuffed and dusty, evidently used to hard work and to walking. But there was something about them ... Everyone else I had interviewed seemed to have something to hide, or something on their conscience; everyone (except Joseph of Arimathea) had been uncomfortable talking to me. These two seemed relaxed, confident. Of course, they could be putting on a good act, but unlike everyone else they seemed happy.

I got out my recorder and switched it on. This didn't seem to bother them.

"Why do they call you Simon the Leper?" I asked, for the skin on his face and hands looked perfect, with no sign of pale, leprous tissue or even healed scars.

"I was a leper once, for five years," he replied, "and an outcast from my home and village, squatting with the other lepers and begging as close to the roadside as I dared. Then Jesus came and healed me."

"Jesus healed you?" I felt pleased. It was one thing listening to stories, probably exaggerated, about Jesus healing people, but here was a first-hand witness.

"It was two years ago. I was begging beside the Jericho road, and I saw this party of men coming up the hill towards Jerusalem. James here was one of them. Jesus wasn't so well-known then, and I had no idea who he was, but he looked at me as he led the others, and there was something about his face and his eyes - they seemed to look right inside me. I was going to ask for alms in the usual way, but instead I found myself saying, 'If you want to, you can make me clean.' He said, 'I do want to,' and he reached out and took my hand. It was five years since anyone had touched me!" As he said this,

253

there was a catch in Simon's voice, and I could see tears starting in his eyes. This was something more about this Jesus; he had compassion and courage. I would rather go into a battle outnumbered four to one than touch a man with that dreadful disease of leprosy.

"Then he said, 'Be clean!'" continued Simon, "and I felt a sort of tingling in my hand where he held me. That was very strange because I'd lost the feeling in that hand. This tingling spread up my arm and over my whole body. It was as if I could feel my skin being healed. When I looked at my hands and arms all the white patches had gone. Jesus' disciples were crowding round, but I hardly noticed them. I just stared at my hands; the skin looked so fresh – and young!"

"Go on," I said, for Simon had stopped speaking and was looking at his hands as if reliving that moment.

"Jesus told me to show myself to our local priest to confirm that I'd been cleansed and then change my clothes and shave my hair and bathe, and make the necessary offerings. Then he went on with his disciples, and I came back to the village and did all those things – and here I am."

I was quite glad that one of the women brought in a tray with a coffee jug and placed it on the table. It gave me a few moments to digest this account. Simon certainly looked as if he were telling the truth, and the account sounded like something he was remembering. But did I really believe him? It would have been nice to have had some before and after photographs.

"So that is why Jesus stayed with you before he was arrested?" I said at last.

James poured out three mugs of coffee and handed one to me.

"Of course I welcomed him every time he came to Jerusalem. But this last time it was a big party: Jesus and the Twelve, and some other close followers and half-a-dozen

Three Days in Jerusalem

women, and a lot of ordinary pilgrims coming from all over to the Passover. A crowd like that can get through a lot of food in one day. But the whole village chipped in, and we found room for everyone to sleep in one house or another."

"And then he was arrested and crucified," I said.

"That was bad," said James, "especially as we all ran away when Jesus was arrested. We were so sure he was the Messiah; we just thought if anyone tried to attack him, he'd call down fire from heaven. But Jesus wasn't like that, and when he just let himself be arrested we all panicked."

There was another pause, so I prompted him: "And so a complete stranger had to bury him."

"Yes, we hadn't ever realised that there were members of our Council that thought so much of Jesus." Then he added, looking shamefaced, "We were so frightened, we didn't even dare go to see him crucified. It was some of our women who watched and told us what had happened."

"Everyone who I talk to," I said, carefully, "says that you disciples stole Jesus' body so that you could pretend he had risen from the dead."

James looked me in the face and gave a broad smile. It was a natural smile, his eyes crinkled at the corners; it seemed as if his whole face lit up. "We don't need to pretend. Jesus really has risen from the dead. We've all seen him."

He looked and sounded perfectly sincere.

"That's a very big claim," I said. "Why do you expect anyone to believe you?"

"Perhaps I don't," said James, thoughtfully. "You know, several times before he was arrested, Jesus told us he was going to be executed and then rise from death. But we never believed him."

"Obviously, you would have to say that," I said. "It sounds as if Jesus planned it with you in advance, or maybe he hinted to you what he wanted you to do."

"Jesus was quite clear that God would raise him from the dead," asserted James.

"But perhaps you felt that your god needed a helping hand?" I suggested.

James shook his head. "No. We didn't believe it at first. We didn't believe the women when they came and told us."

"The women?"

Simon broke in. "I think, James, that we should perhaps ask Mary to speak to the Prefect."

James hesitated, then nodded. Simon went to the inner doorway and spoke a few words. One of the women I'd seen disappearing through that doorway came in hesitantly and stood in front of me. She looked at the floor and held her hands demurely crossed in front of her. She was young and had an attractive face, a face that looked both lively and happy.

"This is Mary of Magdala," said Simon. "Mary, this is the Prefect, Rufus. He wants to know about Jesus rising from the dead."

"I saw him," said Mary, quietly. "He spoke to me. He called me by name."

I wondered why Simon and James should be so anxious to bring this woman forward as a prime witness. Everyone knows that women's testimony is unreliable and should be practically discounted in a court of law. But then, I'd been a bit surprised to learn that Jesus had women amongst his party; it certainly made it seem less like a war party. Everything I heard about Jesus was puzzling.

Simon must have seen me frowning, for he now said, "Mary, I think you should begin at the crucifixion and tell the Prefect your story from there."

"We watched the crucifixion," said Mary. "We thought if the men would go, they'd be arrested, but no-one would bother about us. There was me, and James' mother" (she gestured towards James) "She's also called Mary. Then there

Three Days in Jerusalem

was Salome and Jesus' own mother Mary, and one or two others. Later on John did come and stand with us." (I remembered from the file that one of Jesus' closest followers was called John) "We watched Jesus die." She stopped, obviously close to tears, then gathered herself and went on. "Mary, Jesus' mother was ready to faint, so we got John and Salome to take her back into the city. The other Mary and I stayed where we were. A long time later, we saw a well-dressed man with three or four others come out of the city with the Centurion. The soldiers took Jesus' body down from the cross and these men carried him away to where there were new tombs cut into the rock."

"Do you know who this man was?" I asked.

"Not at the time," said Mary. "We could see he was well-dressed. He looked important."

"It was some days later that we learnt he was Joseph of Arimathea," said James.

"We watched the men cover the body with a cloth and carry it into the tomb and roll a great, round stone in front of the door. There was a whole row of tombs, so we counted them. They put Jesus in the third one along."

I nodded; that certainly matched the position of Jesus' tomb.

"By this time, it was almost sunset - when the Sabbath begins."

"That's our holy day," explained James, "the seventh day of the week."

I nodded again.

"So we had to hurry back into the city ..."

"Where were you hiding in the city?" I interrupted, for there was no information about that in the file.

"We scattered after the arrest," said James, quickly. "Some of us came back here; some went to friends in Jerusalem."

I looked at him, and he stared defiantly back at me. I shrugged my shoulders. It wasn't particularly important. I still had the option of arresting these people and interrogating them properly if I chose. I looked back at Mary and told her to go on.

"During the Sabbath, we women talked it over and decided to go to the tomb and pay our last respects. The burial had been so rushed and clumsy. We found some spices to anoint the body. We couldn't go during the Sabbath, of course, so the next day we got up while it was still dark. We went to the city gates and had to wait there for the guard to open them at sunrise. So the sun was just coming up as we approached the tombs, and we suddenly thought of the huge stone in front of the tomb! It was silly of us, I know, but we'd been thinking about anointing the body and we simply hadn't thought about how we would get into the tomb. We wondered if we could move it ourselves or if one of us should go back and ask the men to help."

"You could have asked the guard at the tomb," I said.

Mary looked puzzled. "Guard?"

"Was there a guard at the tomb?" asked James.

I looked at them closely. Their surprise seemed to be genuine. "You didn't know about the guard?"

They shook their heads. Simon said, "Nobody has said anything to us about a guard."

"A squad of the Temple Police were on watch at the tomb," I explained. "They claim that they fell asleep and you disciples came and stole the body."

James looked even more surprised. "We were scattered all over the place. And we were scared. I didn't know whether any of the others had been arrested. None of us thought of trying to steal Jesus' body – he wouldn't have wanted us to."

"And you didn't see the guards, Mary?" I asked.

Three Days in Jerusalem

"We didn't see anyone," she replied, "but when we got to the tomb, we saw that the stone had been rolled away from the door. We were surprised and a bit scared. We counted the tombs to make sure we were at the right one. Then I looked inside the tomb, very carefully. There was enough light to see the rock shelf where the body ought to have been placed. I could see there wasn't a body there, and I could just make out the grave cloths. Then I got the fright of my life!"

She paused for a few seconds, her eyes wide as she relived the moment. "There was a man there! He was over to the right; that's why I hadn't seen him at first. He had a white robe and he looked very young. I backed out quickly and I heard him say, 'Don't be frightened. You're looking for Jesus. He's not here. He has risen!'

"This young man came to the door of the tomb. He really looked like a ghost! We panicked and started to run away; and we heard him shout, 'Tell his disciples, go to Galilee! He'll meet them there!' But we just ran as hard as we could.

"We got back into the city, and then we started to calm down a bit. We went back to... to where we'd been staying and found Peter and John" (I recognised Peter as being another of the twelve closest followers) "and we told them what had happened. They set off running to the tomb. I decided to follow them, but I was too out of breath to run. By the time I got there they'd looked in the tomb and they were looking around, and they looked in the other tombs, but they were empty of course. There was no sign of the young man.

"Eventually Peter and John walked off, back towards the city, and I just sat down on a rock and burst into tears." She looked at me shyly, so I nodded encouragingly. "It was all just too much. Then someone spoke from behind me and asked why I was crying. I thought it must be somebody who looked after the tombs, so I asked him where he had taken Jesus. Then he spoke my name 'Mary' and I turned and there he was!

It was Jesus, standing there, alive!" I saw that she was starting to get tears once more. "And... and he said to me, 'Go and tell my brothers,' and... I hardly knew what I was doing... but I ran to find John and Peter and tell them... and they didn't believe me." She stopped, and now the tears really were flowing. Simon took her by the arm and led her gently out of the room.

I didn't believe her, either - a hysterical woman, heartbroken of course (I understood that), but she could have seen anyone and mistaken them for Jesus, the state she was in. But it didn't get me any nearer to the solution of my enquiry: who *had* taken the body of Jesus?

I looked at James.

"We've all seen him," he said, firmly.

"Tell me about it," I said.

"After they had been to the tomb, Peter and John decided to get us all together and tell us what had happened. They thought maybe some of us had taken Jesus' body. It took them most of that day, and it was evening before we met up at – in a house in the city. And Peter started off by telling us that *he* had seen Jesus, only for a few minutes, but they'd spoken together."

"What did they talk about?" I asked.

"Peter wouldn't tell us. But he was the one who denied Jesus."

"What do you mean, 'denied Jesus'?"

"After Jesus was arrested, Peter followed them to the High Priest's house. Someone there recognised him as being one of us, but he lost his nerve and swore he'd never had anything to do with Jesus. When he realised what he'd done, he broke down. So we think Jesus wanted to forgive him, privately."

I nodded. I wasn't sure if any of this made sense but I thought it was best to let James tell the story his way.

"Then Cleopas and his son charged in. They weren't part of the Twelve but they were in Jesus' group. They'd decided to

Three Days in Jerusalem

go back to their home in Emmaus; that's a village a few miles west of Jerusalem. They told us that Jesus had hitched a lift with them. They hadn't recognised him, but they'd talked on the journey and, when they got to Emmaus, they invited Jesus in for supper. They asked him to give thanks to God at the beginning of the meal, and he did that and broke the bread to share it out. When they saw him do that they realised it was Jesus – something about the way his hands moved. Then he disappeared, and they got the car out and rushed back to tell us."

"Jesus disappeared?" I interrupted.

"That's what they said. They'd just told us this when Jesus was there with us! We hadn't seen him come in. Anyway, we'd barred the door. But he was there. We thought we were seeing a ghost but he told us to touch him, and we did." James stopped, as if the memory was overwhelming him.

"Go on," I said.

"You know," said James, "it *was* Jesus, but he was different, as though he was more alive than before. He looked more alive than anyone else in that room. He told us off for not believing him. Because, you know, he'd warned us a long time ago that he was going to be crucified and then raised from the dead. We just hadn't taken it in."

"Did you see this 'more alive' Jesus?" I asked Simon.

Simon shook his head. "No, I wasn't there, but I do believe it."

James spoke again. "We weren't all there. We hadn't been able to find one of the Twelve, Thomas, the Twin. He'd gone to ground somewhere. He turned up after a few days, and then we all met up again one evening. Thomas was arguing with us. He simply would not believe unless he saw it with his own eyes. And Jesus came again and made Thomas touch him, and of course Thomas had to believe then."

"I'm not sure I believe you," I said. "I'd like some firmer evidence than eyewitness testimony."

"It's all we've got," said James, cheerfully.

"Why didn't this Jesus appear to the Governor or to the High Priest? They're convinced that you stole the body."

"Would they be convinced if Jesus did appear to them? Maybe they've closed their minds so tight that they wouldn't believe or they just wouldn't see him."

"Where are the rest of you twelve disciples?"

"In Galilee, or on their way there. Jesus told us to go back to Galilee and he'd meet up with us there. We thought it would be safer to go in small groups," replied James.

"You believe that Jesus rose from the dead," I said, carefully. "So what? Who do you suppose this Jesus is?"

"He is the Messiah," said Simon, immediately.

"I could charge you with treason against the Emperor for saying that."

"Jesus didn't want to overthrow the Emperor, or any other king or ruler," said James. "He never trained us to be his army or even his bodyguard. He once said, 'The Kingdom of God is inside you'."

That was one of Jesus' sayings that Crescens had reported. And nothing I'd found in this investigation suggested anything else but that Jesus' movement, unlike most Jewish movements, was peaceful and not even hostile to us Romans.

There was one more question to ask. "Are you both ritually pure?"

Again their reactions seemed genuine: surprise, puzzlement. James started to say, "Yes. Why...?" while Simon's face suddenly cleared and he laughed. "You think we stole Jesus' body and would need to be purified after contact with the corpse."

"Well, did you?"

Three Days in Jerusalem

They both shook their heads. "No," said James quietly, "We didn't steal Jesus' body and we don't need purification."

I switched off my recorder and stood up.

"Well, you've given me a lot to think about. Thank you for your co-operation."

. . . .

The football match was still going on, on a patch of waste ground, as I walked back to the Audax. Ursus was refereeing but, as soon as he saw me, he stopped the game, called the boys round and made them agree to share the ball fairly. Then he tossed it up. The game was renewed and he walked over to me.

"Who's winning?" I asked.

"Six-all at the moment, Boss. Nobody wants to be goalkeeper. But they're good lads; one or two of them have got talent."

We set off back to the city.

. . . .

When we entered the office in the Antonia, I was glad to see that Crescens was sitting at the computer, wearing headphones and typing. I'd told him to start transcribing the interviews I'd already recorded. He waved his hand as we came in, went on typing for a few moments, then stopped and pulled off the headphones.

"The Prefect wants to see you, sir," he said, "and he's hopping mad."

"Petronius? What's he got to be mad about? Oh all right, I'll go and see him."

I walked along to Petronius' office, where his secretary ushered me in as soon as I arrived. Petronius certainly looked angry. He stood up as I walked into his office and glared at me.

"What the hell do you think you're doing?"

"Conducting an investigation," I said, as calmly as I could.

"Haven't you understood any of what we've been telling you about the situation here? Haven't you realised that Judea is a hotbed of rebellion, terrorism and religious fanaticism? That Pilate has spent ten years keeping the lid on this place? And now you come stirring things up - pestering the High Priest. Haven't you grasped that we need Caiaphas on our side? It's only the priests who carry any weight with these Jews. A word from Caiaphas could bring the whole hornet's nest down on us. Haven't you got *any* common sense?"

"In what way have I pestered the High Priest?' I asked, homing in on the only significant thing that Petronius had said.

"You interviewed him yesterday. Why do you want to see him again?"

"Seeing him twice is hardly pestering," I said. "I need to discuss with him some of the information we have received."

"Well, what have you discovered?"

I answered that question with a look that he obviously interpreted correctly. "Do I get to see the High Priest?" I asked.

"Yes, you do, at the Governor's residence, at one o'clock."

"Two to one, eh?" I said thoughtfully. "Is that all?"

Petronius had calmed down by now, but he simply nodded in reply.

I, on the other hand, was feeling angry. I'd never wanted to come to Jerusalem, but I was certainly not going to let a petty official and a jumped-up priest from a minor province obstruct my enquiries. Fortunately, by the time I'd returned to our office, the others had had coffee and sandwiches sent in. A

Three Days in Jerusalem

mug of coffee and a tomato sandwich helped me to calm down.

"I didn't find anything out of the ordinary at the tomb, sir," said Crescens, "but I've had another report from the forensic lab. They say that the shroud and the head cloth have both got scorch marks on them, as if they've been held too close to a fire."

"I suppose that fits in with that Temple guard who claimed the stone got hot," I said.

"We've had two messages from Galilee," Crescens continued, laying two sheets of paper on the desk.

I looked at the first. It was a message from a Centurion in a place called Capernaum, saying that some of Jesus' followers had returned to the village that morning: Simon Peter; James and John, brothers; Thomas, a twin; Nathanael and two others, names unknown. Should any action be taken against them? I was glad to see that someone in this case was on the ball.

"Whereabouts is Capernaum?" I asked.

Crescens spread out a map on the table.

"This is the lake of Galilee," he said, pointing with a long, bony finger. "This is Capernaum. Apparently it's a fishing village on the north bank of the lake."

"That's Herod the Tetrarch's territory?"

"Yes, sir,"

I thought for a few moments. "If these men have carried Jesus' body back to Galilee, they would need to be purified. Can they carry out the ritual in Galilee or will they have to come back here to the Temple?"

"I don't know," replied Crescens, while Ursus shrugged his shoulders.

"I'll ask the High Priest. Meantime, tell this Centurion to keep them under observation and report if they *do* undergo the ritual."

I handed the paper back to Crescens and looked at the second sheet. This was from an official called a *basilikos*, whatever that meant, in Herod's court, reporting somewhat cryptically that an agent had reported a gathering of a group some four days ago, estimated at five hundred people, in the hills about twelve miles north of Capernaum. The group had been addressed by a man who some claimed to be the Jesus who had been crucified in Jerusalem just before the Passover.

"Hmmm, what do we make of that?" I said, passing the paper to Ursus.

This time it was Crescens who shrugged. "Without a good quality photograph – nothing much."

"Could have been one of Jesus' brothers," suggested Ursus.

"Except that they were here yesterday and they obviously did not believe that Jesus was alive," (I paused for a moment, recalling the scene) "and they didn't sound as if they wanted to continue Jesus' movement, if that was the idea behind this 'gathering'."

I looked at my watch. "I have an interview with the Governor and the High Priest. You two carry on here."

. . . .

I walked down to the Governor's residence once more and was shown into Pilate's office straight away. Caiaphas was already there, seated by the side of the desk in a chair with arm rests. Pilate stood up to greet me, but the High Priest remained firmly seated. "Still," I thought, "He hasn't kept me waiting this time. I must have stirred him up a bit." The thought gave me some satisfaction.

There was a tray of coffee on the desk, and Pilate at once poured me a cup. He looked tense and anxious. Caiaphas, I

Three Days in Jerusalem

noticed, was drinking from a glass of wine, just as Joseph of Arimathea had done. His lips were set in a firm line.

"The High Priest," said Pilate, as he sat down again, "is concerned that you want to interview him again."

"I gave you all the information I possess yesterday," said Caiaphas. "I do not understand why you have taken no action against Jesus' disciples, and I am a busy man. I cannot spare any more time on this incident which should be regarded as closed."

"My investigation will be closed when I submit my report to the Legate of Syria," I replied. "When the Legate has read my report, he will decide whether or not the incident should be regarded as closed." I knew that my position as official investigator was strong, and I saw no harm in making that clear to the High Priest.

"You see, High Priest," said Pilate, in a conciliatory tone, "this investigation has been ordered by the Legate. I have no authority to intervene in any way. Indeed, I have to give the Prefect here my full cooperation." I made a mental note that Pilate had not mentioned that it was he who had reported the matter to Legate Vitellius in the first place.

"Surely you can make representations to the Legate," said Caiaphas, with a touch of anger in his voice. "I will fully support you. The sooner this whole business is closed the better for the situation here in Jerusalem."

"What exactly concerns you about the situation, High Priest?" I asked.

"Why, that the followers of this Jesus will continue to claim that he has risen from the dead and that that proves he is the Messiah. They will totally undermine my High Priestly authority and the place of the Temple itself. There will be dissension between Jesus' supporters and loyal Jews. And in Judea, dissension means riots and bloodshed."

"You see, Rufus," said Pilate, and now there was almost a note of pleading in his voice, "I was given the strictest instructions from the Emperor himself to keep the peace here in Judea. Caesar has been very gracious in allowing the Jews complete freedom to practise their religion. I have to cooperate with the High Priest in order to make sure that Jewish religious beliefs are not compromised. Any violation can lead to riots. Believe me, I have seen it happen."

I actually felt sorry for Pilate. He'd been given a thankless, barely-possible situation and had managed it for ten years. He didn't need me coming in and stirring things up. But I had been given a task to do myself. I would just as soon never have heard of this Jesus character, but I had, and I didn't intend either Pilate or Caiaphas to stop me doing my job.

"There are certain aspects of this case that are difficult to make sense of," I said, "and there is no evidence that the followers of Jesus were the ones who stole his body. In fact, there is no evidence that *anyone* stole the body."

The High Priest said something that sounded like 'Tchah!' Then he said, "Who else but Jesus' disciples would want to steal his body?"

"Who indeed," I responded. "Tell me, High Priest, if the disciples stole the body and took it back to Galilee, would they be able to undergo the ritual of purification there, or would they have to come back to the Temple?"

"We have priests in Galilee who are authorised to carry out purification and other necessary rituals."

"Your Temple Police have been checking up on people here and we have some of Jesus' disciples under observation in Galilee. So far there are no reports of anyone seeking purification for an unidentified corpse."

"As I told you yesterday, Jesus disciples might well flout our rituals, as Jesus himself did," said Caiaphas, coldly.

"Everything I hear about this Jesus indicates that he was a man of peace," I said. "He wouldn't want his followers to get involved in riots, so I don't see why you are so bothered about them."

"He claimed to be the Messiah!" retorted Caiaphas.

"Perhaps. But not a war-like Messiah. He came into Jerusalem on a donkey, not a war-horse."

"He was pretending to fulfil a prophecy."

"Then surely that prophecy was telling you that this Messiah would be a man of peace."

"I see you still do not understand," said Caiaphas, scornfully. "You need to be born a Jew to understand our Jewish beliefs. I tell you we have to stamp out all trace of Jesus and his disciples or there will be trouble."

"Is that why you felt it necessary to bribe the guards at Jesus' tomb?" I asked, as casually as I could.

The High Priest's expression did not change, but he gripped the arms of his chair tightly. Pilate looked both surprised and shocked - genuinely surprised I thought, which was reassuring; it tended to indicate that he hadn't known about the bribe.

Nobody said anything for a few moments. I let the silence continue. Silence is one of the best tools in the interrogator's kit. People hate silence. Sooner or later someone feels obliged to break the silence. As long as it wasn't me or Pilate, I could expect to learn something.

Unfortunately, it was Pilate who spoke first.

"Bribe the guards? I thought you Jews had strict laws against bribery. Caiaphas, what's going on?"

Caiaphas was thinking. I could see that much - probably trying to decide whether to choose denial or explanation. Eventually he went for explanation.

"The story told by the guards was fantastic, clearly an invention. I simply wished Captain Micah to persuade them to come up with a more plausible account."

"What story?" asked Pilate, still puzzled. "What did they tell you?"

Caiaphas looked at me. I had been looking at him steadily since I had asked my question. I inclined my head, indicating that the ball was in his court.

Caiaphas took a deep breath and said, "The guards had made up a fantasy story about light and heat coming from the tomb. They opened the tomb. The body was gone."

There was another silence.

"But that means..." began Pilate, then hesitated. "So you're saying Jesus *did* rise from the dead?"

"No," said Caiaphas coldly. "I am saying that the guards reported that the body disappeared."

There was another silence.

"Why would the guards want to steal Jesus' body?" I asked.

There was another silence.

"Presumably," said Pilate slowly, "the guards were cooperating with Jesus' disciples to steal the body and claim that he had risen from the dead." He turned to Caiaphas. "Why didn't you put the guards under close arrest? Why didn't you hand them over to me? My questioners would have got the truth out of them."

"I did not want them tortured," said Caiaphas.

There was another silence.

"Let me suggest a scenario," I said. "The body of Jesus disappears from the tomb. His disciples think he has risen from the dead and start to publicise this. Their movement begins to recruit more followers. In due course the authorities produce the body of Jesus, making it plain that the story of his resurrection is false. The movement collapses in ridicule. The

Three Days in Jerusalem

original disciples are humiliated and have to crawl back to their homes in disgrace. Judaea enjoys a good laugh at their expense and everyone settles down peacefully under the rule of the Roman Governor and the Jewish High Priest."

Caiaphas' expression began to change as I said this - from anger to astonishment.

"You are not suggesting that *I* had the body of Jesus removed from the tomb?"

"It seems a plausible scenario," I replied.

"I assure you, Prefect, that I had nothing to do with such a scenario - nor did my priests, nor the Temple Police."

There was another silence. I let it run as long as I could and once again it was Pilate who spoke.

"I see what you mean, Rufus, about this affair being difficult to make sense of."

I nodded. By this time I'd decided that I had got as much as I could expect out of Caiaphas for the moment, and perhaps I'd got all that he knew. And I had at least made his position awkward by making sure that Pilate knew about the bribes. That might make him more cooperative in future. I stood up.

"Thank you, Gentlemen. I trust you will inform me of any other evidence that comes to your attention."

"Of course, Rufus, of course," replied Pilate.

. . . .

I had been rather pleased with my scenario for ridiculing Jesus' followers out of existence. It was disappointing that Caiaphas and his priests had not thought of it. No sense of humour, I suppose. Otherwise, my chief feeling as I walked back to the Antonia was one of frustration. This case was oddly twisted. Every official involved seemed to have done something that was doubtful, if not actually illegal; everyone connected with Jesus that I'd met seemed to have a clear conscience.

"Right," I said to Ursus and Crescens when I got back to the office, "we've got a report to write, and at the moment we haven't got any suspects and I'm not even sure if we've got a crime. Let's go through it systematically from the top. A man who seems to be innocent but may be guilty is crucified. He dies on the cross that same day, Friday."

"The Centurion in charge of the crucifixion is sure that he's really dead," said Ursus, "and he seems to be a reliable witness."

"The man has no friends or relatives at the execution and his body is handed over to a respected member of the community for burial," I continued.

"The forensic evidence confirms which tomb the body was placed in," said Crescens.

"Next morning, Saturday, or the Sabbath, the Captain of the Temple Police confirms that the body is still in the tomb. The tomb is closed, sealed and guarded."

"The Temple guards are unreliable, both as witnesses and sentries," said Ursus.

"Nothing happens until just before dawn next morning when the guards report that there was light and heat coming from inside the tomb. They open the tomb and find that the body is gone."

"But the grave cloths are left behind, bloodstained and scorched," added Crescens.

"Close inspection of the tomb, by a qualified SCO, demonstrates that there is only one entry to and exit from the tomb - the one that was guarded. The guards leave their post and report to their Captain, who is somehow persuaded not to punish them. Soon after that, some women, followers of the dead man, come to the tomb where they meet a young man in white."

Crescens hadn't yet heard this part of the story but he immediately picked up one point. "So there was a period of time when the tomb was open and unattended, between the guards leaving it and the women arriving."

"Yes," I agreed, "but by that time, the body had already gone. Then there's this young man in white. Who was he? He seems to be independent of everyone else." I paused, but neither Ursus nor Crescens said anything. "The women panic and run away. Captain Micah arrives with the guards, inspects the empty tomb; then they go away. One of the women brings two of Jesus' disciples to the tomb and then *they* go away. But the woman stays around and afterwards claims to have seen Jesus alive."

"It was a very busy tomb at that time," said Crescens, sarcastically.

"The tomb seems to have been left open and unguarded, but untouched, until the garrison Prefect is informed three days later. It's been guarded by Roman soldiers ever since, so we can be sure that it has not been tampered with except by official investigators.

"Jesus' followers claim to have seen Jesus alive (they say, 'more than alive') on at least four occasions, apart from the woman" (I paused to think for a moment) "maybe five occasions if this report from Galilee is correct. Nobody except Jesus' disciples claim to have seen him. Everyone else believes that Jesus' followers stole the body precisely so that they could claim Jesus had risen from the dead – and that is exactly what they are doing."

"But the evidence from the guards is that Jesus' followers did not come near the tomb," said Crescens. "The body just disappeared – in a heat and light show."

"The guards must be in on it," said Ursus. "They must have been bribed, or they're secret followers of Jesus themselves."

"The guards have been bribed all right," I said, "but by the High Priest, not by Jesus' followers."

"What about Jesus' brothers?" asked Crescens.

"They don't seem to be involved. They came here to take the body back to Galilee for a family burial. It doesn't sound as if they expected their brother to rise from the dead."

"Unless they were very clever and stole the body," suggested Crescens, "then came all innocent to claim it."

"I didn't get the impression they were that clever," I said.

After a pause, I went on. "Whoever took the body, left the grave cloths behind, so they must have wanted to give the impression that the body passed through the shroud," (I looked at Crescens) "unless you want us to take your 'just disappeared' seriously."

"I've listened to the recording of your interview with the guards," said Crescens. "If they colluded with the disciples to steal the body, they've invented two stories: one, that they fell asleep and let someone steal the body; two, that the body simply disappeared. That doesn't sound likely to me. Why didn't they just fix on one story?"

"The sleeping guard story was never plausible," I said. "No one could have moved that stone without waking them. The body-snatchers would have had to take out the guards first. In fact, why didn't the guards claim that they had been overpowered by the disciples? A sleeping guard can't give evidence that the disciples stole the body. I think it would suit the High Priest better to have eyewitnesses of the theft."

"The guards said that they had wine," said Ursus. "Maybe it was drugged."

"No," said Crescens. "I've had forensics check the dregs in the bottle. Just ordinary wine, probably from a Jerusalem vineyard, not even particularly strong."

Three Days in Jerusalem

"In any case, the evidence is that the guards did *not* fall asleep," I said, "at least, not all of them at once. They kept watch in rotation."

"Is there any reason why this High Priest would want to remove the body?" asked Crescens.

"Only to stop the disciples stealing it," I answered. "It would be no use him hiding the body. He would need to be able to say that he had the body in his possession if Jesus' followers make a public announcement that he has risen from the dead."

"They haven't done that publicly, yet," said Crescens.

"No, but someone has started rumours." Suddenly I remembered something Caiaphas had said. "You know, Caiaphas told me that the fact that Jesus was crucified and died proved that he was *not* the Messiah, so why do his followers go on believing that he is?"

"Because they believe that Jesus rose from the dead," said Crescens. "You know, Sir, I can't think of any explanation of this light and heat that the Temple Guards reported."

"You think it happened when Jesus rose from the dead?" I asked, sarcastically.

Crescens replied with a question of his own, "You know what Sherlock Holmes would have said?"

"No, I don't know what Sherlock Holmes would have said," I retorted.

"He said that, 'when you have eliminated the impossible, whatever remains, *however improbable*, must be the truth'."

Found in Translation

The Stowaway

> *We move forward many centuries into the future. Man is reaching out into space, colonising new planets. The advances in technology astonish us. But does mankind still need a Saviour?*

"Attention, please! All passengers and crew. This is the Captain speaking. We are responding to a distress call from our colony on Airamas Four. In approximately half an hour we will be dropping out of hyperspace in order to launch a Medical Support Shuttle to transport medical supplies to the colony. We will then resume course to New Shiloh. We will be able to make up the time lost so that we will arrive at New Shiloh on schedule. All passengers please proceed to your cabins ready for the drop to sub-light speed. All crew to deceleration stations. Thank you."

Sue Thomas had paused in the act of changing out of her waitress uniform of frilly apron and black dress into her pale blue crew overalls to listen to the Captain's voice over the ship's public address system. An idea had come into her head. Hurriedly, she pulled on her overalls and zipped them up - made sure her ID badge was pinned to the front. It was mad, of course, stupid even and impulsive. But her father used to say, "Grab a chance with both hands and you won't be sorry for what might have been." Almost without thinking, she opened her locker, pulled out a kitbag and began stuffing her few possessions into it.

Sue went out into the corridor and headed for a flight of steps that led down into the engineering section of the starliner. One or two crew members passed her, but they were heading for their deceleration stations and, assuming she was doing the same, took no notice of her. She reached the engineering deck and turned forward until she came to a door marked 'Shuttle Bay'. The notice also read 'No Admittance to Unauthorised Personnel. Flight safety regulations must be observed'. Underneath was a signature and below that, the printed word 'Captain'. But Sue was both too excited and too nervous to study the notice. Cautiously she opened the door and stepped inside.

She was in what seemed an enormous compartment, compared with most of the tiny rooms and narrow corridors of the Philippia. There was a row of cylindrical shapes, of different sizes, that Sue knew must be the shuttles used for transferring passengers and goods. Which was the one she wanted?

The nearest one, and the smallest, was marked 'MSS' in large letters on the side. What was it the Captain had said? "Medical Support Shuttle". That must be it: MSS. The hatch in the side of the shuttle was open and she could see someone was moving inside. That was no use to her. She had to remain hidden. She sidled quietly along the wall of the Shuttle Bay to try to get nearer to the MSS.

It was as well that she did, for the door she had entered by a moment before opened and a man and a woman came in. Like her, they were wearing crew overalls and were carrying large plastic boxes. They paid no attention to Sue, or perhaps did not see her, but walked straight to the hatch of the MSS and began to pass their burdens through to the person inside. Sue sidled further, until she could dash across to the rear end of the MSS and crouch behind it. Her heart was thumping within her chest, but she need not have worried. The two crew members, with another crewman, presumably the one who had been inside the shuttle, walked away, out through the door, and disappeared.

Sue looked around. She could see no-one, although she could hear voices and mechanical noises from the far end of

The Stowaway

the Bay, out of her sight, behind the other shuttles. Seizing her chance, she slipped round and clambered through the hatchway into the shuttle. To her relief, it was empty.

However, it was a good deal smaller and more cramped than she had expected. There was a control panel with the usual array of screens, instruments, dials, switches and levers. There were two seats facing the control panel, with barely room for her to squeeze in behind them. In the bulkhead behind the seats were two more hatches, side-by-side. One was marked 'Airlock'; the other was marked 'Storage'. Sue opened the storage hatch and looked inside. There were the boxes she had seen the two crew members carrying. They had been neatly stacked at one side and secured with straps. There was just room for Sue to step in beside them. She pulled the door to and was glad to notice that it had a handle on the inside. She pulled the door until it shut with a decisive click. Sue caught her breath as the light dimmed, but fortunately it did not go out completely. She would have hated to be in the dark.

There was nowhere to sit down, and scarcely room to drop her kitbag at her feet. It was quiet, except for a low humming and a gentle vibration - something to do with the shuttle's machinery, she supposed. At least her heart was settling down to a more normal rhythm. And there was still time to change her mind. Sue reflected for a few moments. After she had been made redundant from her job on Earth, looking for work in a colony on a new planet had seemed a brilliant idea, and working her passage as a waitress on a starliner had seemed the best way to get into space for a penniless nineteen-year-old with few qualifications. What she hadn't bargained for was that the Philippia operated a strict class system for passengers. The First Class restaurant was quiet, leisurely and posh, with generous tips from wealthy passengers. The Second Class was pretty good as well, or so she had been told. But the Third Class restaurant was crowded; the food was fast and greasy, the adults were rude, and the children were out of control. Of course, she had had to start at the bottom, in Third Class.

What was more, their destination, New Shiloh, was, in spite of its name, an old-established colony, and she had been told that the job prospects there were no better than on Earth. She might end up having to stay on the Philippia for the return passage to Earth. Airamas Four, on the other hand, was a new colony, only established a couple of years ago, and there were sure to be opportunities for a bright young woman. She was doing the right thing, Sue decided.

Her thoughts were broken into by a sudden movement of the shuttle. People were climbing aboard. She heard voices, and the main hatch slammed shut. The shuttle moved again. Suddenly, Sue felt as if she was falling; she felt sick and giddy and lights seemed to flash inside her head. She knew what it was; the Philippia had dropped out of hyperspace. A few seconds later, she felt herself pressed against the rear bulkhead of the storage compartment. The shuttle was moving, accelerating forwards. The pressure eased and then Sue felt the sensation of falling again. The shuttle had left the artificial gravity field of the Philippia and she, and everything else aboard it, was now weightless. Sue hadn't bargained for that. There was nothing to hold onto, except the straps securing the boxes, and she felt sick and giddy again. Fortunately, the compartment was so small that she could not drift around, and in a little while she began to get used to the feeling and even began to enjoy it.

It was very quiet, except for the faint humming, and she could occasionally hear voices from the cramped control cabin in front of her little compartment. Two men's voices, she thought; presumably those two seats were now occupied.

Presently, she began to feel the cold. Once she noticed it, Sue realised that the storage compartment had always been cold; she had just been too excited and tense to notice it. Now

The Stowaway

she began to shiver. She had a warm jacket in her kitbag and, with some difficulty in the confined space, and fearful of making any noise, she managed to pull it out of the bag and struggle into it. That was better.

Then she heard the men's voices again. One of them sounded a little louder, as if the speaker was worried. A third voice broke in. They must be speaking to the Philippia by radio, or perhaps to the base on Airamas Four. Sue hoped they would soon be landing. Instead she was surprised when one of the voices spoke very clearly and in much louder tones,

"*Come out!*"

Sue held her breath. "That means me," she thought.

The voice came again. "I said, come out! *Now!*"

There was no help for it. Sue pressed on the handle and opened the hatch.

"All right, I give up. What now?" she said, with her brightest smile.

She saw a man wearing blue crew overalls, with a badge of a red cross on a white background which identified him as a member of the medical staff, standing, or rather floating, in the narrow space behind the seats. He grabbed her arm and pulled her out of the cold compartment. She floated in the zero-g and her head banged against the ceiling. The man guided her hand to a grab handle on the ceiling and worked his way past her to look into the storage compartment. Satisfied that she was alone and that all was well with the stores, he closed the hatch. Then he worked his way back to his seat and pressed a button on the instrument panel.

"MSS to Philippia," he said. "Medical Officer Sesom reporting. I confirm we have one stowaway on board. It is a woman."

A voice came back from the panel, "Philippia to MSS. Understood. Establish her identity. And we need to know her weight."

Sue looked anxiously at the back of the Medical Officer's head. He had hair of very pale yellow, and she had noticed that he had no eyebrows, typical of the Dionian race. She thought that she had seen him in the Philippia's Sick Bay when she had had her crew medical check-up. All she was able to see of the other man, presumably the shuttle pilot, was the black hair on his head.

"Please identify yourself," said the Medical Officer. In spite of the 'please' it was definitely a command, not a request.

"My name's Sue Thomas."

"How much do you weigh?"

Sue had been running through in her mind how she would explain herself, but this was absolutely the last question she expected to be asked. She giggled in her surprise. "Is that the first thing you usually ask a girl?"

"It is very important," insisted the Medical Officer. "How much do you weigh?"

Sue thought quickly and decided on an honest answer. "8 stone, 9 pounds."

"What is your position on the Philippia?"

"I'm a waitress, in the Third Class restaurant."

Sesom turned back to the instrument panel. "Philippia from MSS. The stowaway is Sue Thomas, Third Class waitress, weight 55 kilograms."

"Thank you, MSS," said the Voice from the control panel. "We'll do the calculation and come back to you."

Sue was not very pleased to be described as a third class waitress, but she only said, "Well, you've caught me. What happens to me now?"

Sesom did not answer her directly. Instead he asked a counter-question: "Why did you stow away on this shuttle?"

"I lost my job on Earth and things weren't working out for me. I'd heard there were lots of opportunities in the space colonies, so I was working my passage on the Philippia. When

The Stowaway

I heard about this shuttle going to Airamas I thought it would be a quick way to get to a new colony, so I just stowed away. It was a bit mad, I know but..." Sue's voice faltered. The Medical Officer was looking at her over his shoulder with an expression on his face that she couldn't quite read, but it made her feel very uncomfortable. "You still haven't told me what's going to happen. Do I have to pay a fine or something?"

"How did you get on board?" Again he was avoiding her questions. Why?

"I just sneaked into the Shuttle Bay and came aboard when no-one seemed to be looking. I knew I would be breaking some kind of rule, but I just couldn't resist the chance of a better life."

"You must have come through the door to the Shuttle Bay. Did you not read the notice?" asked Sesom.

"What notice?" said Sue. She hadn't seen any notice - or had she?

"The one that says, 'No Admittance to Unauthorised Personnel'."

"Oh that, yes," Sue remembered. She had seen a notice like that. But she had not stopped to read it. "Well there are lots of notices like that, all over the Philippia."

"This one was signed personally by the Captain," said the Medical Officer, sternly.

For the first time, Sue began to feel a little ashamed and even more anxious. The Medical Officer made it sound as if she had somehow let the Captain down.

"Why won't you tell me what's going to happen to me? Is it a fine? Or something worse?"

The Voice from the instrument panel broke in on them. "Philippia to MSS. Come in, please."

The black-headed pilot answered, "MSS receiving you. Davidson answering."

"We have calculated the effects of the additional weight of your stowaway," said the Voice. "The Shuttle now has insufficient fuel for a safe landing. You have gone too far to turn back. The MSS *must* begin deceleration in ten minutes. You must take action before that time. Do you understand what you have to do?"

"Yes, Philippia, I understand," replied the pilot. "This is Davidson, signing out."

"What was all that about?" asked Sue.

"That was the Captain telling us what we have to do to you," said the Medical Officer.

"Well?"

Sesom did not reply immediately. When he began, after a few moments, he spoke slowly, as if he did not like what he was saying, as if he was explaining it to himself as well as to Sue. "In a few minutes Lieutenant Davidson will have to start the main motor and slow the shuttle down before we enter Airamas Four's atmosphere. If we come in too fast we will burn up. The shuttle was loaded with just enough fuel to slow down and enter the air safely. Your extra weight means we need extra fuel, which we do not have. In other words, we do not have sufficient fuel to slow down. We will burn up when we enter the atmosphere."

"Can't we go back to the Philippia?"

"No, we do not have sufficient fuel for that. And the Philippia has already accelerated back into hyperspace."

A sudden thought struck Sue. No, that was too awful; he couldn't mean... "You mean, if we burn up, we're going to - die?"

"Do you know why this shuttle is going to Airamas Four?" asked Sesom.

"No, not really. Something about medical supplies."

"This is the MSS, the Medical Support Shuttle," explained the Medical Officer. "As its name suggests, it is only used to

The Stowaway

deliver supplies or equipment in a medical emergency situation. There has been an outbreak of IPLF in the Airamas Four colony. Already, five people have died. We are carrying antiviral medication to treat people infected and vaccines to protect everyone else. If this shuttle does not land safely, everyone on Airamas Four will die. This shuttle must land safely. It can only do so if we jettison the extra weight."

"Jettison?" The word was not familiar to Sue - what could it mean? Suddenly she began to understand. "You, you can't mean..."

The Medical Officer spoke very slowly, carefully and clearly. "The Captain expects us to put you into the airlock, open the outer door and send you into space. That way, you die, but the shuttle lands safely and many lives are saved."

Sue felt panic rising in her throat. "No. That's, that's cruel. Can't you jettison something else? Some equipment? Something my weight?"

"This is the Medical Support Shuttle," said Sesom, in a calm, matter of fact voice, as if he had made a comment on the weather, not just pronounced a death sentence. "It has been stripped down to the bare minimum of equipment needed to land safely. There is nothing we can jettison."

Sue felt distressed, close to tears, but angry as well. "You want to kill me!" she said accusingly. "And the Captain - he wants you to kill me. He's waiting on the Philippia for you to call and say you've killed me."

"Nobody wants to kill you," said the Medical Officer, coldly. "It is the laws of physics that say we have insufficient fuel to land safely, and it is those same laws that say we cannot get back to the Philippia."

"But I didn't do anything," said Sue, almost wailing. "I just wanted a better life. I didn't do anything wrong!"

"You went through a door marked, 'No Admittance'. You broke a rule made by the Captain himself."

"I didn't know what the rule was for."

"Then you certainly ought to have obeyed it." For the first time, Sesom began to sound angry. "Do you think the Captain makes rules for fun? You disobeyed his direct order. It is logical that you should be the one to die."

"I'm sorry," cried Sue, desperately, and now her eyes did fill with tears. "I didn't know. I'd do anything to go back - anything."

"You cannot go back and there is nothing you can do. You cannot change the laws of physics."

"I'm sorry," repeated Sue. "I don't want to die. Isn't there anything you can do?"

Lieutenant Davidson spoke. As he spoke, his fingers worked at the keyboard and controls in front of him. "Just one thing," he said.

He worked his way out of the pilot's seat into the space behind the seats. "Sit there and don't move. Strap yourself in. Don't touch anything."

Sue struggled between the seats and settled herself in the pilot's seat. Almost blind because of the tears, she fumbled for the straps.

Davidson spoke again. "Sesom, I've programmed the Autopilot. In exactly five minutes it will start the shuttle motor. The Autopilot will slow down the shuttle and guide it in to a safe landing. Goodbye."

Sue looked round and saw Davidson open the hatch marked 'Airlock' and climb through it. The hatch shut. Moments later there was a sound of rushing air and the MSS swayed wildly. Then it steadied down.

The Voice from the Philippia came from the control panel, "This is Philippia calling MSS. Davidson, report, please. Have you taken appropriate action?"

Notes on the Stories

The Big Picnic

This story is based on John 6:5-13

The Pearl

Jesus said, "Again, the Kingdom of Heaven is like a merchant looking for fine pearls. When he found one of great value, he went away and sold everything he had and bought it."

(Matt 13:45-46)

The Coin

Based on Mark 12:13-17

The design and inscription on the denarius is known from examples of the coin recovered by archaeologists.

Contact

This story is completely fictional but I have tried to make it as authentic as possible by reading books about the Falklands conflict of 1982. Two books that were especially useful were:

> Martin Middlebrook (1987) *Task Force: the Falklands War, 1982*
> Mark Eyles-Thomas (2007) *Sod That for a Game of Soldiers.*

Military Terms used in Contact:

Bergen	Term used by the British Army for the backpack containing sleeping bag, spare clothing and personal kit
GPMG	General Purpose Machine-Gun
Non-com	Non-Commissioned Officer (e.g. Corporal, Sergeant)
OC	Officer Commanding
Recce	Reconnaissance

Found in Translation

SBS	Special Boat Service, a unit of the Royal Marines, specialising in covert operations and reconnaissance
SLR	Self-Loading Rifle, the infantryman's personal weapon during the Falklands conflict
TAB	Tactical Advance to Battle; used by the Parachute Regiment to mean the same as "yomp"
Yomp	March with heavy equipment over difficult terrain.

The Donkey

Scriptures quoted by the disciples are:

Micah 5:2 (as quoted in Matthew 2:6)
Isaiah 53:4 (as quoted in Matthew 8:17)
Isaiah 61:1
Zechariah 9:9

The Test

This story is based on the temptation passages in Matthew 4:1-11 and Luke 4:1-13. The scripture quotations are from Deuteronomy 8:3, 6:16, 6:13, Psalm 91:11-12.

The Broken Leg

The story of Jesus and the woman taken in adultery can be found in John 8:1-11.

Although this story is fiction, the incident of the woman with the broken leg actually happened, in 1969, when I was a student nurse at a hospital in London.

Notes on the Stories

Teabreak

This story is based on the *Emmaus Road* incident in Luke 24:13-32

The Bible passages that the young man was referring to are: Psalm 16:10, Isaiah 53:4-12.

In the Hands of the Prophets

Herod was born about 73 BC and died probably in 4 BC. He was not a Jew but came from Idumaea. He supported the Romans in their campaigns in Palestine and was eventually made King of Judea, Samaria and Galilee in 37 BC. Herod was not an independent ruler; he was what the Romans called a *client king*. He held his position only with the consent of the Roman Emperor. When Herod died, his son Archelaus had to go to Rome to ask the Emperor Augustus to make him king in succession. The Jews did not like Archelaus and sent a deputation to the Emperor to argue against him being made king. This is thought to be the basis for Jesus' *Parable of the Ten Minas* (Luke 19:11-27). In the event, Augustus divided Herod's territory into three: Archelaus was given Judea (Matthew 2:19-23), but soon had to be replaced by a Roman governor. Another son, Herod Antipas, was made Tetrarch of Galilee, while a third son, Philip was made Tetrarch of Iturea (Luke 3:1)

In his later years, Herod became increasingly unstable and paranoid. He executed one of his wives, Mariamne, and several of his sons, so his massacre of the boys in Bethlehem is quite in character.

Berekiah's Biblical quotations are from Micah 5:2 and Isaiah 11:1. It seems to be fairly certain that the Magi (Matthew 2:1-12) were astrologers; they were certainly not kings. Various astronomical explanations have been suggested for the Star of Bethlehem and I have simply selected one of them for the purpose of this story.

Found in Translation

None so Blind

Based on Acts 13:4-12

In addition, this story uses the following passages:

Acts 2:22-24, 36, 3:19, 17:24-31, 22:2-9, 26:4-18, I Corinthians 15:3-8, Galatians 5:22-23

The Genesis Project

According to legend, there are seven archangels, although only two, Gabriel and Michael, are named in the Bible. Raphael and Uriel are two more names that appear regularly in mythology but the names of the other three vary from source to source. Metatron is, among other characteristics, identified as being the scribe of heaven, so that is why he appears as secretary in this story.

In the United Kingdom, ACAS is the Advisory, Conciliation and Arbitration Service. Its aim is to improve organisations and working life through better employment relations.

Ferry Meadows is the name of Peterborough's recreational park, near where I live. Readers please feel free to substitute an appropriate local name.

A Jar of Water

The circular crests, worn by Philistine warriors on their helmets, are known from ancient Egyptian illustrations. It is not certain what they were made of, perhaps horsehair, perhaps feathers. I had to make a choice for the story, so I simply picked horsehair.

The Song

This story contains numerous quotations from and references to the Song of Songs.

Notes on the Stories

Other Scripture passages used are: I Samuel 8:11-18, Psalm 122:1-2, 125:1, Proverbs 6:10-11, 12:11, 25:15, 29:26, 31:10

Gentled Horses

Based on Matthew 11:28-30

I first came across the verb 'to gentle' in connection with training horses in Owen Wister's prototype western novel *The Virginian* (published 1902) but it is still in use by horse trainers and can be found in a modern dictionary.

Strictly speaking, this story contains an anachronism, for the bishop's Bible would certainly have been an Authorised Version, in which Jesus says, 'I am *meek*...' However, most modern translations use the word 'gentle'.

Found in Translation

In 1955 Arthur C Clarke, a brilliant and prolific writer of Science Fiction, published a short story called The Star in which a space expedition visits the remnants of a supernova (a star which has exploded) and finds, on a lonely planet, the remains of a civilisation destroyed in the explosion. The expedition's astrophysicist, a Jesuit priest, calculates that the supernova was in fact the Star of Bethlehem. The story thus raises the question of how a loving God can allow, or cause, suffering. The priest in the story finds his faith sorely troubled.

Clarke's story is pure fiction. There is no evidence that the Star of Bethlehem was a supernova. If it was a natural phenomenon, there are other plausible explanations. The trouble is that, in fiction, one can produce any evidence needed to support one's own opinion. So this little story is my, greatly belated, riposte to The Star with evidence on the opposite side.

"Space, the Final Frontier" is (of course) the opening line from *Star Trek* (1966 onwards) by Gene Roddenberry.

Found in Translation

"Look how the floor of heaven is thick inlaid with patens of bright gold" is from *The Merchant of Venice*, Act V, Scene 1, William Shakespeare.

Three Days in Jerusalem

In chapter two of his book *The God Delusion*, the well-known atheist Richard Dawkins claimed that the question of whether or not Jesus rose from the dead was a strictly scientific question with a strictly scientific answer and should be settled (if relevant evidence ever became available) by purely and entirely scientific methods. So I wondered how it would turn out if the resurrection were to be investigated by a Roman officer who had the support of all the apparatus of modern forensic science.

At the end of the story, Crescens quotes from A Conan Doyle, The Sign of Four (1890) chapter 6.

The ritual for cleansing from contact with dead body is set out in Numbers 19:11f.